Alison Barnard

A Walk in the Rain

An erotic lesbian novel

Alison Barnard
A Walk in the Rain

PART ONE

"No, Lisa. I won't do it. It's a terrible idea." Jessa Hanson frowned and paced the room angrily as she spoke.

Lisa Guthrie, her talent agent, looked at her over the tops of her glasses and tried not to smile, because Jessa could be so predictable at times. She leaned against the breakfast bar in the open-plan living space of Jessa's London flat and spoke calmly to her favorite client. "Yes, it *is* a good idea. Just as it was a good idea to cooperate with the biography and keep some sort of creative control. It's the best way to cut down on sensationalism. Your life story is dramatic: first openly lesbian female to be musical director of a major orchestra, one of the youngest people ever to be musical director of a North American orchestra, first classical musician to have a number one pop CD, first biography of a musician to top the non-fiction best-seller charts on both sides of the Atlantic – you're a star."

"I hate that word." Jessa's frown turned into a scowl. "And, with the exception of the fact that I'll be musical director of the TSO, which won't even happen for almost a year, none of that had anything to do with me. The CD was only a pop sensation because I worked with Norah Jones."

"Your name and image were on the front of the CD . . ."

"That was a bad idea: I produced it and played on some of the tracks because she wanted to go in a new direction and I'd enjoyed writing with her, but I should never have consented to the cover photo. It gave the wrong impression . . ."

"Jessa, get over it. The photo showed your navel and caused a bit of a stir in the classical community, but you're obviously still being taken seriously, or you wouldn't have such a great season lined up – not to mention a two-year contract with the Toronto Symphony Orchestra. In fact, answer this: as your manager, have I ever asked you to do something which turned out to be bad for your career?"

Jessa looked at the floor, embarrassed by the question. Lisa was so much more than her manager. Lisa had been a big sister, surrogate mother, agent, even financial advisor at times. It was true that she was well-compensated for that nowadays, but that had not always been the case and Jessa owed more to her than she did to anyone else in her life. Yet Lisa never mentioned all the personal things she'd done for Jessa, only ever reminding her, as now, of the professional decisions, and only when she thought Jessa was being unreasonable in reaction to one of her suggestions.

"No," she admitted with a sigh. "You've made some wacky but prescient decisions about the direction in which I should take my career. And if you think I should retain creative control over the film adaptation of my life story then you're probably right. What I object to is the way you're suggesting I do it. The next two months are going to be busy and stressful: a week in New York, then a week in Toronto, not only conducting, but doing publicity spots when the announcement is made, then Berlin for a week and then back to London. I don't need the added stress of an egotistical actress following me around and constantly distracting me from what I have to accomplish!" Jessa's voice had started to rise as she'd spoken the last sentence and it ended just short of a whine.

"Jessa, you don't know that she's egotistical . . ."

"She's an actress! And a successful one at that! Do you know any successful actresses who aren't egotistical and, in a sick dichotomy, terrified of being themselves? Pretending to be someone else for a living is *not* a healthy impulse!"

"You don't know Shara. She's emotionally stable and her life is not her work. *She* is not her career."

"Oh, it's 'Shara' is it? How do you know so much about what she's like?"

"Because I've met her a few times."

"Oh." Jessa turned away, but not before Lisa had seen the hurt on her face. Surround Jessa with other musicians and scores and she was supremely confident, but at her core was the insecurity born of being abandoned by her parents when she had been a child-like six-teen. In the aftermath she'd become streetwise and outwardly tough, but she remained acutely sensitive to betrayal by the few people she allowed to get close to her.

"Jessa, I would never ask you to spend weeks at a time, especially at such a crucial time in your career, with someone I thought could be bad for you. At the same time, I could not dismiss an opportunity to influence this film. The only way I could be a good manager, and a good friend, was to meet Shara Quinn and see if she was the sort of person it would be worth your time to allow to see what it's really like to walk in your shoes. She's worked with the director before and he has a reputation for allowing his actors to have input into the projects – especially those actors whose judgment he trusts. If you allow Shara to get an honest feel for your life and ca-reer, it could make all the difference, but only if she's intelligent and perceptive enough to see beyond the glamor and the hardship that go hand in hand with your schedule. Having spoken to her for extended periods, I can tell you, without reservation, that she is."

"How many times did you meet her?" Jessa was distracted by Li-sa's mention of extended periods, since Lisa was notorious for siz-ing people up very quickly and accurately. She wondered if, per-haps, Lisa had had initial reservations about this woman, which would not be a good sign.

"Three times." Jessa raised her eyebrows. "The first time was an introductory lunch with her boyfriend – a man named Derek Finch with the same need for attention as a small child. Since it was im-possible to discuss much beyond the bare bones of what she wanted to do while he was there, especially since he wasn't happy about having her on the road for six weeks, she asked if we could meet again. The next time we had lunch in my office and then she issued a reciprocal invitation to her home for dinner and we'd got along really well, so I accepted."

"What, are you dating this woman?" Jessa was not happy and she knew that the jealousy she felt was unreasonable, but Lisa was notoriously antisocial, her job requiring so many business meals that she jealously guarded the time she had with her partner and her extended family. The feeling of sibling rivalry that Jessa felt towards this unknown actress who had lured Lisa into a private dinner was childish and sad, but Jessa felt it anyway.

"Jessa, don't be a baby. Straight women don't 'date', we have meals with friends."

"Are you sure she's straight? Remember the designer who wanted me to use her shirts and then took advantage of a fitting . . ."

"Jessa, she's straight. I met her boyfriend. Besides, that's part of the reason she wants to do this and live in your world. Her best friend is a lesbian, but she's a private citizen and Shara wants to understand the added pressures of celebrity and lesbianism on the life of a musician, composer and conductor."

"I'm not a celebrity – not in the way she is. I'm not illicitly photographed in my undies for 'Heat' magazine and I don't go to film premieres . . ."

"Yes, but you can't wait for a flight in the departure lounge, shop at a department store or go to a classical music concert as an ordinary member of the audience, without causing a disturbance."

"True, but it's not because I'm a dyke. She must experience the same things on ten times the scale, so she doesn't need to spend time with me. Case closed."

"Jessa, it's not just your lesbianism, it's your schedule: travel, practice, promotion, socializing and recording. She wants to experience those things with you instead of imagining what it's like."

Jessa sighed. "So what's the plan? She books into hotels wherever I am and I have to face her from the time I sit down to breakfast?"

For the first time, Lisa looked uncomfortable. "Not exactly."

Jessa's eyes narrowed. She knew from experience that she would not like whatever Lisa said next. "So what, exactly?"

"She'll be living with you . . ."

"No! Absolutely not. My living space is critical to the way I work. I will not have some spoiled egomaniac painting her nails and whingeing when I'm trying to practice or write – or even read. No way."

"Jessa, it's the only way. And it's not going to be such a hardship. You'll be staying in Stephan's loft in New York and that's huge with two bedrooms. In Toronto they've leased you a penthouse flat that's got two bedrooms as well and in Berlin you'll be using the guest flat on Meinekestrasse – and you certainly won't be tripping over each other in that."

"Lisa, I write in the middle of the night and I can't tolerate distractions. Most people who are *not* overindulged actresses can't stand hearing the same six bars played over and over again on a piano as I work out the little kinks in a composition – especially not at two or three in the morning!"

"That's exactly the kind of thing she needs to know, if she's going to play you in a film."

"This entire idea is ridiculous . . ."

"It will make the film more accurate."

"I mean the idea of a film is ridiculous. I'm still alive, for fuck's sake. If anyone wants to know what I'm like they can come to a performance – unless they happen to live in Asia this year, I'm pretty damn accessible. I'm even in Argentina in February. And if they want to know more about me than they can read in the program, that bloody book has more about my life than I want anyone to know."

"But most people don't read."

"Which is what's wrong with the world today," Jessa sneered. "We both know that my life simply is not interesting enough to keep anyone from falling asleep in a darkened theater."

"Unless they're enthralled by Shara Quinn," Lisa joked.

"And that's another thing: the woman couldn't look less like me, if she tried! I've seen her on the telly: she's twee with long hair and gray eyes."

"They're hazel – but that's not the point. She's an actress. Her hair will be cut for the role and she's quite looking forward to wearing a cut-away coat and having camera angles make her look taller than she is."

"God. Six weeks with an actress. Does she even understand what

I do? Has she ever heard a symphony?"

It was Lisa's turn to sigh. "You really need to let go of your preju-dices, Jessa. She enjoys symphonic music from the classical period, but she prefers chamber music to music written for a full orchestra, and opera to either. Do you really think I'd ask you to live with someone who didn't love music?"

"I didn't think you'd ask me to live with anyone," Jessa replied quietly.

"She's not Stephanie. She doesn't want to be Stephanie. She's a nice woman who wants to do a good job. Perhaps you need to live with someone, even as a friend, who reminds you that companion-ship doesn't always come with an expensive price tag."

"I don't want any new friends," Jessa's final objection sounded lame, even to her own ears.

"Perhaps that's the best time to acquire one," Lisa replied firmly. "Now, I have a meeting with a film producer about using that piece you wrote last winter in the score for his film. It could turn into a pretty major project for you and you have that gap between Buenos Aires and Toronto next year."

"It's called time off," Jessa responded wryly. "You should try it some time. I'm serious, you know."

"About what?" Lisa asked innocently.

"About everything. You need to work less, I would like to have next spring and early summer off, since I'm moving to Canada for my first steady job in autumn *and*, and this is important, if your ac-tress turns out to be a pain in the arse, or interferes with my work in any way, she will be out of my life in a hurry."

"Is that all?" Lisa drawled the question and raised one inquiring eyebrow.

"No, that's not all." Jessa walked over to her and hugged her. "Thank you. I know you only want what's best for me and you are the only person in my life who that has ever been true of."

Lisa hugged her back. "You are so welcome, Jessa." Her voice sounded choked, because she knew that Jessa had not realized the loneliness and tale of betrayal implicit in that statement, coming as it did from a woman of thirty-three.

PART TWO

Shara Quinn put down the baton and rolled her shoulders to loosen the kinked muscles, letting the second movement of Beethoven's Fifth Symphony start without her. In the recording, André Previn continued to do an excellent job and the Royal Philharmonic Orchestra didn't notice her absence. It wasn't one of Jessa Hanson's signature pieces, so Shara would not be called upon to conduct it for the film, but a musician friend had suggested it as a great piece to practice on, because the tempo throughout was easier to track than in Holst's *Planets* or others that had been included in Jessa's best-selling recordings. "It will allow you to perfect your right-hand technique, so you don't have to think about tempo and you can concentrate on everything else," Julian had told her in what he'd thought was a reassuring tone.

At the time, all Shara could think was that what she'd thought would be the "fun" part of the project: dressing in drag and waving a baton, was turning out to be more of a challenge than faking virtuoso piano performances. She was a decent piano player and could manage simple pieces on the violin without too many mistakes, especially since she'd been practicing for months just as a way of getting an edge in the audition for the role. She'd known that she wasn't the physical type Peter Garofolo had been looking for when he'd been working with casting directors on the principal role for his new film, but she'd never wanted anything this badly, so from the time she'd heard rumors of the film rights to Jessa Hanson's biography having been acquired, she'd engaged tutors and started brushing up on her skills. She doubted that any actor could be fluent in eight instruments as Jessa Hanson was, but she was competent at one and could get by on violin and guitar, so she intended to milk that for all it was worth. She'd also worked with a voice coach to temporarily obliterate the Irish accent that had been key to her breakthrough film role in Hollywood. Authenticity had got her her first big break and Oscar nomination, and she hoped that musical authenticity would do it again.

She sighed and turned off the music. She needed to work out the tension in her muscles, so she put on shorts, t-shirt and trainers and went for a run on the treadmill. She resented the fact that nowadays she ran more on the treadmill than outdoors, but she hated being recognized when she was running, so although this came in a distant second to running outdoors, it was slightly ahead of being pointed at or, worse, being stopped in the middle of her run.

She could hardly wait to give up her leased house in the Hollywood Hills and head back to London, despite the fact that Derek loved it here. He'd given up his gardening business to be near her and because he didn't need the money, but his constant presence was starting to grate. A month ago when she'd taken a three-week stretch in London as an opportunity to speak to Jessa's agent about access to the subject of the film, he'd invited himself along and proceeded to behave like an absolute prat.

She really needed to do something about him, but he did provide companionship and sex when she needed it, and he wanted nothing from her that he wouldn't have wanted if she'd been an unknown civil servant with a modest salary. She knew it was a terrible reason to stay in a relationship, but she hated the thought of being single and dating.

"Hiya babes." As though conjured up by her negative thoughts, Derek appeared at the door to the exercise room, his hair flopping boyishly over his forehead and his lean body looking California casual in blue jeans and a translucent white cotton shirt. His feet were bare and he was holding two of his healthy yoghurt-shakes in his hands. "I thought I'd make you an after-workout treat."

"Thanks," Shara said, polishing off the bottle of mineral water she'd taken from the small fridge in the corner of the room and reaching for the shake. "What're you doing today?" Derek's professional idleness fascinated her, despite an innate distaste for people who didn't work for a living that would no doubt make her very pedestrian and working-class in the eyes of Derek's friends in England and the little clique he spent time with here. They weren't famous, but they were rich – the children and grandchildren of Hollywood legends and powerful investors, who rated their acquaintances according to the table they were assigned at the trendy restaurant of the moment.

"Brent is driving up the coast to visit an artist he's sponsoring for a new show." Brent Heywood owned an unprofitable art gallery in Venice Beach that Shara thought was little more than an excuse to have parties to celebrate the openings of exhibitions which were raved about in unprofitable boutique magazines run by people with names like "Tiffany" "Tory" and "Justin", but ignored by the mainstream art world. Those patrons of the arts, avant-garde "journalists" and the artists themselves, all seemed to be part of a Southern Californian elite of beautiful young people with trust funds. Despite the difference in nationality, it was disturbing how easily they and Derek had found each other and how seamlessly he'd integrated into their social sphere.

Shara imagined that the drive to "the coast" meant a beach house owned by the artist's parents, where Brent, Derek and at least one flawlessly tanned female would sip champagne, or indulge in a discreet amount of some recreational drug and listen to music by an unknown band with a demo CD that had been paid for by patrons such as Brent and which was highly acclaimed in a small, glossy (but largely unread) music magazine whose editor was one of Brent's social acquaintances.

Derek would get home just before dinner, exhausted and withdrawn, or energetic, chatty and horny, depending on the drug and the company. There was no doubt that Derek attracted the attention of the women he socialized with, but she was sure that he never cheated on her. Derek loved her, so she tried her best to appreciate that and not dwell on the emptiness she sometimes felt in their relationship.

She was convinced that she just wasn't the "relationship" type, because this restlessness had been a characteristic of her interactions with all her previous boyfriends. Derek, at least, was just the sort of person she'd have come up with if she had to imagine a personality that balanced hers. He was laid-back where she was intense, he would rather do something physically demanding whereas she was happiest with things that were cerebral. He enjoyed the spotlight and loved having her on his arm at red-carpet events and she hated that aspect of her career. He thought little about appearances and she was completely paranoid about the way she appeared in public, he thought work was something you did because you had to and she had a tendency to focus on it to the exclusion of everything else; he was outgoing and social while Shara always preferred to stay home with a book and good music on the stereo. On any given day their differences balanced each other out or caused almost unbearable friction.

"What about you?" Derek asked. "Any plans? You know you're welcome to join us for the drive if you're not doing anything."

Shara felt a moment of panic, then she remembered that she had a legitimate excuse. "Thanks, babe, but I'm still preparing for my new role. I have a piano lesson this afternoon and then I'm probably going to watch some DVD's of Barenboim and Karajan."

"Isn't it enough that you're going to spend six whole weeks following that woman around? How much can it possibly take to play the role of a lesbian who dresses in men's clothes for work?"

Shara pressed her lips together and her nostrils flared. Derek was often disdainful of her work, but normally he hid it better than this. She struggled to control her impulse to snap at him. "I'll be playing someone who is still alive and who isn't even at the peak of her career. I want to be true to the role and I want my performance to be respectful of the woman I'll be pretending to be. That means musical training and understanding the life of the woman herself. All of that is time-consuming, but it's an honor to be allowed this opportunity and I want to be as close to perfect as I can get."

"That's the story of your life in a nutshell, isn't it, Shara? As close to perfect as you can get?"

"Is that a criticism?"

"No, not really. But it's a tall order for mere mortals to live up to."

"Derek, I'm working hard to get ready for a challenging role. Have I asked anything more of you than to understand why I have to go away for a while?"

"A while? You'll be gone for six weeks! And, as I understand it, you'll be living with a lesbian."

"I won't be 'living' with her in any sense but the technical one, as well you know. I want to understand the routines and pressures of her life and how they affect her emotionally. It's a miracle that someone as private as she is has consented to allow me to do that, because it certainly won't be convenient for her."

"Well I'm glad you considered her convenience, because I don't recall your having considered mine when you took this role."

"Is that what's bothering you? That I didn't ask your permission before reading for a role that has fascinated me from the time I read the biography it's based on? Since when have you shown the kind of interest in my career that would encourage me to discuss future roles with you? Correct me if I'm wrong, but whenever I talk to you about scripts I'm studying, your eyes all but glaze over."

Derek looked slightly guilty, obviously having thought that he'd hidden his boredom better. "Look, all I'm saying is that a six-week absence is something we should have discussed beforehand."

"It's a six-week absence during which you can visit me as often as you like. I can't have overnight visitors, but I understand the woman practices piano for two hours a day, spends time writing music and has two to four hours of orchestra rehearsals every weekday, not to mention two performances a week, so it's not as though I won't be able to get away. Do you want me to be the kind of woman who asks your permission before she takes a trip? We've been together for five years and I've never been that kind of girlfriend."

"Maybe that's the problem. Maybe if your status were more formal, you'd feel more connected with me and you'd discuss things more."

Shara frowned, genuinely confused. "Derek, what are you on about?"

"I mean, if we were married, you'd be my wife, not my girlfriend, and perhaps then you'd consider how your career decisions will affect me."

"I'm an *actress*. I was an actress when you met me. Most of the work I do is in film and that means location shoots that last for weeks and even months. Even when I did guest spots on television, you knew, and accepted, they could be on either side of the Atlantic. When did that start to become a problem for you?"

"I'm thirty-two now and when we were home last month, I realized that most of my friends had settled down and started families. Even over here people are moving on. Brent and Soraya are engaged, did you know? It's just all made me think about things and about the hints my parents have been dropping for years."

Shara put down the glass with the shake, her stomach suddenly feeling sour. "So your friends get married or decide to have children and, as a result, we should do the same and I should start running my career decisions by you for approval. Have I missed anything?"

"You're twisting my words. That's not what I meant ..."

"So tell me what you meant, Derek. We've been living together for almost four years, I thought we were reasonably happy, things have been going well and my career has taken off more than I could have hoped for or predicted. Suddenly you seem resentful of what I see as a huge career opportunity and you see my being a mere girlfriend, when your friends have fiancées or wives, as a *problem*."

"I don't want to fight about this; I just think it's time to take our relationship to the next level ..."

She shook her head in disbelief. "Is that a proposal?"

"Yes, I suppose it is. I want us to be married, Shara, and interact with each other the way married people do ... and have a couple of kids. You'd make a great mother."

Shara felt the half-digested shake rising into her throat and forced herself to take deep breaths. "I can't talk about this now. I've just made an enormous commitment and worked for months to earn the privilege of being allowed to make it. If what you're asking is for me to change my focus now and undo everything I've worked for, then I just can't."

"It doesn't have to be right away, but surely you didn't think we could continue this way indefinitely?"

As a matter of fact, I did. "Can we talk about this when I get back to London? I really need you to bear with me right now. This project means a lot to me."

"Shara, I've just asked you to marry me."

"I know," she said miserably, before stepping around him and hurrying out of the room.

PART THREE

Shara couldn't believe how nervous she was as she approached the reception desk in the converted warehouse. She'd been expecting Jessa to have a swanky Mayfair address, or a mansion in Highgate Village, so she'd been surprised when the cab had dropped her off in front of the block of flats in Clerkenwell, on the northern border of the City of London and the Barbican Center. The Barbican was the home of the London Symphony Orchestra and the entertainment complex hosted art, film, theater and musical events year-round, but while the surrounding area was popular with City traders, bankers and other professionals, it remained more convenient than prestigious, despite the trendy restaurants and galleries that had sprung up all over it during the last ten years.

One expected people like opera divas and world-renowned conductors to live in absolute luxury and wear formal clothing to breakfast, but Shara realized that people probably also expected the same of actresses who they only saw out of character on chat shows or at film premieres – and that was quite silly, really. So Jessa Hanson choosing to live in an inconspicuous building whose only distinguishing features were the floor-to-ceiling windows that dominated the red brick façade, shouldn't be any more surprising than the fact that she preferred to cook for herself.

She hesitantly walked up to the reception desk, no doubt already having attracted the attention of the man behind it by loitering outside for several minutes. She wasn't worried about being recognized, because she looked as unlike her movie-star persona as Jessa's address was from a Mayfair mansion.

"Good afternoon, I'm here to see Jessa Hanson?" She heard the hesitation in her own voice.

The doorman made little effort to hide his skepticism. He gave her a quick once-over. Her hair was short and artificially darkened, worn like a sable cap that moved softly when she did. She was wearing lightly tinted Armani sunglasses that disguised her signature hazel eyes and her face was bare of makeup except for the translucent gloss that emphasized the soft fullness of her lips. She was also more casually dressed than she ever was during promotional appearances, in low-slung jeans worn with a wide black belt and thonged sandals with three-inch heels. It was a warm day and she wasn't wearing a jacket, just a white cotton top that followed the contours of her body from elbows to collarbone, its wide neck showing off the flawless skin of her throat and the gold cross hanging from a fine gold chain that she wore whenever she wasn't working. The top hugged the shape of her breasts and her flat stomach, stopping just short of her navel to reveal the small silver hoop that pierced the skin just above it and glinted in the recessed lighting of the lobby. There was a cavernous bag slung over her shoulder.

Shara knew that she looked younger than her twenty-nine years and flushed faintly as the doorman's reaction made her wonder if Jessa Hanson had female groupies who regularly tried to gain unauthorized access to her home.

As though reading her mind, the doorman said politely, "Good afternoon, Miss. I'm afraid all visitors must be announced. May I have your full name and Miss Hanson's unit number, please?"

"It's Shara Quinn and unit seven." Shara knew she sounded slightly haughty, but that was just in defensive reaction to her embarrassment at having been mistaken for some kind of stalker.

"Oh ... right." It was the burly doorman's turn to look slightly abashed and Shara wasn't sure if it was because he recognized her name or because he was thinking about his previous attitude towards one of Jessa's guests. "I'll just ring ahead and announce you." He picked up a phone that had been hidden by the desk and said, "Miss Shara Quinn is here," then listened for a few seconds before adding, "Right away, Miss Hanson."

Now the soul of discreet professionalism, he looked back at Shara. "Miss Quinn, if you'll just go through the door on your right, you'll see the lift straight ahead. Take it to the penthouse level and Miss Hanson will meet you there."

"Thank you," Shara said, before turning towards the previously unnoticed door. There was a mechanical click as the doorman released the lock and Shara realized that despite the casual appearance of the building, security was closely attended to.

She fidgeted in the short, silent ride up to the fourth floor, looking critically at her appearance in the tinted glass mirror that made up the back wall of the spacious lift. Suddenly, she felt naked without proper makeup and the rest of her hair. She'd been pleased that the dye hadn't dulled the healthy shine of it, but she still barely recognized herself, even though it had been four days since the drastic instructions to her hairdresser.

The lift dinged softly before the doors hissed open to reveal a small foyer with a dried flower arrangement on a marble-topped cherry table. The walls were papered in white linen and the floor was carpeted in hunter green pile so deep that it made her want to take off her shoes and wriggle her toes in it. The front door was of the same deep cherry wood as the table and just before it opened, Shara realized she had no idea what to expect. She'd read Jessa Hanson's life story, read the script that covered the years from age eighteen to twenty-six, with flashbacks to sixteen, listened to recordings of her musical performances and seen dozens of still photographs of a pretty woman with large dark eyes, a polite smile and a petulant frown, but she'd never seen a moving image of that woman. Jessa had been videotaped for numerous news and music channel features, but all the video footage was being compiled on a DVD that should arrive at Shara's home the following day, leaving her with no realistic physical impression of the woman she would be pretending to be in less than two months.

Jessa opened the door and felt as though her heart had suddenly stopped. She'd known that Shara Quinn was pretty: her face had been plastered on movie posters all over London and Jessa had seen news footage of her arriving at the Academy Awards ceremony, although she hadn't won. Jessa had been battling a bout of the insomnia that periodically plagued her and she'd rented the DVD, curious about the Irish actress who had made such a splash in America. The film had been good and Shara had been superb as the abused wife of an English physicist who ended up tried for treason after she'd sold the results of his research to the highest bidder. Jessa admired the talent of the actress who'd taken home the best actress award, but she still thought Shara should have won instead.

When the door had opened, she'd prepared herself for the sight of shiny dark blond hair, framing beautiful hazel eyes and pretty lips. She'd prepared herself to see a spoiled actress, egotistical enough to think she could portray the most painful years of Jessa's life, despite the fact that they looked nothing alike and had nothing in common. Instead she looked at a woman whose eyes were of indeterminate color behind smoky gray lenses, but the near-terror in their wide depths communicated itself clearly to Jessa. Her hair was shiny and short, and her full pink lips were curved into a hesitant smile that dimpled her cheeks. Jessa's heart seemed to stop beating and her breath caught in her throat.

"Hiya, you must be Jessa. I'm Shara." Her voice was lower than Jessa had expected, although she'd heard it before on the best that Bang & Olufsen had to offer.

Jessa's heart started to pound and despite its distracting internal noise, Jessa forced herself to focus on not making a complete prat of herself. "I am. Thanks for stopping by today. I know, it's short notice, but I wanted to get our first meeting out of the way, and I have so much to do before I go on tour." She stepped aside. "Come on in."

Shara was sure she looked as gormless as she felt. Why hadn't someone told her that Jessa Hanson was gorgeous? And even if she was gorgeous, why did seeing her make Shara feel as though the world had tilted on its axis? She lived in LA where the proportion of abnormally stunning people was ridiculously high, but this had never happened to her before – and certainly not when she'd met another woman.

She walked through a short hallway and into a wide open living space, catching a whiff of a subtle perfume as she passed Jessa. At first she didn't even notice her surroundings because she couldn't get past her original impression of Jessa.

Jessa had answered the door wearing bronze linen trousers and a white, lacy tank top that hugged her body. She was tanned and her skin was smooth and healthy. Shara could see the lean muscles under the skin of her slender arms and strong shoulders, and the tank top left a lot of her smooth abdomen bare. In fact, Shara worried that the drawstring trousers would slip off Jessa's slim hips. She was surprised to find that the thought had an odd effect on her heart rate.

But what had really stolen Shara's breath away had been her first look into Jessa's eyes. They were brown, but despite the tint of her sunglasses, Shara could see that they were a different kind of brown from what she'd expected after looking at photographs. They were like molten chocolate with cinnamon and Shara wondered what they would look like in the sunlight. Jessa's eyelashes were long and dense and Shara suspected that that owed nothing to artifice. She'd found herself wanting to take off her sunglasses to look more closely at those amazing eyes, but the impulse terrified her. However improbably, the woman had taken one look at Shara and Shara had lost the plot.

She'd assumed Jessa was saying something sensible in response to her greeting, but she couldn't hear it, because Jessa Hanson's beautiful eyes held deep apprehension as she'd faced the woman who would haunt her life over the better part of two months. Being the cause of such apprehension had touched Shara deeply. She'd read enough about her to know that Jessa was a bit of a loner, so the loss of privacy involved in agreeing to Shara's proposal would be huge.

Suddenly, when she was still standing outside the door, Shara had been scared that she wasn't doing the right thing; she'd wanted to apologize; she'd wanted to say that she'd changed her mind and would find another way to research the role. But Jessa had stood aside and gestured for Shara to precede her into the flat and Shara's legs mindlessly obeyed before her brain could come back on-line and direct them to do otherwise.

Shara's first impression of the room was of light and space. It was much larger than she'd expected. One wall was dominated by

22

floor-to-ceiling windows, and at the end of the room closest to the front door was a grand piano. There were plants strategically placed between the windows, and the almost imperceptible movement of their leaves added to the impression that the room was open to the outdoors.

The gleaming cover of the piano reflected the light and the outlines of the plants and the room was silent despite the cool air that, along with the motion of the leaves, suggested the flat was centrally air-conditioned, although the ducts were artfully concealed.

At the far end of the room was a breakfast bar and, beyond that, an open-plan kitchen. Had it not been for the traditional Tibetan rugs scattered on the polished oak floor, Shara could have imagined that the room could be used for rollerblading – it was that large. Several feet in front of the breakfast bar and more or less near the windows there were low, caramel-colored sofas and off-white recliners around a carved wood coffee table, and Shara noticed high-end stereo speakers placed throughout the room; no effort was made to conceal them, because their design fit the casually modern feel of the place.

The wall opposite the windows was curved and covered with custom-made bookcases. There seemed to be an eclectic collection of scores, reference books and CD's – the only indication of Jessa's profession, apart from the piano. At the lip of the curve was a sleek, almost impossibly slim, stereo system, and in a gap between the bookcases, in the middle of the wall where it was almost flat, was a wide, rectangular mirror that added to the sense of space. Although intrigued by the books and CD's, Shara found herself being drawn to the windows. She'd noticed the high brick wall across the street when she'd alighted from the taxi and she'd assumed it closed off the grounds of yet another dull office block. Instead, the inside of the wall was ivy-covered and it enclosed gardens and perfectly preserved historic buildings, including a church, between which wound centuries-old cobbled walkways. Shara gasped and took off her sunglasses to better appreciate the unexpected sight.

Jessa saw her looking and said, "It's the Charterhouse. A medieval monastery that was almost completely destroyed by the Great Fire of London, but which has been meticulously restored. Most people don't know it's here," she added unnecessarily.

Shara turned towards her, her eyes sparkling. "Your home is gorgeous." She said it simply and sincerely.

Jessa's mouth opened and then closed without emitting a sound. She was captivated by those eyes. Shara Quinn's eyes were like nothing she'd seen before. They looked gray, but with a hint of green and there was a suggestion of gold around the pupils. *No, you're gorgeous*, Jessa thought. She'd opened her mouth to say the words, then realized that Shara probably heard them every day, given what she did for a living. She willed herself to thank Shara politely for the compliment, but when she spoke, the words that came out were, "Your eyes ... they're like a sunrise." She had no idea where that had come from and as soon as she'd finished speaking, she blushed in a way she couldn't remember having done since the onset of puberty.

Shara couldn't speak. Jessa's words had made her feel as though she'd received a jolt to her system, warming her skin and making her heart race. She looked up at Jessa, now without the barrier of her sunglasses and feeling much more vulnerable. But seeing the mortification in Jessa's expression, she knew she had to say something. "You make me want ... to ... to say thanks."

Jessa's humiliation turned to anger. "Well, don't do me any favors ..."

"No!" It was Shara's turn to look embarrassed. "I meant that when someone says something nice about the way I look, it always makes me feel like a fraud to thank them for it. After all, my appearance is to a very large extent a genetic accident. I have eyes like my father along with his fine, baby hair. I have a smile like my mother and I'm short, the way she was. If those things happen to be appealing to someone else, I never feel as though it is my place to accept the compliment ... but with you, I *want* to deserve it." As she lamely trailed off, Shara's initial embarrassment escalated to mortification that matched Jessa's.

PART FOUR

Now you know how easy you Hollywood types have it," Jessa teased. She'd joked more in the last hour than she had in months, simply for the reward of hearing Shara laugh.

After the initial awkwardness, Shara had said quietly, "Why don't we start again? I'm Shara. Thank you for agreeing to let me follow you around this summer. I'll try not to get in your way, but I really want to be true to what you accomplished in your early twenties and the life you live now."

Jessa had smiled ruefully. "I'm Jessa. I won't tell you I'm enthusiastic about your following me around, but I do want you to accurately portray what my life is like now."

She hadn't mentioned the portrayal of what she'd gone through in the years that would be the focus of the film and Shara didn't say anything further. She knew, instinctively, that that was the part of her job that triggered Jessa's lack of enthusiasm. She also knew that she could be very persuasive. She had every intention of winning Jessa over, but she had enough insight to know that saying so would not help her efforts with Jessa.

"Good," she'd said instead. At the time she'd thought that the natural thing to do after declaring an unofficial truce would be to shake hands, but she'd been reluctant to initiate physical contact of any kind. It was an odd wariness that made her have to concentrate on schooling her features to avoid frowning.

Shara was a tactile person, probably because of her determination to overcome a childhood where physical displays of affection — hugs, kisses, reassuring touches — had been scarce. Her father was what could kindly be described as old-fashioned, one step removed from "spare the rod and spoil the child". But while he hadn't been physically abusive, he was definitely of the opinion that "children should be seen and not heard", should "speak when spoken to" and should "get on with their studies" without input, beyond criticism for any perceived drop in standards, from the adults in their lives. He'd been emotionally absent, except to provide his brand of advice on how a life should be conducted: frugality, austerity and faith, just about summed up his value system. As a minister he spoke about love and Shara knew he felt it for her, but it had never been mentioned between them. She supposed all that would have been mitigated by the presence and affection of her mother, but her mother had died when she was seven and her father had never remarried.

"May I offer you a drink?" Jessa had noted the anxiety that Shara thought she'd hidden and she acknowledged to herself that Shara was in a bit of an awkward situation — even if it was one of her own making.

"Yes, please." Shara had looked relieved and Jessa's attitude softened further.

"I know it's only afternoon, but I'd suggest something alcoholic. All this meeting of new people can be nerve-wracking. I'd join you, but I'm driving later."

Shara's smile made Jessa glad she'd made the offer. Over the next hour and a half, Shara had had two glasses of wine and Jessa had gone over her travel itinerary. They'd expressed surprise that they'd never run into each other in New York because they enjoyed many of the same restaurants. They'd chatted about Toronto that each had spent several weeks in, Jessa while she'd considered the job with the TSO and Shara while she'd been filming a TV movie in "Hollywood North". They both looked forward to seeing Toronto again, although that was obviously the performance series that caused Jessa the most anxiety.

"I'm sure the audience will love you," Shara had assured her, the empathy in her hazel eyes warming Jessa. "Where will you be staying and will you have time to play?"

Jessa grinned. "On to the important stuff? I have no idea. They've rented me a furnished flat ... apartment." She'd shrugged. As long as the piano they provided was properly tuned, she could adjust to most things.

"So, not the Sutton Place, then?" Shara had mentioned the name of a Toronto hotel that was popular with visiting film stars, especially during the annual international film festival, eliciting the "Hollywood types" comment.

"Oh, don't try to pull the 'deprived musician' stunt. You're a conductor. That's the job with the highest percentage of prima donnas outside the opera world."

It was Jessa's turn to laugh. "My profession is almost 100 per cent male. Can men be prima donnas?"

"The worst," Shara said, her eyes wide. Jessa loved the way her Irish accent made the two words sound. "I once worked with an actor who would not come to the set because there was the wrong brand of mineral water in his trailer. We were filming in Colorado, almost a hundred miles from the closest town – and believe me, that town, population seventy-five, did not have San Pellegrino in stock. We had to film around him for half a day while they hired a helicopter to fly in bloody water."

"I know conductors who are musical prima donnas and have walked out on rehearsals for various reasons – and I was in the audience when Kurt Masur walked out of a performance of the New York Philharmonic at Avery Fisher Hall because the audience was coughing too much. But I don't have a story even close to that."

Shara chuckled. "Can't say I blame him. I've wanted to walk out in a strop a few times myself. Attending a concert is not a basic human right. If you have the flu and can't stop hacking, your attendance is not mandatory. It's so bloody selfish to force other members of the audience to listen to you clear your throat, cough and sneeze, especially during quiet passages where we want, need, to be completely focused on the music."

She was so earnest when she said it that Jessa felt something melt inside her. She desperately wanted to maintain her dislike of everything Shara Quinn stood for, but the woman was gorgeous, funny and spoke about music with genuine passion. "Look, if you don't have any plans, would you like to come with me to my afternoon appointment? It's at a school in Stoke Newington, where I've been sponsoring an extracurricular music program. Well, it's an arts program, but my focus is on the music."

Jessa couldn't believe she'd made the offer and Shara looked startled. Jessa immediately grew defensive. "You don't have to come, you know. I was only ..."

"I'd love to," Shara interrupted, while her mind calculated how late she might be getting home and how she was going to explain to Derek that, rather than showing up late for the barbecue with friends that he was hosting, she'd be missing it altogether.

"Really?" Jessa's eyes sparkled, but then she sensed Shara's carefully hidden ambivalence and realized she'd put her on the spot. "I don't want you to feel an obligation to come just because I've suggested it. I try to drop in on them once a month, schedule permitting, so if you want to have an idea of the sort of things I get up to in my spare time, you can come next month. The only difference is that today I have to give a talk to a group of parents with children who aren't in the program yet. It's very casual and I always have instruments available so the kids can touch them and listen to them. It's nothing particularly exciting, so if you have other plans ..."

"Nothing that can't be changed," Shara said firmly. From a research perspective, seeing Jessa promoting her art with a group of youngsters and parents would be invaluableHele. She ignored the nagging thought that Derek was going to see her absence as symbolic and punish her emotionally for it. And she ignored the even more troubling thought that more time spent in Jessa's company was possibly a greater factor in her decision than any desire to do more research. Shara's professional life isolated her and she had few close friends. To make it worse, the ones she had were scattered across two continents and they, too, had busy lives, so she didn't often get to spend time with them. And it was hard to make new friends when people looked at her and saw the famous actress rather than the woman underneath. With Jessa there was no doubt that the offer to spend more time was aimed at the woman not the actress, whom Jessa seemed to despise on principle. Jessa had extended the invitation as a professional courtesy and Shara had accepted it as such, but both knew it was more of an offer to prolong an afternoon of good company into the early evening for two people who were surprised by how well they got along.

"And another thing," Jessa's voice interrupted Shara's thoughts, "I don't want you taking the piss out of Petula."

Shara looked huffy. "You think I would make fun of a child who's learning to play an instrument?"

"Petula is not a child – although she's less than a year old ..."

Shara's eyes grew wide. "You have a baby?" Her mind boggled at the idea that someone so famous had hidden a pregnancy from the world. She looked around the room and frowned. There was none of the paraphernalia associated with having a baby in the flat. Nor did Jessa's body look as though she had had a baby in the last year. Shara flushed slightly at the realization that she'd noticed that much.

"Petula is not a baby ... although I think she's a babe." She was openly teasing now and Shara glared at her. She laughed at Shara's annoyance before she relented. "Petula's my car. Very 60s retro, and probably not what you're used to, but she's fun to drive. I know you live in Hollywood where it's all Ferraris and DeLoreans ..."

"I drive a very ordinary BMW," Shara replied and Jessa laughed. Shara immediately knew what she was laughing at and smiled. "Ok, so it's not all that ordinary to be able to afford a BMW, but it's a small one that didn't cost the earth." She frowned. "I hate being conspicuous."

"Odd choice of career then, wasn't it?"

"I can't say that I started out to be a, quote, 'movie star'. I fell in love with literature, especially plays like those of Chekhov and Pirandello – and yes, Shakespeare. I was your typical geek who wanted to act. I expected, no hoped, to end up as a crusty, aging former West End character actress giving acerbic quotes to acting students at a good drama school. Most of all I wanted to crawl out of my life into someone else's for minutes or hours at a time." She looked away, hiding a sudden vulnerability.

"Anyway, I never expected to be able to afford the Hollywood lifestyle and Derek says that I still haven't accepted that I can. I prefer to think of it as not wanting to change who I am because of what I do. When I was attending cattle calls for bit parts in BBC dramas and apprenticing as a stage manager so I could have a day job that kept me closer to the profession than waiting on tables, I couldn't afford a car. I promised myself that if I ever got a steady gig, I'd buy myself a shiny black BMW with heating that worked and which would not leave me stranded by the side of the motorway as my last car had when it finally died." She shrugged and then turned back to Jessa. "But I have to admit that I've never named the bloody thing." Her teasing statement again lightened the mood, but Jessa remained moved by what she had said.

"Hmm, well, have you ever considered that your car left you stranded because she felt used? Because you'd never loved her enough to name her?" Jessa teased.

"Even if I'd considered it, I would have dismissed it as neurosis." Shara gave as good as she got, making Jessa laugh again and she found that she liked being able to do that.

"Come on, let's get out of here. Do you need to use the phone?"

"No, I can use my mobile. I'm so used to the stupid thing that I no longer remember people's telephone numbers."

"Petula's in the basement car park. By the way, she's named after Petula Clark, who I was introduced to during my formative years by a mad Swedish nanny who loved British pop, but who had moved to Germany in 1971 where her access to British pop was limited, leaving her in a sort of musical time warp. My fondest musical memories of that time are of my music teacher playing Beethoven's Sonata *Pathétique* to me, because I was sad and he wanted to show how music can express our feelings, and of Pia dancing around the drawing room to *Downtown*. I've loved Petula Clark ever since."

Shara grinned. "And Beethoven, no doubt."

Jessa winked at her. "He's not bad, but I was not about to call my beloved Mini Cooper ragtop anything that sounded even remotely like *Ludwig*."

PART FIVE

Despite her display of nerves before they'd set off for the school, Jessa seemed completely at home as she chatted to a group of opinionated pre-teens about the joys of classical music. Shara, still in her "disguise" and introduced simply as Jessa's friend, observed from a chair near the wall, tempted to write notes with regard to Jessa's body language as she responded to challenging questions from the children. Jessa had draped a white cotton blouse over the tank top, but Shara thought that she still looked more like a rock musician than a classical conductor.

The parents in the room were largely silent. Some of them were fans of Jessa's and somewhat intimidated, or just pleased that she would even talk to their musically reluctant offspring. Others were clearly uncomfortable with the matter, having earlier asked questions about the costs of instruments and lessons, or the time required away from academic studies. The woman who'd introduced Jessa had stepped in to answer the more general questions explaining sadly that the instruments would be provided by the local council and the program's sponsors, but the lessons would require some financial commitments from the parents, despite the assistance of volunteer professionals such as Jessa.

Shara hid a smile as one particularly persistent boy spoke up again, "So to be a conductor, you have to read the music of *all* the musicians, but if they're reading it too and playing it, what's your job?"

Jessa didn't bother to hide her own smile. "Music, written music, is not as exact as, say, physics." There were mocking murmurs of relief from the other children. "It seems that way when you first start to learn it," she went on quickly when her original interrogator seemed about to argue with her, "but there is actually a bit of room for interpretation with things like tempo. The conductor's job is to interpret everything that is written by the composer and work with the musicians to bring his or her interpretation to life. So the orchestra could play without a conductor, but it would take many hours of rehearsal to agree on all the different interpretations that each brings to the performance. Even then, the final performance will differ from what a particular conductor might have envisioned. It would be technically correct if we're talking about a major professional orchestra, but it would be different."

"Does that mean you have to be able to play all the instruments in the orchestra?" a girl at the front asked in wonder.

Jessa shook her head. "Certainly not as well as the members of the orchestra play them, but I have to understand what they sound like and how they work together in the musical composition."

"And you have to make sure everybody plays it all properly?" There was grudging respect in the voice of the boy who'd originally thought conductors were redundant.

Jessa smiled at him and winked, "Well I like to think of it that way, but, in fact, every one of those musicians is a consummate professional. They don't need help from me to play properly, but to provide a uniformed interpretation that is the same for every other musician in the orchestra."

"What would be so different?" Another boy was frowning, still confused.

"Ok," Jessa said, "who can whistle?" Almost every hand shot up in the air. "I'm the composer and I'm going to write down an instruction for the whistlers." She reached for a notepad and wrote on it, then pointed to one of the girls near the front. "Your hand was up, do this." She gestured towards the notepad which said, "whistle loudly". The girl pursed her lips and whistled.

Jessa nodded appreciatively. "Thank you." She turned to the group again and picked out a girl at the back. "Now you. Please follow this instruction." The girl put four fingers in her mouth and whistled loudly.

Jessa nodded and turned to the boy who'd asked the question. "Now you." The boy formed a circle with his thumb and forefinger, inserted it between his teeth and produced a shrill, deafening whistle. There was a smattering of spontaneous applause.

"So there you have it," Jessa explained. "Three people whistling without making any effort to be quiet, yet we have three completely different sounds. A similar thing happens with any subjective instruction like 'pianissimo'. Do you know what that means?" Three or four hands went up and Jessa allowed a boy from the back row to answer.

"Yet, even among professionals, there might be very slight differences in what is understood as 'pianissimo' and those differences can change the sound of one instrument relative to the rest – and thereby the emotion that it being expressed by a piece of music."

"How do you become a conductor?" The question came from a girl seated on the side of the group, whom Shara hadn't noticed previously. "Only, my dad has all these classical CD's and I've never seen a lady conductor before you; and I've never, ever seen a black conductor, lady or man." The girl's dark eyes were fixed on Jessa, the expression in their depths a mixture of curiosity, skepticism and hope.

"There are some black conductors," Jessa confirmed, "but not nearly enough of them." She mentioned a young black conductor who had recently appeared at the Edinburgh festival. "The reality is that if you lived in Germany instead of the UK, you'd probably have heard of him, although he's British. We need more young people of all races, and both sexes, to get excited about music and about conducting. That's one of the reasons I think this program is so great." She looked at the girl, who looked less skeptical following Jessa's honest, if not reassuring, answer. "Are you learning to play an instrument now?"

The girl nodded. "Piano, but I'm teaching myself the guitar, with information I got on the Internet."

Jessa grinned. "Well I hope we don't lose you to rock stardom."

"Especially when you can become a classical star like Jessa," Shara teased, making a few people look around to see who had spoken, although most just laughed – especially when Jessa blushed at the comment.

"I admit to being well known within the relatively narrow circles of classical musicians, but nothing like my friend who made the comment." Turnabout was fair play, Jessa thought. "Ladies and gentlemen, in case you didn't recognize her, that was Shara Quinn, academy award nominee for *Against the State*."

There was a collective gasp and then everyone turned to look more closely at the petite woman with the Irish accent. Jessa grinned as Shara fumbled around fielding questions and giving self-deprecating responses to lavish compliments.

Eventually, Jessa rescued her. "The point is, 'stardom' is an artificial state, largely created by the media. Miss Quinn is an actress, who trained for years and worked on relatively obscure projects in order to perfect her craft. The most enduring stars – in any creative medium – tend to have a talent that they work at and nurture. Most have made tremendous sacrifices for their art."

The conversation wandered back to music, but there was renewed excitement and Jessa thought the minor detour had added glamor to an endeavor that, at its heart, was intended to persuade a group of kids that they should give up time spent doing things with their friends, playing games or watching television and dedicate it to learning a craft which promised only moderate compensation if taken up as a profession, and whose rewards would only come years later with proficiency.

PART SIX

The sun was dipping toward the horizon as Jessa drove towards Highgate Village to take Shara home. They hadn't spoken much after Shara had given Jessa her address and driving directions, each going over the afternoon's events in her own mind. Shara found herself surprisingly moved by what she'd experienced. Jessa's generosity of spirit had been completely at odds with Shara's expectation that she would be a prima donna. As Shara continued to ponder that, Jessa muttered, "Unbelievable" and braked to avoid a liveried minicab that lurched in front of her. Shara smiled; Jessa was a good driver who confidently maneuvered through the evening traffic and showed remarkable patience with the recklessness and inattention of some of the other drivers on the road.

Shara turned to look at her and kept on looking. The late afternoon sun slanted into the convertible and burnished Jessa's skin, turning it a luminous gold. It lightened the irises of her eyes to amber and caused her eyelashes to create a slashing shadow across her cheekbone as she turned her head slightly to check her wing mirror before smoothly changing lanes to get away from the minicab.

Shara knew she was staring, so she looked around for a distraction. The car was show-room clean, except for an Oakley case with Jessa's abandoned sunglasses, and an unopened roll of mints. There was nothing obvious to fiddle with, so she turned on the stereo, curious as to what music Jessa listened to when she was driving. The sound of a Bach concerto filled the air and Shara smiled. "I like your taste in music, but how come the music doesn't sound as good in my car?"

Jessa looked self-conscious. "I had the car stereo designed especially for me. You like Bach?"

"Yeah. But I'm surprised to hear something as pedestrian as the *Brandenburg Concertos* playing in your car. I expected something more intricate and modern, Shostakovich, maybe?"

Jessa grinned. "I get intricate and modern from the other drivers, thanks. I like beautiful and relaxing from my car stereo. Not that I'm ruling out Shostakovich. In fact, when I drive out to my place in the country, I enjoy listening to his *Preludes and Fugues*." She looked at Shara briefly before turning her attention back to the road. "What about you? What do you listen to when you drive?"

"Usually something a damn sight livelier than you, that's for sure!"

"Such as?"

"Opera overtures or excerpts, mainly, and if I listen to Shostakovich, it's more likely to be the third or fifth symphony. The rest of the time it isn't classical music at all, although I'm sure that'll make you think I'm a Philistine."

Jessa felt slightly guilty as Shara's mocking statement triggered the memory of her conversation with Lisa. "It depends on what non-classical music – are we talking Sarah McLachlan or Britney Spears?"

Shara laughed, "*We* are talking Pink Floyd, if you must know. Sarah McLachlan suffers from the same problem as Johann Sebastian," she gestured towards the stereo, "too soothing – at least, unless she's making me cry – neither of which is really what I want when I'm driving."

"What's wrong with soothing?" Jessa downshifted and then accelerated past a people-carrier that had pulled out in front of her only to slow down as though the driver were looking for a parking space.

"This!" Shara replied as she glared at the oblivious driver of the people-carrier. "Idiotic, inconsiderate drivers I can't summon the energy to honk or make rude gestures at, if the music is too relaxing." The Bach piece had ended several minutes earlier and had been replaced by the sound of a solo violin. "I mean, here we are listening to Paganini and it's being ruined by my murderous thoughts about other drivers!"

Jessa laughed and Shara smiled at the sound. "That's because the *Caprice* is too lively," Jessa suggested.

"I'd have to drive with nothing but funeral dirges playing, if that's the case!"

Jessa chuckled. "Probably. But what you've said fits into my theory about traffic accidents."

"Oh yeah, what's that?"

"That more accidents are caused by driving under the influence of music than drugs or alcohol."

"You're joking, right?"

"No, I'm serious. Most boy-racers are listening to loud dance music or rock music. I think there'd be a lot less dangerous driving and fewer accidents, if everyone were forced to listen to Chopin whilst driving."

Shara couldn't help herself, she burst out laughing.

"Laugh all you like, but the NHS could save billions in A&E visits and emergency operations if they followed my suggestion. Do you know that Chopin wrote almost all of his music for the piano? Mostly solo piano? Who wants to peel off or overtake round a corner whilst listening to a solo piano?"

The rest of the trip to Shara's house was taken up with Jessa's tongue-in-cheek explanation of how her theory could be put into practice with Shara asking her questions and finding out that Jessa had put quite a bit of thought into the idea. Eventually Shara joined in and started suggesting Orwellian ways to force soothing music into cars and with Jessa making approving noises and congratulating her for having seen the light.

"That's me on the left." Shara pointed to a Georgian house set back from the road, with a red brick driveway and apron, edged by a neat lawn and artfully placed flowering shrubs.

Jessa pulled into the driveway and when she'd stopped the car she turned to face Shara. "I've had fun," she said simply.

"Me, too." Shara smiled at Jessa, taking in the wind-ruffled hair and warm brown eyes of the woman who made her unaccountably nervous. "Thanks for inviting me along. I know you didn't have to."

Jessa looked away and shrugged. "You're not as bad as I thought, so I felt as though we should spend a bit more time together to give you a chance to see that I'm not the bitch I acted like when we first met."

"You probably had good reason to think the worst," Shara conceded graciously. "Being in the public eye seems to exaggerate the frequency with which people live down to one's expectations. But I really don't have any ulterior motives, Jessa. I just want to understand the routines of your life so I can do justice to you on screen."

Jessa turned back towards her, vulnerability etched on her features. "But I'm a ... flawed human being, Shara. And I'm not sure that having you ... understand the real me ... is in my best interest, if all you want the information for is so you can expose my flaws to millions of strangers."

Shara felt a rush of tenderness and she put a reassuring hand on Jessa's arm. "Oh Jessa, how can you think that? You've read the biography. It's detailed, yes, but it certainly doesn't do any more than hint at the person you are. What I show millions of people will be no more than they could have gleaned from reading the book. No doubt some will come away with a sense of the woman you are, but most will just see the events of your life ten years ago and that's more than enough. With any luck it will reflect some of the choices they've made in their own lives and some of the things people have done to them and they'll be moved by it, but anything I learn about you will be so that I don't show things that are *not* who you are. I don't want to spend time with you so I can expose more of you than you revealed to your biographer."

Jessa stared intently at her for several seconds and then she seemed to come to a decision and she relaxed, nodded enigmatically and looked away. "Okay. Fair enough." Then one corner of her mouth lifted in a small smile and she asked, "Can you cook?"

Shara was taken aback by the question and wondered what that had to do with Jessa letting her into her life, only to have its intimate details played out on the big screen and millions of subsequent DVD's. "What, beans on toast, or five-course gourmet meals?"

"Both."

"Well, I can do more than the first and not as much as the second . . . well, maybe I could manage the second, but I probably only have one thing I could do well for each course. Why?"

"Because if you take part in my pre-tour retreat, I don't want you whingeing about my cooking."

"What pre-tour retreat?"

"Whenever I travel for more than two weeks at a time, I go away for a few days beforehand – to clear my head and to just remind myself of who I am, you know? I go to a place I own in the country where the only music is what I make myself on an old upright piano or a guitar and the only food is what I cook myself. There's a generator for electricity and to work the pump from the well so there's running water, but there isn't much else. In the winter heat is provided by wood-burning stoves or fireplaces – there's no central heating. In fact, there are few mod cons except for the satellite phone I take up. Do you think you can handle it?"

"Of course I can handle it! Just what do you take me for, some hothouse flower? Don't answer that," she hurried on, when Jessa opened her mouth to reply.

"Okay then; I plan to go there four days before I fly to New York."

"And I'm invited?"

"If you think you can hack it."

"Okay, but I have one question: how is the bathroom heated? I know it doesn't matter, since it's warm now, but I'm curious about exactly how rustic your little retreat is."

Jessa smiled. "I forgot to say. There's an electric heater on the wall. Oh, and the guest bedroom is a bit cramped because I store seasonal stuff in there, so I'll even give you the good bedroom."

"It's a deal then." Shara grinned at Jessa, feeling a tingle of excitement in her stomach that seemed out of all proportion to a weekend spent roughing it in the company of a temperamental musician.

"You'd better go in. Unless you collect Porsches, I'll warrant you have guests."

Shara looked around. They'd pulled up behind her car and Derek's car was probably behind the closed doors of the double garage, but to their left and directly in front of the garage, there were two Porsche Boxsters and a Carrera. There were also cars parked along the street, which was unusual for the quiet cul-de-sac in which she lived.

Shara grimaced. "Derek's friends. I don't have any friends who drive sports cars. All the same, I'd better get in there and offer my apologies for blowing them off . . ."

"I'm sure you'll charm them into forgiving you," Jessa replied lightly, but somehow the mention of Derek had changed the atmosphere between them.

"Thanks again, Jessa. I'll ring you during the week so we can make arrangements for the trip to your place in the country."

Jessa smiled, but it seemed forced. "Okay, you have my numbers."

Shara nodded and headed for the front door. She could feel Jessa's eyes on her back and hoped she wouldn't trip. It was only as she put her key in the lock that she considered what Derek's reaction might be towards her spending her last few days in England in some remote cottage with Jessa Hanson.

PART SEVEN

Apprehension gripped Jessa as she pulled into the neat bricked driveway of Shara Quinn's home. In the time that had elapsed since they'd spent the afternoon together, they'd barely spoken – not because they hadn't wanted to, but because both had been snowed under with the details of personal lives that had to be put on hold for more than a month and professional arrangements that had to be tailored to a complicated travel agenda. Shara was to film some promotional interviews for a "making of" documentary while she was in New York and, of course, there had been Derek.

When they'd spoken, Jessa had got the feeling that Derek had not taken the news of Shara's road trip well and the pre-tour retreat had only made the situation worse. Shara hadn't said anything at first, but Jessa had picked up on the fact that something was wrong and, in typical fashion, had said accusingly, "Look, Shara, if you've changed your mind about the cottage, just say so. Don't worry that it's going to affect my decision about the tour."

"I haven't changed my mind. It's just that it's … complicated things for me."

Jessa had opened her mouth to suggest how Shara might quickly rectify the situation, but she'd hesitated. Something in Shara's voice had made her sound almost cornered, as though she'd been close to breaking point and trying to hide it. Jessa had wrapped her hand more tightly around the receiver. She did not want to be affected by Shara Quinn's vulnerability. "Okay, let me rephrase that. If coming away with me will make your life more stressful than staying at home until it's time to leave for the airport, then I'll understand, but I've always found that being out there makes all the stuff that causes my stress seem suddenly abstract. And the guy who takes care of the cottage for me, Leonard, has a goat named Harry, who never gets to meet new people because Leonard is a bit of a loner; so if I get on your nerves, there will be the option of more charming company."

Despite the unaccountable tears that had filled her eyes, Shara had laughed. The gentleness in Jessa's suddenly lowered voice and the deliberate injection of humor to relieve the sadness she thought she'd hidden, warmed her and made her want to thank Jessa. She hadn't, because she'd instinctively known that Jessa would deny having done anything. "Are you actually admitting that a goat is more charming than you are?"

"Harry is not just any goat. He has a very outgoing personality, although he also has a penchant for eating any clothes left hanging too low on the line . . . But nobody's perfect."

Shara had laughed again and they'd gone on to talk about the details of the trip. Jessa had advised Shara to bring hiking boots or sturdy walking shoes, as well as at least one pair of old jeans and a jumper, along with rain gear, because, even in summer, the weather was unpredictable and it could get chilly at night. The conversation had ended on a positive note. Nevertheless, they'd only spoken once since, when Shara had called to make sure Jessa remembered her address and to confirm the time Jessa would be picking her up.

The rain was falling in sheets and Jessa sat in the Land Rover and stared through it at Shara's front door. Shara and Derek's front door. With every sweep of the windshield wipers, the door came into sharp focus and then softened and blurred again for a second in the deluge that nature had seen fit to deliver on the very day that Jessa had a four-hour drive ahead of her. Her feelings about the trip seemed to vacillate with the same rapidity as the view through the windshield. It wasn't that she dreaded having Shara in her hideaway for four days. In fact, it was just the opposite: she found herself feeling undeniable excitement at the prospect and that terrified her.

The door opened and Shara emerged, struggling with a cooler

bag, a tote bag and a huge rucksack.

"Shit." Jessa left the engine running and opened the door of the Land Rover. There was no way Shara was going to get all that stowed without help. She jumped down and trotted to the front door. "You certainly don't travel light," she remarked, heaving the rucksack up onto one shoulder as Shara locked the door.

"I've packed food."

"You know you didn't have to," Jessa said, turning away from Shara and hurrying back to the truck. She opened the back door and moved some cartons around to make room for Shara's things.

Shara appeared at her elbow carrying the other bags. "I wanted to. Besides, if I'm going to be cooking, I want to make sure I have everything I need."

Jessa grunted something unintelligible and then said gruffly, "Get into the car. You're getting soaked. I don't want you getting pneumonia on me when we're miles from civilization."

Shara grinned at her, but dashed to the passenger door and climbed into the vehicle, closing the door behind her and fumbling for the seat belt. She clicked it shut just as Jessa got behind the wheel. "My jacket is water-proof. Besides, I'm not gonna get pneumonia from a few drops of rain. I'm of good Irish stock, not like the lily-livered English musicians you're obviously used to spending time with."

Jessa stared at her, unable to hide her surprise. She couldn't think of another woman she knew who wouldn't be whingeing by now. It was six a.m. Shara's hair was soaked, with rain water literally dripping from the ends, and she'd just had to climb into a vehicle that was built for work, not leisure, so it did not cater for the needs of petite women who were used to traveling in German sports cars. Instead, Shara's eyes sparkled and she touched her tongue to the back of her teeth as she smiled widely at Jessa.

Jessa looked bemused. "You're mad."

Shara's smile faded and she shook her head. "No. I think I was going mad, but it's passed now." She hesitated then said honestly, "I rowed with Derek for days over doing this and I can't say last night was the best night of my life. In fact, I can't remember when I last slept more than four or five hours, because I've agonized so much about … everything. But I think I need a few days away from my life even more than you do right now, so when I woke up this morning, I had no doubts."

Looking closely at her, Jessa saw the redness around her eyes and the slightly swollen lids and thought that perhaps Shara had cried herself to sleep the night before. She felt a sudden burning anger that Derek Finch had made Shara's life so difficult when all Shara wanted to do was the job which paid her so handsomely. Although they barely knew each other, she completely understood the uncompromising depth of Shara's work ethic and the fact that she would take every opportunity to hone her craft, even if it meant spending days in a rustic cottage with the woman she was contracted to imitate for the cameras. How could Derek not understand, even expect, her compulsion to do that? Worse, how could he punish her emotionally for doing it?

Jessa fought back the anger and decided not to comment on Shara's reference to her boyfriend. Derek Finch was now safely behind a closed door and Shara didn't have to see him for four days. "Good," Jessa said instead and concentrated on reversing out of the driveway. "Now I hope you're wearing a kidney belt, because Dusty does not offer as smooth a ride as Petula."

"Dusty?" Shara raised an inquiring eyebrow and Jessa pretended to be serious.

"As in Springfield. A bit more butch than Petula, as I'm sure you can tell. She's your classic green Land Rover Defender. A no-nonsense kind of woman, who's practical about the fact that I cheat on her with Petula, because she knows she gives me something no little urban upstart can."

"A way to get to your cottage?"

Jessa grinned. "Got it in one. The motorway doesn't go anywhere near our destination and even the tarmac stops about five miles short. To complicate things further, there's a stream that takes itself a bit too seriously in this sort of weather, so there might be some pretty damp patches to get through."

"Ooo, an adventure." Shara rubbed her hands together, hoping that Jessa would think she was joking when, in fact, she was feeling a very childish, Enid Blyton-inspired, sense of excitement at the thought of heading off into the wilderness with Jessa. The idea of streams bursting their banks and torrential rain, all observed from the warmth of a Land Rover or an isolated cottage with a roaring fire, made her want to hug herself. Then she remembered the neighbor. "So if your place is so far from everything, where does your neighbor live?"

"His main farm buildings are at the end of the tarmac road, but he has a house that's about halfway between there and my place. Both my cottage and the one where he lives used to be tenants' cottages. He makes really fantastic cheese and sells it to gourmet shops, but after his wife died he scaled back the milk production part of the business, I think because it required more workers when all he wanted was solitude. Without the cows he didn't need the land and his sister-in-law persuaded him to sell it to me — not because he needed the money, but because she thought I needed a bolt hole. I do actually spend a bit of time with Leonard when I'm there for extended periods, but neither of us is exactly social." She smiled. "Harry makes up for it."

"I look forward to meeting Harry." Shara smiled back, before they both looked ahead at the tail lights of the early-morning traffic as the sound of the rain drumming on the roof was punctuated by the rhythmic stroke of the windshield wipers.

PART EIGHT

S hara stretched and burrowed her face into the pillow. Through the laundry-fresh scent of the pillowcase, she thought she could catch a trace of Jessa's scent; this was, after all, Jessa's bed. She sighed and slowly allowed her eyes to open. Jessa's bedroom faced east and the head of her bed was directly under the window. The old-fashioned shutters were closed, so although the curtains were open, only slivers of light fell on Shara's prone form as she enjoyed a lie-in. She wondered what time it was. It was impossible to estimate how long she'd been asleep, but she felt so relaxed that she assumed she'd managed the unaccustomed luxury of eight dreamless hours. She glanced at the watch she'd been too tired to take off the night before. 7:00. She was shocked that it was so early, because she felt ready to face the day – ready to see Jessa.

She frowned. Perhaps it hadn't been all that late when they'd come up to bed, but she doubted it. More likely it was the fact that they hadn't drunk any alcohol, which was responsible for her feeling of relaxation and wellbeing this morning. Or the fact that she had absolutely no responsibilities for the next three days. *And you don't have to see Derek*. She tried to brush aside the unwelcome thought, but it persisted.

As though it were possible to leave thoughts of Derek behind by getting out of bed, she pushed off the covers and got up. The room was cool and she shivered, but it was nice to see the promise of sunshine through the thin gaps in the shutters. Yesterday had been wonderful, even with the rain, but she longed to see what the area surrounding the cottage looked like in the sunshine.

Because of an accident on the motorway, they'd arrived at the cottage just before midday, although the low-hanging clouds had made it seem more like dusk. The temperature had been in the teens and Jessa had lit a fire after they'd unpacked the food, and then showed her around her temporary home.

The cottage was simply furnished, but Shara could tell that everything in it had been carefully chosen. Her gaze had drifted over the upright piano with manuscripts scattered across the top and the guitar case next to a small but gorgeous cupboard in one corner. She'd been charmed by the original stone floor in the kitchen, although Jessa told her that, because of it, she'd be glad of the thick rug that covered half of the floor. When Shara had admired the classic Aga, Jessa admitted that it was new, bought the previous winter from a shop in Beauchamp Place, Knightsbridge. "There was a really ordinary electric cooker in the kitchen that decided to die on me one frosty night. I decided to get something reliable that fitted in with the traditional farm kitchen."

"Good choice," Shara had remarked, looking around. The room boasted a sturdy scrubbed table, high-backed chairs with removable cushions, and cream walls accented by door frames and skirting boards in muted gray-green. There were drawings of herbs and flowers in stained driftwood frames, a shelf of well-used, grease-splattered cookbooks and copper-bottomed pots hanging from old-fashioned hooks. The room was cozy without being crowded, and timeless. "Do shops in Knightsbridge deliver in this area?"

Jessa had groaned. "Don't remind me! They put me in touch with one of their contract installers. He had to customize it slightly to use the bottled gas that is the only thing available out here and it had to be installed. He had a daughter at university in the States and I think I bloody paid for the whole thing! His van got as far as the original farmhouse, we loaded the Aga into Dusty and brought it up here, went back for the rest of his crew and then I had to drive them back to the van – all that in gale-force winds and driving snow!"

Shara had looked at the Aga with new respect. "Are you going to show me how to use it? After that story, I'd hate to be the one to break it the way I have so many cookers in the past . . ."

Jessa had stared at her, unable to hide her horror at the thought, then she saw the teasing twinkle in Shara's eyes and they'd both started to giggle. That had set the tone for the afternoon. They'd teased each other and laughed over a light lunch and then Jessa had suggested a walk.

"Out there?" Shara had been horrified. The rain was still falling heavily on the roof, flowing in rivulets over the windows. Several parts of the unpaved road that led to the cottage had been under water and she could have sworn she'd heard the occasional rumble of thunder.

Jessa had grinned at her. "What happened to all that boasting about good Irish stock? Unless you're made of sugar, you're not going to melt. Put on your Wellies and your cagoule and follow me. The clouds have actually lifted in the last hour and I know a great place we can hike to. Trust me, you'll have a good time. Didn't you like to walk in the rain when you were a kid?"

"Yes, but . . ."

"I swear to you, it is just the same now as it was then, only your parents aren't about to spoil your fun."

Despite her reservations, Shara had gone out into the rain with Jessa. They'd followed a trail through the woods for about half a mile and Shara was surprised at how much the canopy of the trees protected them from the downpour. Shara had been walking slightly ahead of Jessa when they'd emerged into an overgrown field on the far side of a particularly dense thicket. The sky seemed to have brightened and the rain had become more of a drizzle. She stopped abruptly and looked around. The whole world looked freshly washed and leaves shivered in shades of emerald as water pearled and dropped from their tips. The silvery sky lent a slightly surreal atmosphere to the scene and she felt the stillness seep into her.

She'd pulled the hood off her head and listened to the whisper of the rain and the patter of water as it dripped off the trees in the woods behind them. She could smell the dampness of the ground under her feet and she'd closed her eyes to concentrate on the faint, heady aroma. Eyes still closed, she'd turned her face up to the sky and welcomed the soft caress of the rain. Her lips curved into a smile and when she'd opened her eyes, they'd looked straight into Jessa's.

She made her way downstairs, still in the pajama bottoms and t-shirt she'd slept in, having paused only to wash her face and brush her teeth.

Jessa wasn't in the spare bedroom and there was no sound in the rest of the cottage. Jessa was obviously awake, because there was a small fire burning in the grate and the smell of freshly-brewed coffee mixed with something unrecognizable, but pleasant and slightly exotic, lingered in the air.

She noticed that the cupboard in the corner was open and there was a hand-woven rug in front of it. She was surprised to see that the beautifully carved doors had concealed what looked like a tiny altar. She saw the wisp of white smoke from the incense burner and identified it as the source of the exotic scent. The front door was ajar and she found Jessa sitting on the front step looking out at the scene in front of the cottage. The cottage was located on a gentle grassy rise dotted with wildflowers, which gave way to the woods they'd walked in, about fifty yards from the front door.

To the left was the rutted driveway where the mud-spattered Land Rover sat, but Jessa's attention seemed to be on the ancient oak tree that stood at the edge of the clearing. She was utterly still, sitting in a pool of early-morning sunshine that burnished her skin and picked out the flecks of silver in her sleep-tousled hair. Jessa's limbs were bare. She'd slept in a vest and faded paisley boxers and hadn't bothered to put anything on over them, despite the fact that the sun had not yet dragged the temperature very far into double digits. Shara felt an almost overwhelming urge to sit on the step behind Jessa and wrap her arms around her waist to pull her into her own warmth. She could almost feel Jessa lean back into her body and smell the clean scent of her hair. Her breasts tingled as she imagined Jessa's weight relaxing into them, yet the feeling that the image invoked was not primarily sexual. *Well it wouldn't be, you're straight* she reminded herself, shaken, nonetheless, by the degree to which she was drawn to Jessa Hanson. *It's because you're literally go-*

ing to inhabit her skin in a few months . . .

"Good morning." Jessa's voice startled her.

"How . . .?"

"I felt the warm air when you opened the door." *And I sensed your presence long before you opened the door.*

"I – I don't want to disturb you if you're meditating."

Jessa didn't turn to face her. "I'm not. Would you like some coffee? There's some on the Aga."

"Yes, please. Would you like me to bring you some?"

Jessa shook her head. "I'll have some herbal tea later. Why don't you get your coffee and come and sit with me?"

Because I'm not sure I can do that without touching you. Shocked at her own thoughts, Shara backed away from the door. "It's . . . it's still a bit chilly this morning. I think I'll have my coffee indoors, but thanks for the offer."

As she withdrew and pulled the door shut behind her, Shara got the feeling that Jessa was smiling.

PART NINE

With one full day still to go, the rest of the world felt a million miles away from the cottage as Shara and Jessa sat down to dinner. It was the warmest night yet and the front and back doors were open, allowing a refreshing breeze to flow through. Both doors were screened, not just to keep Harry out, but also because Jessa confessed that she was not particularly fond of insects. Shara teased her about it and regaled her with insect stories from three months on location in Laos.

"I've never been there." Jessa sat back in her chair and looked intrigued. "I spent several months in Thailand just before Stephanie and I broke up, but we were told that it was too dangerous because of all the unexploded bombs and land mines from the American bombing campaign."

Shara closed her eyes briefly as she savored a bite of the chocolate mousse Jessa had made from scratch. "Mmm ... you are good."

I'd like to show you exactly how good I am, Jessa thought, her nipples hardening at Shara's sensual reaction to the taste and texture of good food. "Thanks," she said instead, looking down at her own plate. "It was the least I could do, since you made such a delicious dinner."

"My pleasure ..." Shara's voice faded as Jessa looked up again. Their eyes met and she found herself unable to look away. They'd lit candles and made a special effort for their final dinner together. Tomorrow there would be the long drive back to London and last-minute packing and they wouldn't see each other again until they met at the airport the following day. Their time together had been special and the decision to celebrate it had been made without a formal discussion.

Jessa was wearing a white cotton shirt with the sleeves rolled up to reveal tanned forearms and her skin seemed to glow against the pale cotton. Her hair had been gelled, but one curl now fell onto her forehead and Shara felt the urge to brush it away. She imagined her fingertips lingering on the smooth skin of Jessa's forehead and something in Jessa's warm, dark eyes told her that Jessa could feel her need for physical contact, however minor. She forced herself to look away because looking at Jessa was making it hard for her to swallow.

She hated when this happened – this physical awareness and tension. Most of the time they were together it wasn't like this. They spent hours comfortably talking about their lives and experiences; she found herself feeling hungry for details of Jessa's life and what made her the woman she was. She told herself it was professional curiosity, but she knew it wasn't. She knew it because she also found herself wanting to share reciprocal details with Jessa, telling Jessa things she'd never told anyone – not even Derek, or her best friend Elise.

The night before, they'd lit a fire outdoors and had a picnic on a blanket under the stars and she'd talked about the trauma of losing her mother. When she'd looked up, Jessa had been crying. Not sobbing and probably not even aware of the two fat tears that glistened on her cheeks. That silent empathy had unlocked something inside of Shara and she'd become aware of a pain that she'd carried for more than twenty years without ever acknowledging it existed. She'd reached for Jessa's hand, offering comfort and receiving it instead. Something had passed between them at that moment that Shara had no reference point for. Some logical part of her brain shouted that she should be scared by that, because whatever connection she had with Jessa Hanson was clearly out of her control, but as they'd continued to hold hands and stare silently into the flames, all she'd felt was safe.

"It's okay, Shara."

Jessa's gentle reassurance forced her to look away from the remnants of chocolate mousse and back at the woman who seemed to be able to shake her to the core. "How do you do that?" Shara asked in a voice just above a whisper.

"You can do it too, you know." Jessa smiled.

"What? Read your mind?"

Jessa nodded. "Some of the time, yeah." She studied Shara's flustered expression for a few seconds before saying, "Tell me more about Laos."

Shara let out the breath she'd been holding and relaxed. "It's where I learned to speak French."

"*French?*"

"Yes, surprisingly. Before the French colonized Vietnam, they thought they could get to China via the Mekong River from Laos. During their brief, failed attempt to do that, they influenced architecture, culture and language. There are many old people in Laos whose first or second language is French. I didn't have a big part in the film, but I had to sit around a lot, waiting to film the scene where I was gruesomely killed, so I hired a French tutor."

"*Comment est-ce-que tu l'as entretenu?*"

How have you kept it up? Shara's eyes widened because Jessa asked the question in flawless, unaccented French.

"*Mon amie Elise a une maison de campagne en Provence et j'y passe quelques jours chaque été. Ça me revient.*" Shara replied before adding in English, "You're full of surprises."

Jessa shrugged. "I had a pretty nomadic childhood, first because my father was in the navy and then later because of my music. Children learn to adapt." She offered Shara a teasing smile, "I can ask for directions to the toilet in many different countries without shouting at the natives in English like the typical Brit abroad."

Shara laughed, "I have to make do with sign language, unless it's English, French, Serbo-Croat or Gaelic."

"*Serbo-Croat?*" Jessa asked in much the same tone she'd asked about Shara's French.

Shara laughed. "Don't ask. I'm sure you have a past relationship you'd rather not talk about."

As if on cue, the satellite phone rang. They both froze and then

Jessa scowled. "That will be for you." If it was Derek on the phone, it would be the third time he'd called in as many days, despite the fact that Shara had told him the telephone number was only to be used in emergencies.

"It's your phone, I think you should answer it." Shara replied evenly, hoping frantically it was someone ringing Jessa.

Jessa pushed the chair back from the table, stood up and stalked into the living room to answer the phone. "Yes?" She knew she was being rude, but she didn't care.

"Hello, I'm calling for my fiancée, Shara Quinn."

Fiancée? Jessa felt her heart begin to pound almost painfully, but her voice remained cool. "How are you?"

Derek hesitated, obviously thrown off by the question. "I'm er . . . fine, thank you. How are you?"

"I'm okay, thanks. In fact, everything here is fine, so I'm pleased to say that I have had no occasion to use the emergency phone in three days."

Shara snatched the telephone away from Jessa, because she knew her well enough to know that if allowed to continue, the conversation would not end well. "Hiya Derek."

She listened for a while as Jessa continued to glare at her, before saying, "No, I don't think so . . . Look, Derek, I think she's got a point. No, it's not because of the cost of the calls . . ." At that, Jessa rolled her eyes, walked away and began clearing the table at considerable risk to the dishes.

Shara moved away from the noise, pushing open the screen to step outside the front door and continue the conversation in private. By the time she came back, Jessa was nowhere to be found. She went out the back door to find Jessa at the end of the small vegetable garden, vigorously working the evening's scraps into the compost heap. "Jessa . . ."

Jessa finished what she was doing and brushed past Shara to walk into the kitchen and wash her hands. The dishes had already been washed and were draining on a rack. She started to dry them.

"Don't you think that your anger is out of all proportion to the situation?" Shara asked her.

"The *situation*? Yes, I suppose anger isn't appropriate. In fact, congratulations are in order, aren't they, since your *fiancé* just rang? What was his emergency? Picking out a pattern for the registry at Harrods?"

"Not that it's any of your business, but Derek only asked me to marry him recently and it just hasn't come up in any of our conversations. I don't know why the hell you're so angry about his calling, even if it wasn't an emergency!" Shara was starting to get annoyed. "What exactly is your problem?"

The plate Jessa had been drying clattered onto the draining board, but, by some miracle, did not break. "Don't pretend you don't know, Shara."

"Know *what?*" Shara was exasperated.

Jessa grabbed Shara's hand. "This!" She placed Shara's hand over her own breast and held it there.

For a split second neither of them moved, then Shara's stunned expression turned to one of horror and she pulled her hand away, just as Jessa released her grip. The sudden lack of resistance made Shara stumble back a few feet before she turned on her heel and ran out of the kitchen. Several seconds later, Jessa heard the door of the master bedroom slam.

PART TEN

Shara lay on the bed and waited for her heartbeat to return to normal. Her body racked with conflicting emotions and physical awareness. She couldn't believe what Jessa had just done. Again she had no reference point for something that had happened between her and Jessa. And this time it was something outrageous. But as the thought came into her head, another thought chased it away: what Jessa had done had not been outrageous by some standards. Unexpected, yes, socially taboo, perhaps – at least in some social circles. But a lesbian alone for four days with a woman who was obviously fascinated with her, had thought that the woman felt more than fascination and forced the issue.

Shara turned onto her stomach and covered her head with a pillow. She couldn't deny that Jessa fascinated her. It wasn't just the woman's unselfconscious beauty, it was her quirky sense of humor, her intelligence, her kindness and the graceful stillness with which she could hold herself. Over the last few days Shara had observed Jessa as she'd meditated, hiked, or curled up with a book on the couch. They'd talked about life and about music. They'd sometimes disagreed and Shara had seen evidence of the fiery temper Jessa had almost allowed free rein in their first encounter. Shara's temper matched Jessa's, but they always seemed to see the humor in their passionate disagreements and would start to giggle mid-argument. Or the argument would end, resolved or with agreement to differ, with no lingering negative feelings. That only added to Shara's fascination with Jessa and the oddly intimate friendship that had sprung up so quickly between them.

Friendship, fascination, *attraction*?

No! Shara rolled onto her back and squeezed her eyes shut. She was straight. Derek wanted to marry her. She had a successful career, a charming, handsome, not to mention independently wealthy, boyfriend. A good life. She was not *attracted* to a woman. It was just empathy. It was what made her a good actress. So what if she found herself drawn to the way Jessa's clothes molded themselves to her body or revealed smooth expanses of skin? So what if she enjoyed looking at Jessa: the expressive eyes, the slightly crooked smile and the soft lips? So what if, when they'd been cooking and she'd felt Jessa's breath on her skin, her body had reacted in an unmistakable and elemental way? Wasn't it only natural to be physically curious about what made the subject of her close observation tick?

Shara rolled on her side and pressed the pillow against her head, before rocking back to stare at the ceiling. *Stop kidding yourself. You're not going to marry Derek. You love him, but you're not even sure you like him. Your life is only good in superficial ways, which is why you couldn't wait to get away from it and from Derek. Your fascination with Jessa Hanson isn't the problem, it's a symptom. And Jessa had no right to exploit it!*

As she lay there her mind focused again on what Jessa had done and she decided that in the light of her emotional vulnerability, Jessa had, indeed, acted outrageously. The more she thought about it the angrier she became and she started to plan the showdown she intended to have with Jessa about it.

She was just working herself into a real temper over what had happened, when the music penetrated her consciousness. It was a solo piano piece, precise, deliberate, gorgeous. Shara's first impression was that Jessa had turned on the stereo, then she remembered that there was no stereo in the cottage. Jessa was playing the piano.

Slowly, Shara felt the anger flow out of her body as Jessa continued to play. She thought the music sounded like Rachmaninov, but she didn't know enough to be sure. What she did know was that

Jessa had a formidable talent as a pianist. She didn't make a conscious decision to move, but she found herself being pulled towards the compelling sound that Jessa was coaxing from what had looked like an ordinary upright piano before Jessa turned her attention to it.

She closed her eyes and imagined Jessa's long, slender fingers racing over the keys with effortless skill.

She cut off that train of thought as soon as it started and almost raced down the stairs to the living room. She hesitated in the doorway and just stared at Jessa, whose eyes were closed and whose brow was slightly furrowed as she played. As Shara watched, her fingers stilled on the keys and she lifted her hands. Her frown faded, although her eyes remained closed.

Eventually, her fingers drifted down towards the keys and the opening bars of Chopin's prelude number 15 in D flat major drifted towards Shara. The piece was called *The Raindrop*. Shara had played it in the past, but never from memory and never like this. Under Jessa's skilled fingers the piano imitated the insistent sound of rainfall.

Jessa's head fell forward, but in the soft light of the lamp near the sofa, Shara could see the small smile on her face and knew that Jessa was remembering their first day and their walk in the rain. She also knew that Jessa was doing it to replace the memory of what had just happened between them with something better.

Shara, too, found herself dragged back to that rainy afternoon.

They hadn't spoken much, although Jessa had pointed out a clump of bushes where a family of rabbits lived. She'd said that on sunny days, if she stayed really still and was very patient, they would eventually come out to play or feed. They'd crossed another wooded area and when they came out on the other side they could see a cottage that was about the same size as Jessa's. Leonard hadn't been at home, but Shara had met Harry. Jessa had handed her some slices of apple she'd brought along in a plastic bag in her pocket and Shara had fed them to Harry, immediately earning his affection.

Shortly afterward, they'd begun the walk back. Harry had set out with them, but the rain had started to fall more heavily and with a protesting "baa!" he'd turned around and, to Shara's amusement, run back to the lean-to at the side of the cottage where he'd been lying down when they'd first seen him.

"He doesn't like to get wet, which is why he has to sleep outdoors. In the winter, Leonard lets him sleep in one of the farm buildings. Harry doesn't like cows, but he hates baths more, so he isn't exactly sweet-smelling."

Shara insisted that she hadn't noticed and Jessa had rolled her eyes. They'd joked as they'd walked away from the cottage, but Shara could see why Jessa liked Harry, with his pot-belly, vocal demands to be scratched behind the head and his aversion to baths.

As they'd walked through the woods, they'd again grown quiet and Shara had simply enjoyed the rain on her face, the rhythm of their feet on the ground and the feeling of her own heart beating as the sweet, rain-washed air filled her lungs.

Through all these things she'd remained acutely aware of her companion. Jessa's long legs eating up the distance and the grace with which she navigated obstacles in the path. She obviously knew the area very well and led Shara to a small clearing on a hilltop that offered panoramic views of the rolling hills around them. Visibility wasn't particularly good, so they couldn't see the cottage and Jessa had obviously been disappointed. "Next time," she'd said.

Shara had grinned inanely at Jessa's assumption that she'd be invited back to the place Jessa had referred to as her special spot.

"How many people have you brought here?" she'd asked on impulse.

The question seemed to startle Jessa. She'd paused and looked into the distance before turning her head so she could look directly into Shara's eyes. "No one but you," she'd replied softly.

PART ELEVEN

They'd stood on the craggy hilltop just looking at each other for several minutes before Jessa had said, "Come on, I know a short-cut back to the cottage. But it's a bit rough; you'll have to prove what a tough Irish woman you are." Without waiting for Shara, she'd walked off to the right and jumped off the rocky edge.

Shara had gasped. Jessa had bent her knees when she'd landed on an outcropping of rock just below where they'd stood and when she'd straightened, Shara could see her from the chest up, so she'd only jumped about three feet. Nevertheless, when Shara looked down, she could see that the ledge was only about two feet wide and beyond that was a steep rocky path that she would risk rolling down if she missed her footing when she jumped. It would have been bad enough if Jessa hadn't been taking up space on the slanted, rocky shelf. Shara had decided that it would be madness to jump and risk breaking something, miles away from help and a month before filming was to begin. "Uh-uh. I'll walk back the way we came."

"You'll get lost. Come on, don't be a baby."

"What if I slip? It's at least twenty yards to the bottom of that hill, there are rocks everywhere and I don't think I'd enjoy having the trees at the bottom stopping me from rolling, either!"

"Shara, you're not up here alone. Trust me. Take my hand, I won't let you fall." She reached up, but still Shara hesitated. "Darling, I won't let you get hurt." Jessa was no longer teasing because she sensed that Shara's unease was genuine.

Shara had searched Jessa's features and seen only honesty and re-assurance. As much as Jessa joked with her, she'd known that this time she was serious. She'd grasped the proffered hand, surprised by its warmth but not by its strength.

She'd looked away from Jessa only long enough to gauge the distance and then she'd jumped, bending her knees when she landed as she'd seen Jessa do. Her boots had slipped on some small, loose stones and Jessa had held her to prevent her from slipping further, although she'd been in no danger of tumbling down the path.

She'd looked gratefully at Jessa, surprised to find their faces only inches apart. "Thank you." Shara's voice had trembled as she'd looked at Jessa, her eyes roaming over Jessa's smooth skin, faintly flushed from the brisk climb, and the warm brown eyes with their lashes spiked with the rain.

"My pleasure." Jessa had been so close that Shara had felt the whisper of her breath on her face. Shara's gaze focused on the lips that had spoken the words so softly and a small sound escaped from her throat at the strength of the urge she felt to press her own mouth against them. She'd turned blindly away and would have fallen if Jessa had not pulled her back.

She'd refused to meet Jessa's eyes, but could feel them on her face. They were both breathing audibly. She'd wanted to think it was because of the close call, but the throbbing of her pulse points told her otherwise. What she'd felt had been the rush of arousal, not the rush of adrenaline.

As the final notes of *The Raindrop* sounded, she remembered that moment of acute physical awareness in the rain and walked, inexorably drawn, towards the woman who had played the piece so exquisitely.

"I'm sorry." Jessa's voice reached her across the sudden silence and it never occurred to Shara to wonder how Jessa knew she was in the room. "You're my guest and I should have just let it go."

"Jessa, there's nothing to let go," she lied desperately.

Jessa still wasn't looking at her, but she saw Jessa close her eyes. Shara wanted to cry.

"Fine," Jessa said stiffly.

"Jessa, if you pursue this, I won't be able to travel with you. Is that what you want? Because if it is, all you have to do is say so."

"According to you, there's nothing to pursue," Jessa retorted sarcastically. She turned to face Shara, but when she saw the lost, pained expression on Shara's face, her expression softened. "Okay, Shara, we'll do things your way. But since Chopin will probably remind me of you for the rest of my life, would you like to play something for me?"

"What was the piece you played earlier?"

"Rachmaninov's *Variations on a theme by Chopin*."

"It was wonderful."

"Thanks." Jessa moved to one end of the piano stool, making room for Shara. "Now, what are you going to play for me?"

"A nocturne? Although, I have to warn you, I haven't played this from memory for years and, even then, I was never even close to being as good as you."

"That's why I'm here. To enjoy the music you make and to help you with your technique, if you think you need it."

For some reason that statement made Shara shiver before she sat next to Jessa, close enough for their thighs to touch. After what had gone on between them, she knew that Jessa would not force her to deal with whatever it was that drew them together, so she relaxed, enjoyed their closeness and began to play Chopin's Nocturne no. 2 in E flat major, with almost no hesitation.

PART TWELVE

By the time they got to Shara's home it was as dark as it ever got in London. This time the traffic was not to blame for their late arrival, nor had they overslept.

Shara had been up by 7:00 and had gone downstairs to find Jessa sitting in a full lotus position in front of the altar with her hands resting on her thighs, her eyes closed and her lips slightly parted. Jessa's posture was perfect and the only movement in her body was the barely perceptible rise and fall of her stomach as she breathed. A day earlier, Shara had asked her if she swallowed when she was meditating and she'd explained that she'd been taught to touch the tip of her tongue to the roof of her mouth to inhibit the production of saliva, but after a few years she usually slipped quite easily into a meditative state and it simply was not an issue.

Remembering that conversation and so many others about things that were important to each of them, Shara had left Jessa to meditate and walked into the kitchen to make coffee. She'd known by then that Jessa didn't drink any stimulants or alcohol on the days she meditated and that included every day she was at the cottage, but there was a limit to what Shara would give up for a film.

She had also set out the infuser and Jessa's favorite earthenware mug and filled the kettle with water, so that Jessa could have her herbal tea as soon as she was ready, then gone up to shower while the coffee was brewing.

Later that morning they'd walked down to see Harry, their pace unhurried despite the threatening skies. Shara had secretly hoped that it would rain, as it had on their first day, but in keeping with the muted turbulence of their relationship, the gray clouds had obscured the sun and raced each other across the sky, but not allowed themselves to release their burden over the wild meadows and woods through which the two women had walked.

They'd returned, famished, with Harry at their heels, made up a picnic lunch in defiance of the clouds and eaten outdoors, only to find that Harry could be a lot more ruinous to an impromptu picnic than an army of ants. They'd laughed about it and Shara had slipped Harry the occasional illicit sandwich or piece of apple, giggling when Jessa had scolded her and Harry, who'd looked suspiciously as though he was smirking.

When they'd gone indoors to put away or compost the remains of their lunch, they'd returned to find Harry making dessert out of the corner of the blanket they'd been sitting on. Jessa had told him off and he'd deliberately turned his back to her, flicked his tail and left. Shara, having watched the whole thing from the front steps, laughed until tears ran down her face, earning herself a stern glare from Jessa, until Jessa suddenly saw the humor in the situation and what had been intended as a reprimand to Shara turned into a snort and a giggle, making Shara laugh even harder. Finally, she managed to say to Jessa, "At least I know what goats do in the absence of a middle finger!"

They'd spent the early afternoon making sure the cottage was squared away. Shutting off taps and switches and making sure that anything perishable was packed up or put in the compost heap. Shara was surprised at how little "real" rubbish there was to take back with them, once they'd separated paper and cardboard and rinsed tins and bottles for recycling, and put the organic things into the compost heap. They'd worked in companionable silence. Jessa said that she usually took dirty linen back to London, but Shara persuaded her to do the laundry at the cottage. Why have a washing machine and dryer and take stuff back to London? She hadn't exactly had to twist Jessa's arm, so she'd felt less guilty about having Jessa do housework that was probably alien to her at home, just so they could spend a few more hours together. By mid-afternoon they'd both run out of excuses and climbed into the Land Rover for the drive home.

The outside security lights were on, but the house itself was in darkness. Since it was after 10:00, Shara surmised that Derek was sulking and so had made sure he wasn't home to greet her. An empty house was marginally better than a petulant boyfriend, but neither prospect made Shara want to hurry out of the Land Rover.

"Thanks for a wonderful mini-holiday . . ."

"I guess I'll see you tomorrow . . ."

They spoke at the same time into the awkward silence that had descended between them, punctuated by the soft sound of the piano from a Shostakovich fugue.

"I'm glad I didn't ruin everything by . . ." Jessa didn't know what to say. *Putting your hand on my breast* would only revive the embarrassment for both of them, but she was too honest to pretend nothing had happened. Should she explain why she'd done it? *I see you trying to ignore and deny the way you look at me and I don't want you to marry some bloke as part of that denial! I know you want to touch me. How could I not, when there are times I want to touch you more than I want to draw breath?* But she knew that to explain would be the verbal equivalent of the physical action which had almost destroyed the atmosphere between them.

"You didn't ruin anything." Shara's simple statement saved Jessa from having to finish what she'd been saying. "Anyway, thanks." With that, she reached for the door handle and jumped to the ground.

Jessa got out and went to the back to help her retrieve her things. "I can help you carry your bags to the house, if you like."

"No, I'm okay. Listen, why don't we unload the rubbish and recyclables here? We have these huge bins and it would probably be easier than hauling everything over to your place."

"Sure. Thanks."

Together they carried the bin-liners and their contents to the side of Shara's house. There was only indirect illumination from the security lights, but it was more than enough to allow them to put things in the appropriate containers.

When they'd finished, Jessa asked, "Do you need a lift to the airport?"

"No, thanks. There's a service I use that's excellent, but it's sweet of you to offer."

"That's me," Jessa said wryly, "sweet."

"You are, you know," Shara insisted, studying Jessa in the dim light.

"I'd better go." Jessa's voice was soft.

"I'll see you tomorrow at about 11:00?" Their flight was at 1:00.

"Yeah." Suddenly Jessa felt self-conscious.

Shara stepped closer and they hugged. For several seconds Jessa closed her eyes and savored the feeling of Shara's warm, firm body pressed against her. She'd longed for this. From the moment Shara Quinn had turned her face up to the rain on that first day, she'd wanted this. When Shara had made that small noise in her throat as they'd stood at the top of the hill and looked at Jessa's mouth as though she'd like to eat her alive, Jessa had wanted it more. And over the next three days, as they'd shared meals, quiet times and lively discussions, she'd grown to want it with almost desperate intensity.

Eventually they pulled apart, but didn't step away from each other. Shara looked up at Jessa and the longing she saw in Jessa's expression made her eyes fill with tears. She made the soft throaty sound that Jessa remembered from that moment in the rain.

Jessa leaned down just as Shara reached up to put her hand behind Jessa's neck and raise her mouth to Jessa's.

As their mouths met for the first time, they both moaned. One kiss turned into two and then three. Jessa's hands roamed restlessly over Shara's back and Shara tangled one hand in Jessa's hair as the other voluntarily did what Jessa had forced it to do only one day earlier. Jessa gasped into Shara's mouth and Shara swallowed the small sound, taking it as encouragement to stroke Jessa's peaked nipple with her thumb.

Less than ten yards away, a car door slammed and they broke apart, breathing heavily and staring at each other in mute shock.

PART THIRTEEN

S hara showed the agent at the desk her boarding pass and was welcomed to the airline lounge. She hadn't seen Jessa in the first class check-in zone, so if she wasn't there, she was either taking advantage of the duty-free shops or she was late. Jessa hadn't struck her as the type of woman who would risk missing a flight to such an important business engagement, or the type to brave the summer hordes for last year's Gucci designs, so Shara looked nervously around the lounge for her travel companion.

Jessa was wearing dark blue jeans, thonged sandals and a pale blue cotton shirt with the sleeves rolled up. Her long legs were stretched out in front of her, crossed at the ankles to show off a perfect pedicure, and resting on a Louis Vuitton bag. Her sunglasses were pushed back into her hair and her nose was buried in a copy of Jeanette Winterson's *Lighthousekeeping*. There was a summer-weight cashmere blazer thrown over the seat next to her, but without it she looked more like a graduate student than a classical musician, let alone a conductor.

A very elegant and very beautiful student, Shara admitted silently.

"It's her best book for a long time, isn't it?"

Jessa's head snapped up and Shara's heart started to pound at the way Jessa's expression changed when she caught sight of her.

Jessa's eyes lit up when she looked at Shara, and she took her time to look. Shara was wearing cream linen trousers and an emerald cotton top that brought out the green in her eyes. The casual jacket that matched her trousers was slung over her arm and her usual, oversized handbag was resting on the carry-on bag she pulled behind her. She, too, had pushed her sunglasses up over her hair and a few soft strands fell onto the lenses. She couldn't help the small smile that automatically curved her lips when she looked at Jessa, despite the apprehension in her wide eyes.

Jessa noticed everything: the high-heeled sandals that added inches to her petite frame, the full breasts under her tailored shirt, the contrast of golden skin against emerald cotton and the hungry way she looked at Jessa's lips before meeting her eyes. Jessa also noticed the way her smile faded, to be replaced by a look of near desperation that prevented Jessa from saying anything in acknowledgement of what had gone on between them the night before.

"Yes, it is. I quite enjoyed *Gut Symmetries* despite what the critics had to say about it," Jessa replied to the comment Shara had made in lieu of a greeting, "but I haven't been too impressed by much since then. Okay, let me qualify that: even on her worst day, Winterson can come out with sentences, paragraphs and ideas that stun me with their brilliance, but she hasn't written anything that pulls those ideas together as well as this for a long time."

"I agree." Shara nodded as she took the seat on the opposite side of Jessa from where the blazer had been flung, "although I preferred her collection of essays on art to *Gut Symmetries*."

"*Art Objects?* Yeah, I didn't always agree with her, but she has a remarkable mind and it was interesting to read her opinions." Unable to resist, she asked Shara, "I don't suppose you've read *Oranges are Not the Only Fruit?*"

"Yes," Shara responded, looking away, "I have. My father wasn't quite as mad as the character's mother, but there were enough similarities to make it quite a disturbing read for me." When she saw Jessa's puzzled look, she continued, "My father is a minister – and a single parent."

Jessa nodded and didn't ask the obvious follow-up question about similarities in the sexual orientations of Shara and the lesbian protagonist of Winterson's first novel. It was so glaring an omission from Shara's reaction to the book that it threw Jessa. *How deeply has she hidden this?* she wondered and looked away from Shara to the huge plasma screen television, thankfully muted.

"Shara, about last night … did things go okay with Derek?" As soon as she'd asked the question Jessa's stomach lurched. Did she really want to hear the answer? Did she want to hear that Shara and her boyfriend, her fiancé, had made up and enjoyed a farewell fuck while Jessa had been lying alone and sleepless in her flat?

It had never occurred to Shara and Jessa that Derek would think they were inside the house. Unfortunately, thinking that his fiancée is alone with a lesbian at 10:30 p.m. with all the lights off is not likely to put a man in a good mood – especially when said fiancée has just spent four days in an isolated cottage with that same lesbian. The house had almost shaken on its foundations with the force with which Derek slammed the front door behind him.

"I'd … I'd better go." Shara's voice had been husky as though she hadn't used it for a long time.

The sound had played along Jessa's nerve endings, but she'd managed to nod. "Do you want me to come wi … come in with you?" Jessa had fumbled for words and heard Shara's indrawn breath. The question that hadn't been spoken had tortured them both. Do you want me to come with you?

"I'll be okay. He'll calm down. He's upset because he feels neglected, but he's got to understand that …" But she hadn't finished, because she hadn't been sure what she'd wanted Derek to understand.

Jessa had reluctantly agreed to leave, but only after Shara promised to text her to say that Derek was taking everything in his stride. "I'm going to go to Starbucks in Hampstead High Street. It's less than ten minutes' drive from here. I'm not going to go home until you text me or phone me to tell me that everything is okay."

Half an hour and a very large chai latte later, Jessa's phone had vibrated.

"Hello?"

"It's okay, Jessa, you can go home. The only reason I didn't ring sooner is that I needed privacy and Derek's been in the room."

"Where is he now?"

"I said I wanted a Thai takeaway. I don't, but it will take him at least half an hour to get it." Jessa could hear a smile in her voice and had surmised that it was a wry one.

"I'm sitting in Dusty outside Starbucks, having my second chai and a sticky pastry."

"Jessa, you haven't had any caffeine for four days! That much caffeine and sugar will keep you up all night."

"Nothing wrong with staying up all night." Jessa's voice had been low, almost hoarse.

"Even if you have a transatlantic flight the next day?" The changing timbre of Jessa's voice had sent a shiver down Shara's spine.

"I want to make love to you, Shara." The words had caused an instant feeling of arousal in Shara and she'd emitted a soft gasp. "If I had my way, I'd make love to you all night long . . . We'd arrive at Heathrow exhausted and you'd still be shaking with little aftershocks from having come so hard."

"Oh, God, Jessa, please don't do this," she'd begged, but her body had been tense with a sexual craving so strong that it made her shake and her hand had gripped the phone so tightly she'd wondered afterward why the hard plastic hadn't shattered.

"Do what? Tell you how I feel? Does it make you uncomfortable to know how much I want you? Are you repelled by the thought?" Shara had said nothing. What she'd felt was not repulsion. "Or are you uncomfortable because you hear me saying what you feel? Do you know what kissing you was like for me, Shara? I felt your soft lips against mine, felt you drawing my tongue into your warm mouth and stroking it with yours, felt your body moving against mine and your hand on my breast and it was the most intense sexual experience of my life." Shara whimpered. "Being in your arms felt *right*: as though it was somewhere I was always meant to be. And while it was happening, my soul told me that you felt everything I felt. Did you feel it, Shara?"

"It doesn't matter what I feel." Jessa had heard the tears in Shara's voice and even the memory of that moment made her hurt. "My life is . . . complicated right now, Jessa, and we, I've just made a commitment to a lot of people."

"Like Derek?" Jessa's words had revealed the raw pain she'd felt.

"Derek is one of the people I owe consideration," Shara had admitted carefully. *And my agent and Peter Garofolo and the hundreds of*

*people who have already been employed by this film project and whose live-
lihoods could be jeopardized by a scandal when production has not even begun. I know Derek and he can be vindictive. He would make what you faced
with Stephanie look like a nursery school picnic.* "Not everything is black
and white, Jessa."

"But some things are. Some things are basic and elemental and
honest." Shara had said nothing, but Jessa could hear her crying
quietly and she'd felt as though her heart was breaking. She'd
known at that moment that Shara wouldn't, or couldn't,
acknowledge what they both felt. She'd known that Shara would
rather live a lie with Derek than face a truth that would shatter everything she believed about herself.

As if to confirm that, Shara had said in a broken voice, "Jessa, if
you pursue this, I won't be able to travel with you." It really was as
simple as that.

- Jessa had wanted to wail, to shout at Shara and the world that the
situation was completely unfair. She'd waited so long to feel this.
After Stephanie it had taken years for her to date in any healthy
way. She'd had relationships and she'd had more bed partners than
most, but she'd always been honest with them and told them that
she wasn't capable of going the girlfriend route. Yet part of her had
always known that one day she'd be ready. It was the supreme irony that when she'd finally met someone who touched her deeply
and made her want ... everything, that woman would be terrified
of her own feelings and unwilling to take a chance on what they had.

She'd closed her eyes and allowed the pain to wash over her. Her
first impulse had been to tell Shara to sod off. To tell her that she
was a coward and could go to hell or go back to her boyfriend with
Jessa's compliments. Then images and sensations flashed through
her memory: Shara's confused awareness at the cottage, Shara
looking at her in the rain and wanting to kiss her without even understanding what she wanted, Shara sitting next to her, playing
Chopin's *Nocturne* and looking at her afterwards with so much
warmth and affection as their bodies touched and generated a heat
that both had savored without words or further action.

Mostly she remembered the way they'd kissed: it was as though,
when they'd touched each other, their control had mutually

snapped. She didn't know who had started it, but she knew that if Derek hadn't come home, they would have finished it. Right there at the side of the house. Neither would have given it a thought and they would have made love. If Shara wanted to deny the power of that, Jessa could understand it, because she'd known she was a lesbian from the age of fourteen and it had completely thrown her.

Stop thinking about yourself, Hanson. Give her time and space.

But as the silence had continued, doubts had started to crowd Jessa's mind.

Maybe you're just a lustful experiment for a bi-curious woman who has no intention of ever doing more than fucking you when her boyfriend isn't about. Either way, it's best just to back off, at least for now.

"Fine. I won't pursue anything except what I've been hired to do in America and Canada, which leaves you free to do your job."

Jessa's voice, carefully modulated, but raspy with suppressed emotion, made Shara press her hand to her stomach. *Oh God, I don't want to hurt her.* But she could see no way out of the impossible situation she was in. "Jessa, I . . ."

"So I guess I'll see you at the airport?" Jessa made a superhuman effort to lighten her tone, but it rang false to the woman who already knew her so well. Nevertheless, Shara was grateful that Jessa was going to make it easy for her to set aside what had happened between them and get on with the tour.

"Yes. Yes, you will."

"Derek is fine." Shara's voice broke into Jessa's thoughts. "He's still sulking," *mainly because I wouldn't fuck him last night – not that he could doubt my protestations of illness when I took one whiff of the Thai food he brought home and puked all over his shoes,* "but he's not planning my demise or anything. He even brought me to the airport."

Jessa nodded. So they were still together and Derek had probably made love to her last night and fallen asleep with her in his arms. She couldn't bring herself to say anything inane or approving, so she said instead, "Can I get you a drink or a snack? I overslept, so I didn't have time for breakfast and now I'm starving."

Shara didn't ask Jessa why she'd overslept or how much trouble she'd had falling asleep the night before.

PART FOURTEEN

It was Thursday morning and Shara was exhausted. They'd arrived at JFK International Airport late on Monday afternoon and Shara had had to be at the TV studio at 6:30 a.m. the next morning to film a promotional interview. She'd then gone with Jessa to the first meeting and rehearsal at Lincoln Center before leaving to go to a studio in Queens to film a clip that would be used in the "Making Of" documentary once the film about Jessa was close to release. The only thing that had lifted her jet-lagged spirits that afternoon had been learning that the working title of it was *Maestra*, which she thought was perfect. They'd had dinner with executives from Jessa's record label at Le Cirque, getting back to the loft exhausted, and slightly tipsy, just before midnight.

The second day had been just as full: Jessa had woken her at 5:00 a.m. so they could go for a run in Central Park accompanied, somewhat disturbingly, by a burly and obviously armed man named Brad. It was distinctly strange to be going to and from a morning jog in a limousine, but Shara had been in the entertainment industry too long to do more than thank her lucky stars that they'd provided mineral water as part of the service.

After breakfast, there had been a full rehearsal with the orchestra and choir, followed by lunch with some corporate sponsors. That had been followed by another rehearsal and then tea at the Plaza with the leader of the orchestra and the Musical Director, an affair that had been little more than a two-hour technical discussion as they'd pored over copies of the score and marked them with pencils. Fascinated though Shara had been by the process, she'd been relieved when Jessa had declined several invitations to socialize that evening, saying she needed an early night.

Except for the times she'd been in a rehearsal or at the teatime meeting, there always seemed to be someone at Jessa's elbow, demanding her attention. By Wednesday afternoon, Shara had been fighting the urge to shout at them to leave Jessa alone.

When the phone rang at 7:00 on Thursday, Shara buried her head under the pillow, but knowing that her job was to understand the way Jessa lived, she dragged herself out of bed and into the bathroom, because she needed to find out who would have called and why – assuming it had been a business call.

She groaned as she towel-dried her hair and caught sight of her bleary eyes in the mirror. She needed at least two more hours of sleep, but she didn't doubt that bloody Jessa would be bright-eyed and perky, even though they'd gone to bed at the same time. Jessa being a morning person was as disconcerting as the way she could flirt with her and send her hormones into overdrive without showing a hint of remorse. She never went far enough for Shara to protest, but she made sure Shara was aware of her attraction. When Shara had asked her why, she'd said simply, "To pretend that I don't feel what I feel would be a lie. Does that make you uncomfortable?"

Shara had paused before answering. What she felt wasn't discomfort, or anything negative. Jessa's open affection, which was everything but physical, made her feel ... cherished. "No," she'd said quietly, "it doesn't."

"Good morning." Jessa didn't look up from her copy of the *New York Times* but Shara could hear the smile in her voice.

"Is it?" Shara asked grumpily as she walked to the kitchen for a cup of the coffee that she knew Jessa would have made for her.

"I think so. I'm with a gorgeous woman in a fantastic flat in one of the greatest cities in the world ..."

"Stop taking the piss ..."

"Okay, the flat is great, as opposed to fantastic, and the city isn't at its best in the summer, but the woman is definitely gorgeous."

Shara flopped down in a chair opposite Jessa and closed her eyes as she sipped her coffee. "Your eyesight is starting to go," she said when she opened her eyes again.

Jessa lowered the paper and looked at Shara. Shara wasn't wearing any makeup, but her lips were soft and pink, her cheeks were slightly flushed from her shower and her gray-green eyes were still heavy-lidded from sleep and framed by naturally long lashes. Her slightly grumpy look only made Jessa find her more adorable. "There's nothing wrong with my eyesight," she said simply.

The appreciation in Jessa's expression, and in her voice, made Shara's stomach do a funny little flip, and she looked down at her cup. "Thank you."

She didn't hear the rustle of the paper to indicate that Jessa had gone back to reading it, so she knew that Jessa was still staring at her. To distract them both, she asked, "Who was the early-morning caller?"

"Lisa. She's in final negotiations for me to score my first film. She'll be here tomorrow and probably stay for the performance on Saturday night. She might go with us to Toronto on Sunday and stay there for a few days as well, but we were mainly talking about the score. If things go as planned, I'll get to see the rough cut of the film when my summer tour is over."

"That's very exciting." Shara was wide awake now. Lisa had told her about the legendary producer-director who had been taken by one of Jessa's compositions and was considering using some of her music for his next film, but this wasn't just about writing original music for the soundtrack, it was about actually scoring the whole thing. It was great news for Jessa's career.

"Yeah, it is." But she didn't sound thrilled. She put down the newspaper and walked towards the glass wall of the loft to look down on the early-morning Tribeca traffic.

"What's the matter?" Shara frowned at her. Despite Jessa's reputation for moodiness, Shara had developed a healthy respect for Jessa's professional patience. With all the demands on her time and the fact that they were in direct conflict with what she needed to do to get ready for her debut with the New York Philharmonic that night, Jessa had remained patient and charming, only politely drawing the line yesterday at another night of socializing with strangers. She'd also told Shara how grateful she was for the career she was having, more so because it had almost come crashing down around her ears eight years ago. It was completely out of character for her to react so indifferently, even negatively, to an opportunity of this magnitude.

The previous night they'd had food delivered, which they'd eaten in near silence, each thinking about the events of an impossibly full day. After dinner, at Jessa's suggestion, they'd walked around Tribeca and Soho, stopping at a café for a glass of wine before going back to the flat to lounge around and listen to music, while talking occasionally, sometimes about music and sometimes about their lives. Jessa could go for hours without speaking and Shara found that she enjoyed the silences between them almost as much as their conversations.

When she'd started to feel tired, she'd been shocked to see that it was 1:00 a.m. Considering how exhausted she'd felt that afternoon, she couldn't believe how late they'd stayed up.

Even more surprising was the way the sexual attraction between them had not been an issue on their first evening alone since they'd left the cottage. It was still there: her body still responded to the sight and the closeness of Jessa, but her craving wasn't just for the physical, so she'd distracted herself by enjoying the sound of Jessa's low voice and the rhythm of her speech, as well as what she'd had to say. She'd talked to Jessa about things and people that mattered to her, basking in Jessa's intelligent empathy. She'd shared funny stories with Jessa because she loved the way Jessa laughed. She'd also found that Jessa could make *her* laugh. For some reason, laughter seemed to bring their sexual attraction closer to the surface, which was dangerous, but not dangerous enough to make her want to give up the heady pleasure of a shared sense of humor. Jessa's light flirting had had a similar, warming effect, but neither had allowed it to escalate.

She felt as though she knew Jessa Hanson in a way she knew few other people and that Jessa knew her equally well. For that reason she was sure that whatever motivated Jessa's reservations about the film score, it wasn't ingratitude or lack of awareness of the project's importance. "Sweetheart, what is it?"

Jessa turned sharply, surprised to hear Shara's voice and see her standing so close to her by the window.

"It's nothing, really."

"Jessa . . ." Shara raised a disbelieving eyebrow.

To her surprise, Jessa flushed and refused to look at her. "I shouldn't even be thinking like this. To express musically the emotion that a film by such a prominent director inspires in me . . . It's the chance of a lifetime."

"But?"

"But, it's someone else's vision. Someone else's creation. What if I muck it up? What if I don't *get* what he's trying to do? Everything else I've written so far has been personal. On the one hand, a small voice inside me hesitates to take on something so overtly commercial, but on the other, I think that art can be created in ordinary media and what ultimately matters is the skill and vision of the artist. Which brings me back to the first problem . . ."

"Sweetheart, stop worrying. You're a gifted composer. I've listened to music you've written, both popular and classical, and if you wanted it to be, scoring a film would be a cakewalk for someone as talented as you. But you won't let it be a cakewalk, you'll work hard and you'll make it better than it has to be. You'll make it the best." She took Jessa's arm and turned her so Jessa was forced to meet her eyes. "I know you and I know that."

Her quiet confidence made Jessa's eyes fill with tears. Jessa pressed her lips together to stop them from trembling as she stood there, caught between Shara's faith and her own doubts. Eventually, she looked away and said, "It might not matter, anyway. The contract isn't signed and if I bugger up tonight's performance badly enough, the problem might be academic."

"Jessa, I was at rehearsal and I heard the first run-through. It was brilliant even before the final rehearsal you're gonna have later this morning. Your relationships with other musicians are like nothing I've ever seen. You deserve your reputation for excellence and you will live up to your own expectations for tonight – which we both know are higher than any film producer's or director's could ever be."

Jessa turned to face her, searching her features for any sign of doubt, but there was none. Shara's absolute belief in her caused a warm trembling in her belly and she felt overwhelmed.

"Come here," Shara said softly and pulled Jessa into her arms to hug her tightly.

As she held Jessa, she said quietly, "Here are the rules: I'm the flighty actress who's supposed to have crises of confidence and decide out of the blue that I'm crap. You are the incredibly gifted conductor who sees music everywhere and whose hands move as she's looking at a jet taking off, because she's composing as she watches and playing the piano in her head. That's who you are, Jessa. It's who you will be, with or without the film contract, with or without the New York Philharmonic." She pulled back to look at Jessa. "Understood?" Her voice was gently teasing and Jessa smiled, despite her earlier misgivings.

"You're amazing."

"No," Shara smiled back at her, "I'm hungry. And if I'm not fed in short order, I'll be dangerous."

Jessa's eyes crinkled at the corners and her smile widened. "Having seen you eat, I'm suitably nervous."

As though realizing at the same time that they were holding each other, each let her arms fall to her sides and stepped back slightly, Shara looking away self-consciously and Jessa looking slightly at a loss.

"Do you want to go out for breakfast?" Shara asked, deciding that food was a safe, neutral topic.

Jessa shrugged. "Why not? I know a great little greasy spoon in Chelsea and we might as well take advantage of having a car and driver at our disposal." She hesitated, before saying softly, "And Shara?"

Shara looked at her, eyebrows raised questioningly.

"Thanks. I'm not used to having anybody . . ." She stopped speaking, suddenly terrified of what she was about to reveal. She'd learned the hard way to deal with her demons on her own. Lisa understood that she had doubts and fears, but Lisa's practical advice to consider her past and her hard work in order to counter insecurities, never quite reached down into that dark place inside her where the terror lurked. That place that Shara had just touched, seemingly without effort.

"I know." Shara's voice was equally soft. "Nor am I. But I expect you'd do the same for me."

Jessa nodded, but suddenly she needed to get away from Shara before she said, or did, something they'd both regret. "I'll go and ring for the car."

"And I'd better put on a pair of shoes," Shara mumbled, acutely aware of the intimacy of what they'd just exchanged. Before Jessa could even pick up the telephone, she had fled to her room.

PART FIFTEEN

A sense of excitement and expectation permeated the air in Avery Fisher Hall. There was the murmur of conversation and the sound of musicians tuning their instruments or practicing and Shara stood in the doorway to take it all in. She breathed deeply and inhaled the faintly exotic smell of hundreds of expensive perfumes blending together in the cool, filtered air to create the aroma of privilege. Tickets for the performance had been sold out for months, which had led Lisa to joke that this had been more like a rock concert than a classical one. Yet this was no rock audience.

The people in the orchestra section were, on average, older than Shara had expected and immaculately turned out, with enough diamond jewelry winking discreetly on the women to give an insurance adjuster nightmares for weeks. Despite the heat on the streets outside, the men looked cool and untouched in crisp evening wear. Shara felt in no danger of being recognized here. She didn't even need her short, artificially darkened, hair as a disguise. Because *Against the State* had been out of theaters for well over two years and all her more recent work had been of the mass-market variety, she doubted this crowd contained many of her fans.

Her decision to sit in the audience, rather than be backstage, for her first live experience of Jessa performing for the public had not been made lightly. She'd been backstage during rehearsals earlier that week, sitting through the technical discussions and the replaying of transitions until Jessa had been satisfied. She'd watched the nods of understanding as Jessa explained to musicians, some decades older than she was, how she wanted something done. She'd sat through the soprano's minor strop, calmed by Jessa with a few well-placed compliments and a serious discussion with the woman about her objections.

At that morning's final rehearsal, she'd allowed herself to imagine what it would be like with all the performers in formal attire and the hall full of paying patrons, rather than friends and a group of students visiting from Juilliard, but her imagination had not done it justice. After the rehearsal she'd admitted to Jessa that she wanted to get a sense of what it was like to see her as well as to "be" her, so she was having trouble deciding which would be the better place to sit that night.

Jessa had grinned at her. "It will be completely manic backstage and not really the best atmosphere for preparing yourself to listen to Mahler." She'd explained that while instruments were being tuned and singers were warming up their voices, a TV crew would be trying to interview anybody they thought was influential and quotable. Last-minute adjustments would be made to hair and makeup as jokes, some off-color, were told to ward off the inevitable nerves. Apart from the TV crew, a few other journalists from classical music stations and magazines, as well as local newspapers, would probably be milling about, many trying to steal the odd word with her. The occasional wealthy patron was also likely to be given some "face time" with the conductor as a privilege paid for by giving tens or hundreds of thousands to support the orchestra or Lincoln Center arts programs.

"Really? But don't *you* need to prepare yourself to perform?"

Jessa had shrugged. "It's all up here," she'd said, pointing to her head, "and when I turn to the orchestra and they look at me, waiting for me to tell them we can start to do what we do best, it moves to here." She'd put a hand over her heart. "All the people and the chaos, even the audience, can't touch either place in me." She'd winked. "But don't tell anyone I said so. That way, when I tell people they've been a lovely audience, they'll think that means more than it does. I'm just happy when they're quiet and I can ignore them."

"So you'd be just as happy to play to an empty room?" Shara had been incredulous. "I get a real thrill from live theater as opposed to film – instant feedback and gratification. Are you saying I have a bigger ego than you?"

"Well, I wasn't going to mention it ..." Shara had slapped her on the arm. "And no, it's not the same to play to an empty room ... but only because concert venues are designed acoustically to have people seated in them, so often they sound too bright or too muddy when empty." She'd looked at Shara's skeptical expression and relented, "Okay, I admit that, when we've just managed to play something perfectly and I can almost see the composer smiling at me, it's great to hear thousands of people applauding in acknowledgement."

"So you *do* like playing for an audience!"

"Yes, sometimes. But not necessarily opening night, or so-called special event, audiences who are often there to be seen rather than because they particularly love the music. It's hard to explain how different audiences affect me ..."

"Do you think I'd get a better feel for that backstage, looking at their faces?"

"I'm sure you'll know from the theater that I barely see their faces on the way in ... I'm pretty far inside myself and I go through the motions until I'm about to start and it all comes sharply into focus. So being backstage would not really give you a sense of what I see or feel audience-wise. If you want to get an idea of why that 'special event' kind of audience doesn't touch me, then you should sit with them." She'd smiled shyly at Shara. "And I admit that it would make me feel better to know that at least one person out there loves music for the purity of it and wants me to do well ... Believes I can do well."

Shara's heart had contracted at Jessa's words. "Baby, there's no doubt in my mind, or my heart," she'd replied, and the decision had been made.

The last time Shara had seen Jessa, she'd been wearing a black dress and Brad had followed her into the dressing room to deposit a garment bag and duffel bag, before stepping out, closing the door behind him and crossing his arms over his muscular chest. It was his job to make sure Jessa wasn't disturbed until she left her dressing room to make her pre-performance rounds – to the rehearsal rooms, where the singers were warming up, to the staging area, where the musicians milled about with press and patrons and, finally, in the wings with just the leader of the orchestra, the journalists with the best access and the group of professionals it took to put on a concert of this size. At that point Brad would mingle with the audience before taking up a position by the door closest to the stage to watch them as they watched Jessa. He'd asked Shara to "stick" with him until she took her seat and instructed her to wait for him to walk her backstage after the performance. She certainly had never entertained the thought of arguing with him.

She smiled at him as she took her seat and he nodded at her. The orchestra was on the stage and the audience was growing quiet. Shara almost held her breath as the door at the side of the stage opened and the concertmaster walked onstage. The audience applauded and he bowed, introduced the orchestra, to the sound of more applause, and bowed again before taking his seat as principal violinist and cueing the oboe to play a sustained A so the rest of the orchestra could tune their instruments to it one final time before the performance began. Shara felt as though the butterflies in her stomach were vibrating to the various instruments that played that strident note or B flat in counterpoint. She couldn't believe how nervous she was when she wasn't the one on stage. Then the door opened again and Jessa strode out and she forgot to be anything but enthralled.

Jessa looked stunning. To describe what she was wearing as "drag", was to miss how utterly female the cut-away coat looked on Jessa. The silvery waistcoat followed the lines of her body and emphasized her slender waist and flat stomach, and the white-on-white of her bespoke linen shirt and bow tie offset her tan and the dramatic makeup that she wore.

Shara had never seen Jessa in makeup, except in photographs, and she licked her lips as she noticed the way Jessa's cheekbones were dramatically highlighted and her lips seemed to pout slightly. Jessa's eyes were emphasized by dark eyeliner, so they looked even bigger and slightly exotic, especially when the stage lights picked out thick eyelashes lengthened by black mascara.

The length of the black coat and the black-on-black formal trousers with their satin stripes down the sides, made Jessa look statuesque, even in the low-heeled black boots that had been polished to a mirror-shine, but they didn't quite hide the womanly curves of her body. The applause was thunderous as Jessa walked confidently to the center of the stage and bowed before looking around the room, smiling politely and bowing again to accept the adulation of the crowd, even before a single note had been played.

Then Jessa looked down to the front of the audience, searching the crowd until she saw Shara. Her smile widened and she gave a small nod that, although barely perceptible, made Shara feel ridiculously special. Almost before the moment had happened, it was over. Jessa turned away to shake hands with the principal violinist and to acknowledge the rest of the orchestra. She then stepped onto the podium and raised the baton.

There was a glistening moment of perfect silence before the distinctive opening notes sounded and the tense, brooding, almost angry, first movement of Mahler's second symphony, *The Resurrection*, began.

Shara was mesmerized. Every movement of Jessa's body was significant and she held nothing back. The physical control and emotional immersion with which she conducted made it impossible for Shara to look away. There was no doubt that Jessa Hanson was a leader – from the moment she stepped to the front of the orchestra, she became the heart and soul of it.

Shara had heard recordings of Mahler's Second before and they almost always seemed to be ever so slightly disjointed, yet as she listened, not only did the orchestra execute every note with spine-tingling precision, but even to her relatively untrained ears each movement flowed into the next, perfectly paced and timed as Jessa seemed to cast a spell, not only over the audience, but over the musicians as well.

It was a symphony that ran the gamut from stark to lush, from haunted to triumphant, from near-desolation to exultation and everything in between. In the quiet passages, Jessa's movements were nuanced and almost delicate, but Shara found her own body tensing as quiet and restrained built up to mini-explosions of musical expression that Mahler seemed to have written for this magnificent orchestra and the woman who conducted it. Shara's stomach flipped when Jessa threw herself into the peaks of the music, an unruly lock of hair bouncing onto her forehead and eventually clinging to the smooth skin that glistened with sweat.

By the time the fourth movement started, Shara threw away her preconceptions and decided that *Urlicht* was one of the most beautiful musical passages she had ever heard. *And Jessa Hanson is one of the most beautiful people I have ever seen.*

After the vocalists came in, Shara felt the hair on her arms stand on end. The haunting soprano solo that became a duet with an offstage violin touched something elemental in her. When the contralto soloist took her place in front of the choir, Shara tore her gaze away from Jessa long enough to pay fleeting homage to the rich timbre of her voice – the ultimate and most intimate musical instrument.

As the final movement, with its tension, doubt, anger and triumph unfolded with the mastery and brilliance that can only result from conductor, orchestra and singers working perfectly together, Shara felt the tension gathering in her body again. One layer of musical intensity built upon another until it culminated in a final triumphant crescendo that made tears well up in her eyes and flow down her cheeks.

PART SIXTEEN

As soon as Shara appeared at the door of the dressing room, Jessa opened her arms and Shara ran into them. Brad discreetly closed the door behind Shara, but he smiled uncharacteristically as he thought, *about time*. He'd overheard enough conversations between the two women and between the shorter one and her absent boyfriend to decide that that particular friendship was going to end with some girl-on-girl action. He'd been doing celebrity security duty too long to expect happily-ever-after, but something about the way those two women looked at each other made him want to hope again.

"You were amazing," Shara murmured into Jessa's neck, inhaling the warm scent of clean skin and perfume that had been heightened by her physical exertion as she'd conducted.

"Thank you." Jessa spoke into the hair just over Shara's ear, without letting go of her. "What an experience! I'm not sure that anything I've done has ever gone so perfectly … There wasn't a moment when I thought the orchestra wasn't doing quite what I'd envisaged or hoped the audience hadn't heard something. Not a moment."

Shara hugged her harder, moved by the sincere wonder in Jessa's voice. "They wanted to be perfect for you as well as for themselves. I overheard a viola player saying that you'd brought something to Mahler that she hadn't known was there and that it blew her away." Shara pulled away slightly so she could see Jessa's face and she smiled at her. "And I think she wants you."

Jessa smiled back. "Well it doesn't matter what she wants. To-night was for you."

Shara stared at her, eyes wide, profoundly moved by Jessa's simple statement. Jessa stared back, taking in the soft, parted lips and the emotion brimming from the hazel eyes. She could smell Shara's perfume and was intoxicated by the fragrance and the feel of the woman in her arms. She wrenched herself away and stumbled backward until she was a few feet from Shara.

Shara looked confused and a bit hurt. "What is it? Have I done something wrong?"

Jessa shook her head, but she didn't say anything. She'd undone her tie and it hung from the open collar of her shirt. Her coat had been flung over a chair, leaving her in formal black trousers and that body-hugging waistcoat. With makeup still emphasizing her eyes and cheekbones, the look of near-desperation made her seem somehow wild and, to Shara's mind, sexual.

"Jessa?"

"You've done nothing wrong, Shara. In fact you do everything right!" With that cryptic comment, Jessa turned away from her and began to remove her cuff links.

"I don't understand. I thought you'd want to . . ."

"Celebrate my triumph? Well, yes, that would be nice. I'd like to come off stage after the best conducting performance of my life, take the woman I love in my arms and bask in the warmth of her support and her joy in what I've accomplished." She turned back to face Shara. "But that's a fairytale, isn't it? I'm here with somebody else's fiancée and if I follow my instincts and kiss her, if I give into what my heart and my body tell me is the right thing to do, then the whole fantasy falls apart, doesn't it?"

Shara didn't know what to say. Her heart was hammering in her chest and her body wanted to cross the small distance between her and Jessa and take the decision out of Jessa's hands by being the one to initiate the kiss. There was no doubt in her mind that she could overcome Jessa's reservations and override her reluctance. She knew that she wanted that kiss as much as, perhaps more than, Jessa did. But had Jessa just said that she *loved* her? *No, that was a general statement and to assume anything else is fanciful*. Yet the thought caused a longing so strong in Shara that she made a small sound and her eyes filled with tears.

She didn't take the few steps that would have brought her back into Jessa's arms because the distance between them was more than just a few feet of carpet. Getting past the physical divide would have lead to an emotional maelstrom whose effects would be felt far beyond the undeniable physical pleasure that would result.

To take those steps would have been to deny the importance of the fact that she was already in a relationship with Derek Finch; to deny that what was happening between her and Jessa was important enough to make the existence of a boyfriend a crucial, destructive factor. She acknowledged that the latter hurt more than the former. She couldn't even tell herself that it would be "just" a kiss, or pretend that it would have to be chaste with Brad outside the door of this publicly located room. She knew, she'd known since their first kiss, that if she and Jessa touched each other again in more than a friendly manner, they wouldn't stop until they'd made love. But then what?

"Cat got your tongue?" Jessa asked her with a sneer, before turning away again to begin unfastening her shirt, after taking off her waistcoat.

A discreet knock sounded and Brad's voice came through the closed door. "Ladies, we have to leave for the reception at the Rainbow Room in half an hour. I've kept the hordes at bay by promising them that you'll be mingling later and they can compliment you on your performance then."

"I ... I'll leave you to change," Shara mumbled, embarrassed by the tears that filled her eyes and spilled down her cheeks. Unable to bear the sharp barb that she expected in response from Jessa, she opened the door and almost knocked Brad over in her haste to get away from Jessa's dressing room.

"*Shit!*" Jessa slammed her hand down on the makeup table and clenched her jaw to prevent herself from breaking down and sobbing. How had she managed to make such a spectacular hash of what should have been one of the brightest points in her career? *Did I actually tell her that I love her? No, of course I didn't. I could have been speaking hypothetically . . .*

"Yeah, right," she said aloud. People have been telling you just about all your life that you have a special talent. Well you must, because it must have taken tremendous skill to be solely responsible for making a happy night unhappy, making one of your sweetest performances turn bitter and upsetting the woman who inspired that performance, all in one minute. The woman you've loved since the day you took her for a walk in the rain.

"Miss Hanson?" Brad's voice, normally gruff, was gentle. "Can I get you something?"

"I'm fine, thanks . . . Or maybe you could get me a bottle of mineral water?"

"Coming right up. But don't under any circumstances leave this room until I return, okay?"

"Sure," Jessa replied in subdued voice as she continued undressing.

By the time Brad returned she had sunk into a kind of semiconscious numbness and was standing in her underwear. Her state of undress didn't faze him, because he'd worked the security detail for models and other unselfconscious types in the past.

"And there were messages for you up front as well as almost a dozen bouquets. I've brought you the cards from the flowers, but what do you want done with them?"

"Send them to the geriatric wing of a local hospital. You choose." Her voice was dull. He handed her the notes. "Maybe these will cheer you up. We leave in twenty minutes, twenty-five tops."

"Thanks, Brad." Jessa managed a smile and after hesitating as though he wanted to say more, he discreetly withdrew.

Jessa flopped into an armchair and looked through the notes, all with envelopes attached, but all opened by Brad as a security precaution. Most of them were from well-wishers with a few post-concert congratulations, but one had been delivered by international courier from London. The sender was "D. Finch". Jessa recognized the Highgate address and unfolded the note, written on embossed stationery.

For some reason, Shara's fiancé had chosen not to wish Jessa luck for her New York Philharmonic conducting debut. Instead he'd taken the opportunity of the performance's famous address to send Jessa a proprietary message. It said simply, "Dear Miss Hanson, Please advise Shara that I will be joining her in Toronto on Sunday."

Jessa laughed mirthlessly. Point taken, Mr. Finch. And thank you for saving me from making a further fool of myself with your fiancée.

PART SEVENTEEN

As it turned out, Derek decided not to fly to Toronto until Monday, but neither the delay in his arrival, nor the presence of Lisa, served to thaw the atmosphere between Shara and Jessa. From the moment Jessa had met Shara by the car as they'd set off for Thursday's reception at the Rainbow Room and thrust Derek's note into her hands, she'd barely spoken to her, except where absolutely necessary.

She kept her promise to allow Shara into her inner circle and keep her fully aware of the details of her life, but it was all done with an aloof politeness that belied the savage anger that smoldered in her dark eyes whenever she looked at Shara.

They'd arrived in Toronto at noon on Sunday. It had been a spectacular day with sailboats skimming across the dark blue water of Lake Ontario and graceful people on rollerblades taking advantage of the sunshine to enjoy the miles of paved pathways along the water's edge. Lisa had booked into the Westin Harbour Castle, which offered views of the lake and the downtown skyline, and was only a few hundred yards along Queen's Quay from the apartment that had been rented for Jessa. She invited them to join her for brunch at her hotel's revolving restaurant, but Jessa declined, pleading a headache.

Not long after Lisa and Shara were seated and had ordered drinks, Lisa asked bluntly. "What's going on between you and Jessa?"

"Absolutely nothing," Shara replied, deciding to be equally blunt, only to have her tone inadvertently reveal her bitterness over how badly wrong things between her and Jessa had gone.

"Doesn't seem that way to me. I know Jessa and it's not like her to be as withdrawn as she's been around you. And when she's not around you, she refuses to talk about you or how your time together is going."

"Maybe it's because she doesn't like me. Have you thought of that?"

The waiter brought their drinks and Lisa sipped hers before replying with a thoughtful look at Shara, "I've never known Jessa to hold back from simply saying that she doesn't like someone. Besides, when I spoke to her on Thursday morning, she gave the opposite impression, so why would she have changed her mind?"

Shara squirmed uncomfortably and took a gulp of her drink, wishing suddenly that she'd gone for something stronger than orange juice. "I think ... I think it has something to do with Derek coming to visit."

"Oh ..." Lisa nodded her understanding before frowning. "But she hasn't met him, has she?" The clear implication was that knowing Derek would have explained a moody, negative reaction to the prospect of seeing him again.

"She's spoken to him a few times ..." Shara admitted and then flushed slightly, because her response had reaffirmed the implication and because it embarrassed her that she couldn't think offhand of one friend or female acquaintance who actually liked Derek.

"Why on earth should it bother her that he's coming? It's not as if she's going to be forced to spend time in his company." She reached into her handbag and took out a few sheets of A4 paper. "Here's our schedule for the next three days." As Shara unfolded the printed document and read it with increasing horror, Lisa nodded. "Yep, that's not a misprint. We start each day with a breakfast show, two radio and one television, we have at least two purely business meetings each day and she's also got a rehearsal every day. To make things worse, she's asked to have the program changed for the first concert and that means inserts in thousands of printed booklets. As the manager of the temperamental artist, I'm working with the Canadian office of the record company to get it done because nobody wants to pay for it. That might be my problem, but it also means Jessa has to work longer with the orchestra to get them up to speed. She has no time off, not even for meals, until Friday morning."

Shit. Derek is going to have a meltdown. "Is there any way Derek can come to the evening events? Jessa made arrangements for me to attend, but I wasn't expecting . . ."

"Didn't he know how busy you were going to be if you were shadowing a musician on tour?" Lisa made no attempt to hide her impatience.

Shara couldn't blame her. It was her job to cope with Jessa's temperamental changes to programs along with a full schedule, but Shara was here as a favor and her boyfriend should not be adding to Lisa's burden.

"Hasn't he done promotional tours with you? This is the same except with the added pressure of rehearsals and live performances."

"I tried to tell him," Shara said miserably, "but he hasn't really seen me for more than a few hours in a week and a half." She shrugged. "I think he was expecting me to at least have my evenings free." Her shoulders slumped. "If you can't, it's okay. I'll just skip the events and spend the time with him." The idea upset her, because she was hoping that constantly being forced into her company would make Jessa relent a bit and they could go back to the friendship they'd had before the events following the first New York concert.

She knew that she should be more excited at the prospect of seeing Derek and less upset at the prospect of not seeing, and making up with, Jessa, but she blamed her feelings on Derek's lack of consideration in springing this trip on them.

"I'll see what I can do," Lisa relented, "but I know that he won't be able to attend the performance on Thursday unless there are returns. Even the promotional seats for that are taken."

Shara was grateful that at least one thing wasn't a complete disaster. "He'll have gone back to London by then," she assured Lisa. "It's his grandmother's birthday party on Friday and he has to be there."

Lisa raised an eyebrow. "He's keen."

Shara felt her face warm again. She could not explain to Lisa why a man who had a family engagement that could not be put off, would fly twice across the Atlantic and cause his girlfriend so much inconvenience on a business trip, just so he could see her for a few hours a day over three days. Lisa assumed the reason was sexual, but Shara suspected it had more to do with power than lust.

"I think he just wants to get some things ... settled ... between us."

Lisa narrowed her eyes and looked at Shara, as though trying to decide what was really going on in her brain, then she shrugged, "Okay, Miss Quinn, but I'd say that sixteen hours on a plane in three days means he's expecting settlement in his favor." Then she smiled. "Shall we order? I'm starving."

When Lisa got back to her suite, she was surprised to find Jessa sitting in the living room, idly flicking through the channels on the television.

"Should I ask how you got in?"

Jessa shrugged. "I have an honest face and I asked nicely?" At Lisa's openly skeptical look she added, "And I gave the concierge two tickets to Saturday night's concert. Street value of four hundred dollars apiece, apparently."

"How's your head?"

Jessa scowled at her. They both knew that Jessa did not have a headache. "How was brunch?"

"Informative. Have you eaten? Would you like me to ring down for something for you from room service?"

"Lisa, I'm not here for the food. What did Shara say?"

Lisa was not surprised by the question. She knew that Jessa's silent anger of the last two days was based on something that ran much deeper than irritation or dislike. Something had happened between them, something that had deeply wounded Jessa. Jessa always wore her heart on her sleeve, so hiding the pain under a veil of anger for the last few days had to have taken a heavy toll. She had no doubt that this conversation would give Jessa a chance to vent about the underlying cause of her anger. Jessa's reticence had been as inexplicable as Shara Quinn's obvious pain when she'd said that

Jessa disliked her.

"She said that you don't like her. Either that or you don't like her boyfriend. Maybe both."

Jessa switched off the television and stood up abruptly, walking over to the sliding glass doors and looking out onto the lake, with its small chain of islands about a mile from the shore. "Maybe she's right."

"So why does it hurt you so much that her boyfriend is coming to visit?" Lisa had never been one to pull her punches, but when Jessa flinched, she wished that in this instance she'd been less direct.

Jessa closed her eyes as though waiting for a wave of pain to pass. When she opened them again they were filled with tears. "I don't understand, Lisa. Sometimes she looks at me as though ... and when we touch, even in the most innocent way, it *moves* me ..." She put a clenched fist over her heart. "And I know she feels it ... feels something. So h-how can she *marry* him?"

Without another word, Lisa walked over to Jessa and put her arms around her, holding her silently as she sobbed.

PART EIGHTEEN

S hara didn't think it was possible, but Monday had proved to be marginally better than Sunday, mainly because she'd spent most of Monday with someone who was neither Jessa nor Derek. On Monday, she'd left rehearsal early to go to the airport to meet Derek, so she had not had a chance to hear the orchestra's first attempt at Jessa's new, untitled composition. It had hurt that Jessa had not shown her the score.

As it turned out, she might as well have stayed for the rehearsal, because Derek missed his flight as a result of an organized protest on the M25. He'd been too impatient to wait for the next direct flight out of Heathrow, so he'd taken one leaving shortly after the one he'd missed, but with a connection in Amsterdam. He hadn't thought to ring Shara, even when he found out that his Amsterdam-Toronto flight would be delayed several hours. By the time he had rung from the plane, she'd already been in a chauffeured car, on her way to the airport to meet him.

Reluctant to face Jessa and with nine hours to kill, Shara had asked the driver to take her to Niagara Falls. He'd asked her if she wanted the radio on as they drove and she'd asked him to put on the local classical music station. She'd bitten her lip when Jessa's voice emanated from the speakers. They were broadcasting highlights from that morning's interview. Jessa was being asked about the rigors of travel and how she coped with homesickness. Jessa's voice had been sad when she'd said that traveling with someone you cared for was the best way to avoid loneliness, but she also used music as a balm when she was on the road. Shara squeezed her eyes shut and tried to ignore the pain – her own and Jessa's.

It had been a relief when the announcer had asked Jessa to introduce the music she most closely associated with her English heritage and Jessa had joked about *God Save the Queen* before introducing *The Lark Ascending* by Vaughan Williams. It was a musical composition that gave Shara goose bumps even without being introduced by Jessa in a voice whose sadness stemmed directly from Shara's actions. As the lone violin soared and told a story of pastoral beauty and musical elegance, Shara had been transported back to a small cottage in the country. Her breath caught on a sob and the small sound seemed to act as a catalyst for the unraveling of the control she'd maintained over a pain that had seared her heart since Jessa had relegated her to a position somewhere between business acquaintance and necessary evil.

When the tears started, they refused to stop. Although she tried with all her strength not to give in to them, sobs shook her body and hurt her throat. The Williams piece ended and the Berlin Philharmonic began the distinctive opening bars of Beethoven's *Eroica*, a symphony whose beauty, strength and complexity could only remind Shara of Jessa. If anything, it made her cry harder.

The piece that followed was a Tchaikovsky waltz. At that point, a succession of sleepless nights, emotional exhaustion, the gentle ride of the luxury car and the soothing music combined to overwhelm her and she fell into an exhausted sleep.

"Miss Quinn?"

Shara opened her eyes and looked uncomprehendingly at the driver, before remembering where she was.

"I thought you could use a cup of coffee. I tried letting you know when we got to the Falls, but you was sleeping so sound that I kept driving to Niagara-on-the-Lake. It's a real pretty town and not as many tourists as they got near the Falls, so if you want to stretch your legs a bit ..." Obviously not used to talking this much to the clients, he looked embarrassed and thrust the coffee cup at her.

"Thanks, Tony. I really appreciate that. I must have been more tired that I realized." She'd said nothing about the tears that had preceded her nap and he'd been too discreet to mention them.

Instead he'd nodded. "It's good for the health to have an afternoon nap. Where I come from, it's considered civilized." He'd been leaning through the open door as he spoke. Then he'd straightened up. "I'll be here with the car. The main street is just there," he pointed past the back of the car, "and my daughter loves the fudge shop. Perhaps you will, too."

She'd sipped the coffee and mingled with the tourists, enjoying her anonymity and the pleasant summer weather. Afterwards, she'd spent almost an hour browsing through the small shops on the pretty main street with its Victorian architecture and posters for the Shaw festival.

Afterwards, they'd driven slowly past Niagara Falls. Shara had rolled the window down to observe the sheer size and force of the natural phenomenon and she'd felt the spray on her skin. Although Tony had offered to stop and let her out to have a closer look, she'd declined to join the thousands of tourists on the footpath along the gorge.

Despite the coffee, she'd fallen asleep again on the way back to Toronto, waking up to find that a summer storm had descended on Greater Toronto and she was starving. "Tony, are you hungry?"

"Yes, Miss, but it's not a problem. I'll eat after I drop you off at the hotel."

"Why don't you let me buy you dinner before we go to the airport?" She'd looked at her watch. "We've got at least two hours to kill before Derek's flight is due to arrive."

"It wouldn't really be proper …"

"I won't tell, if you won't. Come on. I'm hungry and you're hungry and I don't know anything about local restaurants."

"I can make some recommendations …"

"Of touristy places with nouvelle cuisine and a view of the lake?" Shara scoffed gently. "I want to eat somewhere that you'd take your wife and daughter – not some place that's on a list you're supposed to quote from."

Tony laughed. "Okay, but I hope you'll remember me when I need a reference for a new job."

"I'll tell you what. Why don't you take a dinner break for an hour and a half? You'll be off duty and I'll make it up to you by taking you to dinner."

As if to spur him to action, Tony's stomach growled loudly enough for Shara to hear it. "How can I refuse dinner with a beautiful woman and ignore such a persistent stomach?"

They'd had dinner at a small Italian restaurant called "Rocco's Plum Tomato" in a western suburb. The food had been excellent and Shara had enjoyed two glasses of wine. Rocco himself came over to chat to Tony and fuss over Shara – not as a celebrity, but as a "friend" of Tony's.

"Shara, I think you should stop this nonsense and come home with me."

"It's nice to see you too, Derek," Shara had replied mildly.

Derek had stopped short, suddenly realizing that he'd been ranting from the time he emerged from the customs hall. "Sorry, babes," he'd said sheepishly. "I've missed you, Shara." He pulled her to him and hugged her, before pulling back to look at her. She'd looked tired, although he had been the one who'd been traveling for the better part of 24 hours.

Shara had stared back at him and wondered why she'd felt nothing, not even irritation at the self-important tirade Derek had launched into as soon as he'd seen her. There had been no apology for her having to interrupt her trip or wait for him, only a sustained whinge. He was still handsome, even in a wrinkled shirt and khaki trousers, with his hair flopping untidily over his forehead. She'd wondered if rich people bred that casually rumpled elegance into their children. His features were familiar to her, but this had brought no comfort. There'd been a time when just seeing him would have made her smile.

Derek was everything she was not, from his laid-back attitude to life and his upper-class upbringing to his lack of real understanding of people like her who were ambitious, because ambition was a trait he lacked. She gave to charities after reading up on them and determining their level of need, whom they benefited and their politics, while he allowed his accountant to arrange charitable donations because they were a tax advantage. He didn't see the difference.

He made friends easily and gave them up just as easily when someone more interesting came along, where she maintained a few, precious, friendships that she'd had for decades. The only thing Derek took seriously was his connection to his family, which she supposed was natural because his inheritance would surely outstrip his trust fund, no matter how generous that seemed to be. She, on the other hand, had more or less lost touch with her father because she was not what he'd expected, or apparently wanted, in a daughter he'd brought up on his own after his wife died, leaving him alone with a willful toddler. Derek's non-judgmental nature had been what first attracted her, possibly because it was the opposite of her father's, and she tried to hold on to that as she struggled to feel an attraction that had evaporated in the preceding months.

"Is something wrong?"

She'd shaken her head. "No, it's just been a very long day. You must be tired. Come, the car's just outside. The driver's name is Tony and he's looking forward to meeting you."

"You make friends with the oddest people," he'd remarked, following her as she walked away. "But I have to admit that it has been a long day. Did I tell you that I had to travel in steerage to Amsterdam because first class was full?"

"Several times," Shara mumbled. "Here we are," she said loudly and with false cheer when she spotted Tony standing beside the car in the waiting zone.

When the door had closed behind them and Tony started the engine, an uncomfortable silence descended in the car. Shara could feel the weight of it, but she didn't know what to say to break it. She'd remembered a time when they would have been struggling to keep their hands off each other. Now she dreaded the thought of his trying to touch her. There'd be no excuse of physical illness and she could think of nothing to explain why she didn't want to have sex with the man who wanted to spend the rest of his life with her. Yet *she* didn't want *him* – at least not the way she wanted . . . *Jessa*. Shara forced the mental image of Jessa's eyes to fade, but that left only the close confines of the car, with rain pounding on the roof and forcing the windshield wipers to sweep maniacally fast in order to clear a space for the driver to see. Derek's presence seemed to expand to fill the space until it forced the air from Shara's lungs and made it difficult for her to breathe.

Just when she was about to ask Tony to stop the car so she could step out into the downpour for a few gasps of air, Derek twisted his body to face her. "Will you at least tell me what the hell is going on? I travel halfway round the world to see you and all I get is this ... impersonal reception."

Shara flushed and glanced nervously at Tony. "Derek, can we discuss this when we get to the hotel?"

"No. We can discuss it now. What's going on, Shara?"

"This just ... this just isn't a good time for me. I'm tired. I've been working really hard recently getting ready for this role and it's been a full itinerary since we landed in New York ..."

"Working hard? Following that dyke around? Is that what's made you so tired that you can't even show any enthusiasm after I've traveled more than fourteen hours to come to this bloody country to see you?"

Acutely conscious of Tony, who could hear every word, Shara was horrified, especially after hearing the reverence with which Tony spoke of his adopted country. "Derek! Just for the record, from what I've seen of it, this is a beautiful country. And I wish you wouldn't refer to Jessa as a ... *dyke*."

"It's what she is. What's happened? Has she turned you against me?"

Shara's numbness upon seeing Derek was gradually evolving into annoyance and threatening to erupt into rage. She looked out of the car window as she fought to compose herself and gather her thoughts. Traffic was light and they'd already turned east along the lake shore, heading into the city. Straight ahead she could see the glow of light from the downtown skyscrapers, but the skyline and the distinctive shape of the CN Tower were obscured by mist and rain. "Nobody has turned me against you. In case it escaped you, I've spent nine hours *waiting* for you. I've missed a rehearsal, a TV interview and a dinner with the most prestigious classical music record label in the world."

"You make it sound as though you're the musician! None of that shit was anything to do with you. You're *tagging along*! How do you think it makes me feel to know you'd rather spend time with strangers, worse, musicians and recording industry blood-suckers, than with *me*?"

"You don't even *know* these people, yet you're comfortable calling them names ..."

"Nor do you. And would it matter if I did? The fact remains, you would clearly rather spend time with that dyke and her entourage than with me, despite the effort I've made ..."

"And just why *did* you make that effort, Derek?" Shara's hold on her temper was slipping badly. "And don't tell me it was for me, because we both know that would be a load of bollocks. Is it resentment of my career? Are you sorry that my success is not leaving me enough time to pay attention to you? Is that why you've been so dead set against my wanting to do well in this biopic?"

"That's preposterous."

"So tell me why you're here, when I specifically said that it was the city with the tightest schedule and you know that I'd have a lot more time over the next two weeks in Berlin and, most conveniently for you, in London?" Before he could answer, she went on, her voice steadily rising in volume, "Why? Because of some irrational insecurity? Because you think that a month in the company of a lesbian will turn me into one?"

PART NINETEEN

S hara stood outside the door to the apartment and tried to control the trembling in her belly. She felt an almost paralyzing nervousness that she knew was partly due to exhaustion. Her eyes burned from lack of sleep and from the bright summer sunshine that seemed determined to make up for the previous evening's rain, even though it had barely been six in the morning when the taxi had brought her back to Queen's Quay.

When she felt a bit calmer, she put the key in the lock and turned it, feeling her heart pounding in anticipation of a moment that could change her life. She hesitated before pushing the door open and remembered her quarrel with Derek. Remembered his scoffing at the idea of her being a lesbian, even while inside her the realization was taking root and the pieces were falling into place. She'd stopped listening to what he was saying, barely noticing the disdainful expression on his face, because she was preoccupied with a sudden insight into why she'd always been able to remain detached about the men in her life – even Derek. Why she'd always enjoyed sex with them, but had never felt the near-obsessive physical craving she felt for Jessa, even though they'd never made love. The thought caused her heart to ache.

"Why are you acting like this, Shara? How can you possibly question my motives for coming to see you? I tell you that I've missed you and all you seem to want to do is quarrel with me! I thought we could spend some time together and start planning the wedding. Is that so difficult to understand?"

What Derek was saying penetrated her reverie and Shara's jaw had dropped open in shock. "Derek, I haven't accepted your proposal."

"What do you mean?"

"I *mean* you suggested we get married and I never agreed! And even if I had, do you really think that a business trip would have been the best time to work on wedding plans, when you know I'll be back in the UK in less than two weeks? Why are you trying to rush me into this?"

"Forget the crap about your precious *business* trip," he'd said savagely. "Are you implying that you don't want to marry me?"

"I'm not implying it, Derek, I'm *telling* you!" Shara shouted at him. "I don't want, and have never wanted, to marry you. You don't want a wife, you want an acceptable milestone in your life – preferably one who will stay at home, fawn over you and produce offspring at the same intervals as your superficial, status-obsessed, so-called friends! Before you flew over here to make wedding plans, you should have asked me if I *wanted* a wedding, but that would have required empathy, consideration, or at least *some* fucking acknowledgement that my life and wishes carried the same weight as yours!"

As though realizing for the first time the extent to which he'd upset Shara with his presence and assumptions, Derek had relented. "Look, Shara, I'm really sorry if I've made you feel that your opinion doesn't matter, because it does, but surely you see that we need time together . . ."

"Time together isn't going to fix what's wrong with our relationship, Derek. What's been wrong with our relationship for some time." The fight had gone out of Shara, leaving a hollowness in her voice and a deep sadness in her heart. No matter what, she had loved Derek, just not enough – never enough.

"We don't have to get married right away . . ."

"I can't marry you, Derek," Shara had interrupted, her voice tight with suppressed tears.

Genuinely confused and having no experience of rejection or the thwarting of his plans, Derek had stared at her in stunned silence for several seconds before blurting out, "Why?"

"Because I don't love you." Shara fumbled for the door handle and fortunately, the car had stopped outside the Sutton Place Hotel where Derek had reserved a room. She'd stumbled out into the night and walked blindly around the corner, oblivious to the steady rain and with tears streaming down her face. A few people had walked by and stared curiously at her as she leaned against the side of the building and sobbed.

When she'd calmed down a bit, she'd looked around and seen the car, with Tony behind the wheel, parked down the street with its hazard lights flashing. Ever discreet, he was allowing her some privacy, but keeping an eye on her to ensure she hadn't got into trouble in a strange city when she was overwrought. Grateful for his consideration, she'd walked slowly towards the car and got in.

"Where can I take you?" The simple question had been spoken gently.

"I don't know ... I need to think ... Can you recommend a hotel for the night?"

He'd made a call on his cell phone and then said, "I'll take you to the Royal York. The concierge will meet you at the back entrance and escort you to your room. The formalities of checking in will be handled once you're settled."

Shara had nodded in silent gratitude.

The next several hours had been a blur of exhaustion, tears and memories that threatened to tear her soul apart. There were so many happy times she'd shared with Derek, yet there were so many others when their relationship had left her lonely and emotionally unfulfilled. She'd felt so much regret that it had almost suffocated her. Some of it concerned time wasted in a relationship that had quietly died, yet a lot of it concerned a dark-haired woman who now occupied such a huge space in her heart and in her soul and for whom her body yearned in a way that was impossible to ignore and increasingly difficult to turn away from.

She missed Jessa so much that the feeling added to her guilt at having been dishonest with Derek about her fading feelings for him. She wanted to grieve for the loss of her relationship with Derek, but she realized that more of her grief was for losing the safety of knowing exactly what to expect of her future, as long as that future was to be with Derek. Her feelings for Jessa were much more specific: she missed the intimacy of their friendship, the comfort of Jessa's affection and support and the certainty of Jessa's feelings for her. The intensity with which she missed those things made her feelings for Derek pale into insignificance, even as she faced an empty future without either of them.

As dawn had seeped into the night sky, she'd made a decision. She wanted to try to sort things out with Jessa. She wanted a relationship with Jessa, only she feared it might be too late. She knew that Jessa felt hurt and betrayed and the complexity of those feelings made Shara nervous.

Despite Derek's presence in her life, both she and Jessa had been aware that what had developed between them was special and exclusive. They'd never talked about Derek, but both had known that when the tour was over, Shara would have to deal with him and sort out her future. They'd tried to ignore that and concentrate on enjoying each other's company in the artificial atmosphere of the tour. Jessa's belief that Shara had invited Derek to Toronto, when Jessa was enduring the most stress of any time since they'd met and where Shara could have given something back to Jessa by supporting her, would have been heartbreaking even if they'd felt nothing for each other but friendship. And they felt so much more.

Now was the time for Shara to openly acknowledge what she felt. After Derek's little stunt, Shara knew the onus was on her to make the first move. To allow herself to be emotionally vulnerable and tell Jessa that she wanted to be with her. Explain to Jessa that Derek's visit had been as much of a shock to her as it had been to Jessa and to tell her that she'd ended it with Derek and hoped they could be together, not just as friends, but as lovers.

She pushed the door open and knew at once that something was different. She looked around for what was out of place. The first thing she noticed was the violin case on the sofa and the sheets of a score spread over the dining table. *Maybe Jessa was playing last night* she thought, although she knew that wasn't true because the baby grand piano was open and there was a score propped up on it. Jessa had not been playing that violin. Her heart was still pounding, but the reason had changed. She walked further into the flat and noticed the empty bottles of mineral water and the glasses, plural, on the coffee table. Jessa had definitely had company and whoever it was must have stayed very late, if they went through all that mineral water after a dinner party that would not have ended much before eleven o'clock.

She was almost at the doorway to the kitchen when she saw it: a crumpled, rather brief, black dress on the floor outside Jessa's bedroom. She knew it wasn't Jessa's and a soft, pained gasp escaped from her lips.

PART TWENTY

The bedroom door was open and Shara heard a voice that sounded vaguely familiar. "Jessica, you're an animal. You kept me up until almost dawn and you're awake already ... Maybe it's just as well – I need to get home and change my clothes. I can't very well turn up at rehearsal in last night's dress."

"You're welcome to shower here and wear something of mine. I feel guilty about exhausting you – I know I'm demanding and ..."

"Shh ... it was my pleasure. Now, where's my dress?"

Before Shara could move, the woman walked out of the bedroom. Shara knew who she was: Lucia Scattaglia, a violinist with the orchestra.

She and Jessa had a past. When it had become obvious to Shara at the first rehearsal that they knew each other, Jessa had admitted, "I've known Lucia since I was eight. She was the first girl I kissed, but I haven't seen her for over a year; the last time was in Vienna. At the time she was wasting her talent as a member of the Vienna Symphony when she could have been leader of another orchestra, all so that she could stay there and live with a woman she described as the love of her life." Jessa had shrugged sadly. "Maybe there's no such thing, because here she is. It's a shame I won't have space in my schedule to spend any time with her and catch up on events in her life. Still, I'm sure that her decision to leave Vienna will probably be the best thing for her career. She's fantastically talented and deserves a career as a soloist."

It looks as though Jessa found time in her schedule after all . . . Shara thought, bitterly, as pain pressed down on her heart. It didn't help that Lucia was gorgeous, especially in black panties that showed off her golden skin. Her breasts were bare and Shara flushed as she tried not to look at them. They were small and as tanned as the rest of her physically fit body. She was taller than Shara, with short black hair and wide brown eyes that looked at Shara in shock.

"Oh, sorry, I did not realize that Jessica had company . . ."

"I'm not company," Shara replied shortly, desperately blinking back her tears, because she did not want to make a fool of herself in front of the woman and it would have been too easy after the night she'd just had. "Excuse me," she added abruptly and walked blindly towards the door of her room.

"Are you talking to yourself again?" Jessa was smiling as she walked out of the bedroom, her hair still wet from her shower, wearing an unbuttoned pink shirt, cream trousers and no shoes.

Shara turned to stare at her and she knew at once what Shara was thinking. To be fair, she couldn't blame her. It was 6:30 in the morning, she was half-dressed and had quite obviously shared a bedroom with a woman who was practically naked. She also wondered how much of their conversation Shara had heard and how she'd interpreted it. "Shara, I wasn't expecting you back so early . . ." It was absolutely the wrong thing to say, because, while true, it nevertheless made Jessa sound as though she'd been caught doing something she wasn't supposed to.

"Obviously," Shara sneered.

By then, Lucia had struggled hastily into her dress and was slipping her feet into high-heeled sandals that Shara hadn't previously noticed, but which had been abandoned next to the sofa. "Jessica, I shall see you later at rehearsal. Shara . . . er . . . nice to see you again." She didn't wait for a response from Shara, but grabbed her evening bag and violin case and headed for the door. She could sense an impending explosion and she did not want to be there when it happened.

"Yeah, I'll see you, Lucia. And thanks."

Shara made a noise whose emotional significance Lucia found it impossible to gauge, so she slipped out of the door without further comment. As soon as she left, Shara turned away and continued to walk toward her room.

"Shara?" She stopped walking. "Are we going to talk?"

"What's there to talk about?" Her voice was tight. "From the look of things, you'd be better off catching up on your sleep; you've got an interview in two hours and a rehearsal after that."

"Why can't you look at me?"

Because when I do, all I can picture is her hands on you. Her mouth on you. And it tears me up inside. "Why don't you finish getting dressed. I've already had an eyeful of one near-naked woman this morning . . ."

"It bothers you that Lucia spent the night in my bed." It was a statement.

Pain twisted more cruelly in Shara's chest at Jessa's matter-of-fact confirmation of the situation, even though it had been obvious without that. She squeezed her eyes shut but still did not turn to face Jessa.

Nevertheless, Jessa saw the slight stiffening of her spine and misinterpreted its meaning. "It pisses you off to think that I was doing anything other than pining over you while you fucked your fiancé, doesn't it? You don't want me, but you don't want anyone else to have me. You like the idea of having me waiting in the wings to adore you when you've got the time to spare."

Shara could hear the contempt in Jessa's voice and, while she knew it was her own silence that had led Jessa to conclude that she didn't care about her, she also remembered the many ways in which she'd shown Jessa how much she *did* care.

She turned around. The hurt she felt was ripping her apart and she had no outlet for it. She wanted to cry, she wanted to shout and she wanted to lash out. She hated herself for having waited so long to admit her feelings that Jessa had given up and moved on. She hated Derek for forcing the event by showing up in Toronto and making Jessa think she'd wanted to see him. But right now she also hated Jessa for having given up on her so easily. How strong could Jessa's feelings possibly have been if, less than two weeks after their first kiss, she'd jumped into bed with someone else? Could Jessa feel what she felt and still allow another woman's hands to touch her body? Another woman's mouth? She struggled for words to express her pain and anger, but none came. "Go to hell, Jessa!"

Jessa flinched as the bedroom door slammed behind Shara. "I'm already there," she whispered, before turning away and going to her own room.

PART TWENTY-ONE

When Jessa showed up for rehearsal without Shara in tow, Lucia deliberately maneuvered her to the side of the room and asked softly, "Have you sorted everything out with Shara, or does she still believe that we slept together?"

"We did sleep together, Lucia." Jessa's voice was equally low and laced with irony, but Lucia could tell by Jessa's pale complexion and her reddened eyelids that she did not see any humor in the situation.

Lucia made an impatient sound and her eyes flashed with annoyance. "Not the way she thought. Stop being difficult and answer my question."

"Have you always been this bossy?" Jessa asked wearily, acutely aware that they were receiving funny looks from some other musicians who had noticed the conversation and Lisa was openly glaring in their direction. She sighed as she acknowledged that Lucia was going to get an answer even if it meant creating a scene. "No, I didn't explain to Shara that you were working with me on a huge solo for which nobody in the world had even seen a score until two days ago. If she wants to think we were having sex, then let her. She can hardly have a problem with it when that's exactly what she was doing with her fiancé at the time."

"How do you know that?"

"Oh, come on, Lu," Jessa whispered fiercely, leaning closer to Lucia, "she invited him over here and he flew all the way from London. Do you think they spent the night playing cards?"

"Well, you know, they say sex is like bridge: if you don't have a good partner, you'd better have a good hand . . ." Jessa didn't laugh at the joke and Lucia shook her head impatiently. "Jessica, you're assuming she was having sex with him, just as she assumed you were having sex with me. But you didn't have sex with me, because you're in love with her. Isn't it just possible that the same thing happened with her?"

A corner of Jessa's mouth turned up in a smile that didn't quite reach her eyes. "I didn't have sex with you because you didn't ask and because by the time you'd perfected your solo, and yes, that's perfected in my opinion, not yours, it was almost dawn."

"I didn't ask because you were mooning over her. Trust me, Jessica, I know how to push your buttons and if she hadn't been in the picture, I could have persuaded you that a duet was more important than my solo, long before dawn."

This time Jessa really did smile, because Lucia was charming and she was glad to have her back in her life. "I don't deny what I feel, Lu, but if she loved me, she would have spent these four weeks with me and then told him that she couldn't marry him. She certainly wouldn't have invited him to join her while she was on tour with me."

"Perhaps she wanted to be sure of her feelings and the best way to do that was to see him again. Maybe she even wanted to break up with him in person and couldn't wait until the tour was over."

Jessa looked away, because she'd tried to fool herself with that theory shortly after she'd read the note from Derek, but Derek's sending the note to her, not directly to Shara, had been territorial, almost triumphant. Not the action of a man who'd been summoned to receive bad news. "If that's true, then why did she spend the night with him? His flight arrived early yesterday afternoon. Surely that would have given her enough time to end it. How many times would it have been necessary to fuck him before she finally decided it was over and she could come home to me?"

"Excuse me, but we have a few dozen musicians waiting for your attention." Lisa's voice cut in, saving Lucia from having to respond to Jessa's questions. "It's bad enough that you insisted on Lucia for the solo, rather than the first violin, so let's not feed the rumors that she slept with you to get it."

"Lisa, it's good to see that you are still playing the role of Jessica's mamma, because she obviously can't sort out her life for herself. You know very well that I would not sleep with your daughter unless she agreed to marry me. I'm from a good family, remember? And she can no longer assert that it's not legal, as she did all those years ago when I seduced her, because it is nowadays – in Canada, at least."

Lisa smiled at Lucia. She'd always liked the girl and she'd been disappointed when they'd drifted apart and Jessa had started her affair with Stephanie. At the time, she'd thought that some of her displeasure was tied to the fact that Stephanie had persuaded Jessa to hire a publicist, insisting that Lisa could not possibly guide Jessa's career toward the fame and fortune that Stephanie craved.

Unlike Stephanie, Lucia was a gifted musician and a really sweet person. Her family had loved Jessa, all but adopting her once they'd recovered from the shock of discovering that Lucia was a lesbian and her friendship with Jessa was more than platonic. In hindsight, Lisa suspected that that was one of the reasons they'd got involved: Lucia knew her family loved Jessa and they could hardly object, on more than principle, to her being involved with someone they already cared for. Jessa had certainly never seemed to be deeply in love with Lucia. *Not the way she is with Shara*. Lisa felt profound guilt that she'd introduced Jessa to the actress and set in motion something which had proved to be such a disaster.

Two years after the split with her own family, following their discovery of her sexual orientation, reliving the process with a more positive result had helped Jessa to work through, and let go of, a lot of lingering pain and anger. For that, Lisa had been extremely grateful to Lucia and the extended Scattaglia family.

"As long as you two marry in your own time, I couldn't care less, but this conversation is starting to look like a tryst, so I'd suggest you knock it on the head and get to work ..."

"Sì, mamma," Lucia teased. "Although I think you should allow me some leeway since, on Thursday, I shall perform your bambina's composition in a way that will make it the most important classical piece to be premiered this year – maybe even this decade . . ."

Lisa couldn't help herself, she laughed. "That's good to hear. Now, if you can manage to move that ego of yours onto the stage without calling for assistance from a porter, I'd suggest someone start this rehearsal."

Jessa took several seconds to compose herself. It all seemed so irrelevant now: the job she was supposed to take up with this orchestra the following year, the rest of the tour and, especially, the rehearsal she now faced. To make things worse, the piece they were supposed to spend the morning rehearsing wasn't by an eighteenth century master, it was a very personal piece written for a love she knew she'd lost forever. Lost before she'd really had it. At first she'd considered entitling it *Shara*, since she hoped to use it to exorcise the memory of its inspiration from her soul, but she'd decided that naming it after her would only embarrass Shara and elicit mockery from Derek.

Even when it had been untitled, she'd been determined to perform it here – to begin the healing process in the city where she planned to make her home. She knew that it was by far the best thing she'd ever written and it surprised her how quickly and effortlessly it had flowed from her. It was a musical poem: each stanza represented one stage of her short, tempestuous relationship with Shara. The first was hesitant and melodic, dominated by the violin solo that Lucia played as though it emanated directly from her soul rather than her violin, which indicated to Jessa that the love she'd left behind in Vienna had not been forgotten.

The second stanza was an adagio, featuring the cello more than any other instrument. It documented the confusion that had accompanied the acknowledgement of her feelings for Shara. The tempo slowly built up during a vivid passage where the viola carried the melodic theme, celebrating the dizzying minutes when they'd kissed, before closing on a triumphant, percussive high.

The final stanza was underpinned by the same melody as the first, initially heard only in fragments, with a haunting echo on the cello, occasionally emphasized by the oboe. That haunting echo was the sound, in Jessa's heart, of a wonderful, instinctive friendship, overshadowed by the complications of a growing love.

As the piece ended, there was no melodrama, no grand finale. There was only the quiet clarity of an emerging love theme, played by the violins, with harmony from the violas. It was clearly the sound of a woman's heart weeping for something she was absolutely certain of, something she was absolutely certain she'd lost.

After performing it for the first time, the musicians erupted into spontaneous applause. They knew that they'd become part of something exciting that included not only the stunning performance that Lucia delivered, effectively removing any doubt as to why she'd been chosen for it, but also the thrill of a spectacular new composition. It wasn't often that they'd had the chance to be conducted in a piece by its composer and they savored the opportunity to be guided towards an accurate interpretation of every nuance of emotion and technical complexity that had been conjured from her imagination. One star-struck timpanist went so far as to ask Jessa to autograph his score, causing her to blush and eliciting another smattering of applause from his colleagues, who would no doubt tease him about it later.

Lisa noticed that Jessa looked exhausted and suggested a break before they began rehearsing *Planets*. She'd known, upon hearing the untitled piece, that it was a tribute to the woman who had stolen Jessa's heart and then broken it.

Before leaving the auditorium, Jessa told the orchestra that she'd decided to call it *A Walk in the Rain*.

PART TWENTY-TWO

SIX MONTHS LATER

*H*eartsick. *Broken-hearted.* Shara considered what those words meant and what they'd meant to her before she'd met, and spent time with, Jessa Hanson. She supposed they had always been abstract concepts. After all, the heart was a muscle unrelated to emotion: when it stopped beating, you stopped living. It was a simple biological fact. But nothing had been simple since she'd walked away from Jessa in Toronto. Now she knew that a biologically healthy heart could hurt, it could break and, most cruelly of all, when it broke, you survived to endure the pain.

The only thing that had kept her from rushing to the airport that morning had been the knowledge that Derek, too, would be moving heaven and earth to be on the first available flight to London. Instead, she'd spent several hours making arrangements for her departure and for something special she'd been thinking about before her world had fallen apart.

When she was satisfied and after receiving a package via courier, she'd rung Tony and asked him to drive her over the border to catch a flight, connecting in New York City, to Heathrow. For the second time in two days, she'd sat in the back of a car as it headed for Niagara Falls. This time it had gone past the Falls and over a bridge to the USA and Tony had got her a cup of coffee as she waited for the interminable US immigration formalities to be carried out. Once again, Shara thought that Tony's daughter was very blessed to have such a thoughtful, caring father.

An hour later, they were at the Buffalo airport and Shara was saying good-bye to another person she'd come to care for. At least this time she didn't have to pretend that it didn't hurt.

Tony refused to take money from her, but she'd anticipated that and handed him an envelope with "something to cover the cost of the petrol". He'd reluctantly accepted it and Shara had felt better. She'd found out that Tony's daughter was in her final year at the University of Toronto and it had taken hours to do it, but Shara had paid the young woman's tuition bill up to the point of graduation and set up a fund to cover a post-graduate degree, with the stipulation that if she chose not to use it, the contents would go to a scholarship for financially disadvantaged students. The envelope contained a letter to that effect from the university, a short note from Shara and, as a gesture that would make Tony smile, some petrol-money. The note attempted to explain how much Tony's kindness had meant when she was at one of the lowest points in her life, but she was sure she had not succeeded.

She'd spent the next two weeks studying the script for *Maestra*, more determined than ever that her portrayal of Jessa should not betray the woman who had trusted her enough to let her so completely into her life. She knew that Jessa had cared for her and that she had betrayed Jessa's feelings by refusing to acknowledge them at first and then refusing to acknowledge her own, reciprocal feelings later on. In the two weeks after she'd returned to London, she'd relived every second of her time with Jessa, finally deciding that it had been at the moment on the hilltop in the rain that she'd fallen deeply and irrevocably in love with Jessa Hanson.

She'd cried until she'd had no tears left, weeping out her grief for the loss of something she hadn't realized she'd had. She'd played the game of *What if?* until it drove her to the brink of madness. What if she'd kissed Jessa that day? What if she'd hung up on Derek the night of her special dinner with Jessa and invited Jessa into her bed? What if she'd made love with Jessa, touched her, tasted her and given her pleasure? What if she'd admitted that morning in New York that Jessa, after only a few weeks, was the most precious thing in her life and she didn't want to face a future without her?

What if she'd done one or all of those things? Would they be together now, or would she still be alone, except with vivid memories, not just of walks in the woods and long conversations late at night, but memories of lovemaking that would surely have shaken her to the depths of her soul?

After all, Jessa could not have felt what she'd felt, what she still felt, or Jessa could not have given herself to Lucia. It was as simple as that.

What she felt for Jessa was like nothing she'd experienced before; it consumed her. She knew that it had shaped her performance in the film, but it would take the rest of her life for it to work its way out of her soul. Just remembering kissing Jessa, the intimacy of feeling Jessa's mouth on hers, could bring tears to her eyes and make her heart soar in her chest, even though the kiss had had a carnal dimension that made her want Jessa sexually in a way that should probably be considered shameful.

She knew that making love with Jessa would be more than physical: it would be sacred. She could not imagine lying with someone else when she felt so much for Jessa. She sincerely hoped that, with time, that intensity of feeling would pass, because she wanted to live again – not just exist with a broken heart that continued to beat.

It had been a relief to start daily work on the film and she'd been grateful that Peter Garofolo was such a hard taskmaster, because the punishing schedule he'd established had physically exhausted her. It had also been good for her emotionally to try to get inside the head of the woman she loved and react to things as she knew Jessa would.

The part of Stephanie had been played by Keeley Hawes in the most important role of her career to date and Shara had been impressed with the way she'd inhabited the character, making it easy for Shara to portray the reckless infatuation that had led Jessa to commit to doing anything for Stephanie, even if it meant the end of her career – which it almost had.

The hardest scenes were the crowd scenes with the flashbulbs of the mock paparazzi and the extras with their autograph books held out, all shouting demands and questions at her. It had been almost *too* real.

It was almost unheard of for such a major project to begin filming in September and wrap up before the end of the year, but that was exactly what Garofolo had managed to do. Since she was in so many scenes, Shara worked almost as hard as the director. When he'd realized that Shara was interested in more than just playing her role, he'd welcomed her into his world and solicited her feedback as they viewed the day's rushes together. She suspected that, fresh from his third divorce, he'd been interested in more than her experience as a thespian, so she'd told him in no uncertain terms that she and Derek had broken up because she was in love with someone else. Beyond a boyish grin and a shrug, he'd taken the rebuff in his stride. If anything, it had made him take Shara even more seriously and he'd gone so far as to offer her credit as an assistant to the director, if she wanted it - "But no more money!" They'd laughed and she'd told him that she'd settle for directing one of his productions some day. "Deal," he'd replied, holding out his hand for her to shake.

It was the tunnel vision of the project that Shara blamed for the fact that she did not find out about the impact of Jessa's latest composition until the final day of filming. She was getting into the limousine on her way to the wrap party when she heard Jessa's name emanating from the radio that the driver had been listening to as he'd waited for her to emerge from her temporary home in Beverly Hills. "Can you turn that up, please?" She asked, her heart pounding.

"Sure Miss Quinn. Just didn't figure you'd want to hear more about Jessa Hanson after bein' so wrapped up in her for the last little while."

You have no idea just how wrapped up in her I am Shara thought, biting her lip as pain washed over her. Before she could recover, the volume on the radio was turned up and her thoughts were mercifully drowned out.

"That's right, folks, she's done it again. Not only does she hold the record for the highest charting classical music piece in chart history, well not counting a disco version of Beethoven's Fifth in 1976, she now has the record for the only classical piece ever to win both short and long-form video

awards on MTV. Not bad for a chick with a stick!

Now if you've been living in a cave and have no idea what the fuss is about, I'm gonna give you a chance to hear Jessa Hanson conducting the Toronto Symphony Orchestra as they play her phenomenal composition, 'A Walk in the Rain', right after this commercial break."

Shara's head was spinning. Why had no one on the set mentioned this? And why hadn't Elise, or Susan, or any of her friends? The last question answered itself: because they'd all avoided mentioning Jessa after Shara had admitted her feelings to Elise and asked her if she wouldn't mind telling their other friends to just let it be while it was still so raw. She'd tried to make light of it by promising to reveal everything over several vodkas once "it" was all over, but in her heart she hadn't been very confident that it would ever be over. After her confession, she'd been struggling to hold back her tears and Elise had hugged her for a long time, promising to respect her wishes. Fortunately, she'd had plenty to say about Derek and his pushy behavior, so she hadn't felt as though she'd been completely shutting out her friends.

As Shara thought about that, the advertisements ended and the "phenomenal" composition began to play. By the time it ended, Shara was sobbing helplessly and she knew that she would not be going to the wrap party.

PART TWENTY-THREE

Jessa had never felt less like celebrating Christmas in her entire life. Not even her sixteenth Christmas, the first one where she'd been estranged from her family, even though she'd already broken up with the girl who'd precipitated the rift. At the time she'd lost one family, but she'd had another – she'd had Lisa. She'd also had the Scattaglias, if she'd wanted to fly to Italy to spend the holidays with them, which she had done for what they'd called "little Christmas" on the 6th of January. The problem now was that when you lost the person who completed your soul, there was no replacement.

She got out of the taxi tightly clutching the package, trying to absorb the good wishes, positive energy and Christmas spirit its contents symbolized. The kids at the school had heard her mention that she tended to misplace her car keys, so they'd made her a bowl to keep them in. It was fashioned from red clay, but covered on the outside with dozens of brightly painted ceramic tiles. Each tile had been hand-painted by a member of the program, then pressed into the wet clay of the slightly crooked bowl, glazed and fired. When Jessa had seen it, she'd been touched to the point of tears. They'd presented it to her half an hour earlier at the conclusion of their Christmas concert. A concert which had been incredibly good, considering the program had only been started two years earlier.

The last thing they'd played had been *Silent Night*. They'd worked incredibly hard on it, so that they wouldn't need to read the music as they played and they could perform it by candlelight. Even their parents had cooperated and not used flash cameras. The effect had been so beautiful that it had given Jessa goose bumps. It had also made her feel incredibly lonely.

Knowing that the school car park would be full and street parking would be impossible to find, Jessa had decided not to drive and while she'd been waiting for the taxi to arrive to take her home, it had started to snow. As the soft flakes had settled on her coat and her hair, the families, teachers and volunteers streamed out of the school, children's voices filled with excitement at the prospect of a white Christmas. Jessa had wondered if it was snowing where Shara was. Was Shara in Ireland with her family? Or was she in California, pretending to be the woman whose heart she still held?

She knew that Shara was no longer with Derek. Like Stephanie, Derek had used the tabloid press as an instrument of his revenge, presenting himself as the broken-hearted fiancé, wronged by a woman he'd doted on, despite the fact that she wasn't of the same social class. Jessa had felt impotent rage when she'd read the headlines. Despite the way Shara had treated her and the fact that Shara had never given her a chance to explain or redeem herself, she loved Shara Quinn with everything that she was and she never wanted anything bad to touch her life.

Jessa hesitated before she crossed the street to walk into the lobby. Thoughts of Shara would sometimes do that: paralyze her. She'd learned not to fight it. She allowed herself to think of Shara and turned her face up to the sky to accept the icy kisses of the snowflakes, taking comfort from the fact that the woman she loved was somewhere under the same sky.

"Jessa?"

At first she thought she'd imagined it – the sound of Shara tentatively calling her name. She shook her head almost imperceptibly and then started to cross the street. Traffic in Clerkenwell was light on the night before Christmas.

"Jessa! Wait!"

Feeling slightly faint, she turned around, just as Shara stepped away from shadow of the monastery wall where she'd been standing. "Shara." Jessa's voice was faint. She was wondering if she'd finally lost her mind.

"Hiya, Jessa." Shara smiled nervously. Jessa's eyes devoured the sight of her. Her hair was just as short as it had been when they'd first met, but now it was soaked with melted snow. She might have been working in California, but her skin was deathly pale and her eyes looked large and filled with apprehension in the uncertain glow of the streetlight. "I hope I'm not interrupting your holiday celebration and I'll try not to take up too much of your time." She spoke quickly, as though she expected Jessa to interrupt her or walk away. Jessa was surprised by how nervous she sounded and the way her voice shook.

"I'm not celebrating the holiday," Jessa said flatly, noticing as she spoke that Shara, too, seemed to be staring. Her gaze settled on the haphazardly re-wrapped present in Jessa's hands and she looked confused.

Jessa's grip tightened on the package. "It's from the kids you met – at the school?"

Shara nodded jerkily and looked away briefly before asking. "Lucia not spending Christmas with you, then?"

Suddenly, Jessa was angry. All the hurt she'd felt for all those months bubbled up in her chest and threatened to pour out in an eruption of rage. Because of what she thought had happened with Lucia, Shara had turned her back on what they'd had and never looked back. For the rest of the tour and the entire time Jessa had been working on scoring the film, her heart had been consumed by a pain so fierce that it had driven her to focus on her work just to survive. It had also made her sensitive to every nuance of the love story that she'd watched on the screen. Her work had been of a higher standard than she could have dared to hope and the producer had expressed confidence that the original songs and themes she'd composed would achieve chart success. But that project was finished now and her future yawned endlessly before her. Once again the pain of losing Shara was coming to the forefront of her life and yet Shara herself, the woman who'd made the decision to throw everything away, was standing there asking about *Lucia*.

"It wouldn't be any of your business if she were," Jessa said through gritted teeth.

The savagery of her response seemed to literally knock Shara back. She took a step to maintain her balance and then met Jessa's eyes bravely. "You're right," she said in a voice that shook helplessly. "I had no ... right." Her voice was hoarse. "I only came to say that I heard it yesterday. It's wonderful, Jessa. Beautiful. I heard it and it was as if ... as if I was living it all again in vivid ... glorious ..." Her voice broke and she stopped.

She searched Jessa's face and all she saw was anger. Tears filled her eyes, but did not fall. She thought perhaps they'd frozen in her eyes as everything else in her seemed to freeze when she saw the loathing in Jessa's eyes.

"You hate me ..." She said finally.

Jessa turned away, unable to give voice to such an enormous lie.

"Fine," Shara said. Her voice sounded stronger, but when Jessa turned to face her, she could see that Shara was shivering uncontrollably. "Hate me. But that night you're the one who slept with Lucia. You wrote that piece of music, so you felt everything I felt. You even ..." He voice broke again, but she forced herself to continue. "Y-you even called it *A Walk in the Rain*, so I know that moment ... th-the moment ... on the hill ..." This time the shiver seemed to steal her breath.

Jessa frowned. She'd been about to lash out at Shara, ask her if she thought she was stupid and then she saw the way she trembled. She noticed that not only was her hair wet, but that she was underdressed for an English winter and the melting snow appeared to have soaked through her jacket. Not only was her skin pale, but her lips looked bloodless and her teeth were chattering, which was why she'd stopped speaking. "Let's go inside," she said abruptly and reached for Shara's arm.

Shara snatched her arm away. "No."

"You'll catch your death out here! Did you drive?"

"C-c-cab."

"Well, they aren't exactly thick on the ground tonight, so come in and warm up and you can ring for one from my flat." As she spoke she grabbed Shara's arm again and more or less marched her across the street.

"Miss Quinn." The doorman looked stunned to see Shara. She

wasn't surprised. When she'd first arrived, he'd told her that Jessa wasn't at home. When she'd looked skeptical, after all, Jessa could have driven home and taken the lift from the garage, he'd smiled. "I'm not having you on. She left through the lobby and she hasn't come home yet. You're welcome to wait for her here." Embarrassed, because she'd felt like a stalker, even though he wasn't treating her like one this time around, Shara had declined. Now, looking at her, it would have been obvious that she'd chosen to wait for Jessa in the cold. He must think she was completely mad.

"H-hi again," she managed to mumble before Jessa whisked her through the security door and into the lift.

Shara didn't feel very well. She hadn't eaten since the night before. She'd refused lunch on the flight over and she'd been operating on adrenaline from the time she'd heard Jessa's new composition on the radio. She was leaning heavily on Jessa by the time they entered the flat. She could not feel her fingers or toes and then she came to the horribly unromantic realization that she was going to be sick.

"T-toilet ..." she gasped and Jessa led her along a corridor to the most decadent bathroom she had ever not had time to see, where she rushed to the toilet, and retched, although she had nothing to bring up. She sank down onto the bathroom floor, thoroughly humiliated, but too cold and ill to get up. This was not the way she'd planned her reunion with Jessa.

PART TWENTY-FOUR

To Shara's chagrin, Jessa helped her up, closed the lid of the toilet and sat her on it. She was still shivering uncontrollably and Jessa's expression was quickly changing from worried to alarmed.

"You're freezing," Jessa said, frowning. She grabbed a fluffy white robe off a hook and held it out to Shara. "Get out of those wet clothes and put this on. I'll make you some tea." She looked at Shara again and shook her head. "You probably need to go to hospital." She turned away, turned on the taps in the bath and walked out of the room. Shara hoped she wasn't going to ring for an ambulance, or her humiliation would be complete.

Jessa came back into the room after only a few minutes. She'd shed her own jacket and was in her stockinged feet. Shara hadn't moved. She looked helplessly at Jessa, reluctant to admit that her fingers were too numb to undo buttons or zips. Jessa made an impatient sound when she realized what the problem was. "You're not fit to be allowed out on your own," she muttered, before kneeling down in front of Shara to take off her ridiculously high-heeled boots and the thin socks she'd worn under them, neither of which had protected her feet from the cold, wet pavement.

Next she peeled off Shara's wet jacket and dropped it on the floor, on top of her boots and socks. Her blouse followed and then Jessa pulled her to her feet so she could unbutton her jeans and peel them down her legs. Shara sighed as she watched Jessa's head bent over her and felt the tender way she was undressing her. There was nothing sexual about Jessa's actions, but they seemed so much more than just kind. Unable to help herself, Shara reached out and touched Jessa's hair. It was damp from the snow and incredibly soft. "You're so very beautiful," she whispered, before another shiver shook her small frame.

"Shara . . ." *You've turned yourself into a human ice lolly and, even with that, I'm having trouble keeping my hormones under control as I undress you, so behave, okay?* Jessa couldn't say what she felt, so she turned away to sprinkle some bath salts under the steaming tap: lavender to relax and chamomile to heal. Not that she thought aromatherapy was really going to fix what ailed her.

She turned back to face Shara, who had not moved. She wanted to ask her if she was capable of taking off her underwear on her own, but she already knew that the hooks on a bra would be beyond the capabilities of fingers that remained icy despite the warmth of the room. Hesitantly, she took off Shara's bra, unable to disguise her soft intake of breath when she saw Shara's naked breasts; dark nipples puckered from the cold and aureoles tight, the way Jessa imagined they would be if . . .

Shara's teeth chattered, halting Jessa's errant thoughts. She gulped as she peeled down Shara's panties. She was so close that she imagined the soft curls trembled from her breath. Although she herself was far from cold, her legs shook as she stood up, took Shara's half-frozen hand and led her over to the bath. For the first time, she cursed the size of the bathtub, because it meant she had to help Shara climb in and ignore the brush of Shara's naked breast against her arm.

Shara cried out as the warm water touched her frigid skin.

"It's okay, darling. It's just the circulation coming back. It will only be uncomfortable for a few minutes." When Shara was in the bath, with steaming, fragrant water up to her chin, Jessa murmured, "Now, stay there," as though Shara were capable of doing anything else, "and I'll be right back."

She returned with a steaming mug and handed it to Shara. "Drink this. It will settle your stomach and warm you from the inside out."

Shara murmured her thanks and inhaled the scent of ginger from the mug. She was starting to enjoy having Jessa take care of her, now that she wasn't feeling quite so wretched.

"Were you sitting on the pavement?" Jessa was frowning as she looked at the wet and decidedly muddy clothes on the bathroom floor.

Shara looked embarrassed. "I might have been ... for a little while."

"How long were you out there?"

Shara shrugged, but didn't meet Jessa's eyes. "Not sure." She'd stopped shivering and was starting to feel as though she was in some sort of waking dream. She wasn't about to ruin it by admitting to Jessa that she'd been waiting for her for at least three hours – long enough for the cold winter rain to turn to snow. It would make Jessa think she was completely mad.

"Can any of those go in the washing machine? Even if I dry them, they won't be fit to wear unless they've been cleaned."

"Everything but the jacket, I think." Shara couldn't have cared less about her clothes.

Without another word, Jessa picked up the soggy mess from the floor and left the room. Shara closed her eyes and sank into the warm water, her hands cupping the hot mug. She fervently hoped that the change in the rhythm of Jessa's breathing when she'd taken off her bra, meant that a more pleasant image had replaced the one of Shara hanging onto the edge of the toilet and attempting to throw up the meager contents of her stomach.

By the time Shara had finished the tea, she was feeling almost human. Jessa still had not returned and, left alone with her thoughts, she was starting to believe she'd made a huge mistake in coming here at all, not just in waiting outside in the cold for Jessa. What good would it do to confront Jessa about *A Walk in the Rain*? No matter what she'd felt when she'd written it, obviously she'd been able to get over those feelings and go to bed with Lucia. Yet, coming here had proved one thing: Jessa wasn't completely immune to her. Jessa had been concerned about her pathetic state, but the way she'd cared for her and the way she'd looked at her body had clearly implied that her feelings were more than casual.

Shara put down the mug and got out of the bath, pleasantly surprised to find that the floor was heated. She dried herself with a towel that smelled freshly laundered, but with a hint of Jessa's shower gel. She chided herself for lingering and burying her face in it, before placing it back on the heated rail. She shrugged into the robe Jessa had left for her and went in search of her hostess.

Jessa was in the kitchen, ladling soup into two bowls. She looked up when Shara approached. She noticed Shara's flushed skin and pink lips and smiled. "You look as though you might actually live," she said mildly.

Shara's flush deepened. "Sorry about that. And thanks for doing all this. I suppose I must have lost track of time while I waited. Not very bright." She was feeling so awkward that she suddenly wished the floor would open up and swallow her.

"Deciding not to wait in the lobby was definitely not very bright. Were you afraid you'd be recognized?" Jessa took a baguette out of the oven as she spoke and broke it with her hands, French style. She'd already set out a bottle of mineral water and two glasses.

"Not really. I just had some thinking to do and I couldn't, not with the security guard watching me."

Jessa nodded, as though she understood Shara's strange logic. "Come on, have some soup."

Suddenly ravenous, Shara nodded. "Thanks. Smells delicious. How did you make it so quickly?"

"I had vegetable stock in the fridge. I like to cook when I'm at home. Nothing fancy, but at least I know what's in it."

They ate in near-silence. Shara declined a second helping because she dreaded a return of the nausea she'd felt earlier.

"Shara, why are you here?"

The question startled Shara and her spoon clattered into the almost-empty bowl. It was the obvious thing for Jessa to ask, so she didn't know why she hadn't prepared an answer. She looked down at her hands. "I ... because yesterday, just before I went to the wrap party, I heard *A Walk in the Rain* for the first time. I know that sounds strange, now that I know what a big hit it is, but for the last five, six months, I've avoided ... real life."

Jessa looked stunned. It had hurt so much to believe that Shara had heard the music that documented her love, yet felt nothing, done nothing to so much as acknowledge it. As a result, all the accolades, the awards and the sales milestones had only made her bitter. Finding out that, in fact, Shara had never heard the music, threw her completely off balance. *Yesterday*. Shara had heard it yesterday, last night, and it had prompted her to fly more than six thousand miles in twenty-four hours. Jessa's mind reeled and her heart thudded in her chest.

She got up from the table and walked towards the window only to stare blindly out at the snowflakes as they drifted past the street light. Shara's words and their implication kept playing over and over again in her head.

"Jessa, if I'd known ... if I'd known you felt that ... I wouldn't have left. I shouldn't have left. I know that now."

"So why are you here?" Jessa's voice was hoarse.

"I have so many regrets. I couldn't live with any more regrets. Every mistake I've made with you has come from not taking any action. At least, if coming here was a mistake, it will be a mistake I made from doing something, not from avoiding something."

She could see the tension in Jessa's body, but Jessa made no move to face her. She walked towards Jessa. "The first mistake I made was in not begging you to make love to me at the cottage, when everything in me wanted you to." She heard Jessa's soft moan and knew she had her full attention. "The next mistake I made was not telling you in New York that you'd become the most important person in my life. The third mistake I made was not telling Derek to stay away from me until I could come back to London and end it with him. The last mistake I made was in deciding that if you wanted her, perhaps you'd be better off with Lucia. I should have stayed, fought for you, pleaded for you ..." Hot tears stung her eyes, and spilled down her cheeks. "Please, Jessa, have I made another mistake?"

"You don't think that sleeping with Derek that night in Toronto was a mistake, after you'd spent most of the previous day with him?"

"I didn't. His flight didn't come in until almost nine o'clock. I'd spent the day in Niagara Falls and the evening having dinner with the limo driver in Toronto. I'd had a lot of time to think and before we even got to his hotel, I'd broken it off with him. You were still angry with me and I didn't feel ready to face you, so I spent the night at the Royal York hotel. I decided I'd been running away for long enough, which is why I was at your flat so early, only to find ..."

"That I'd spent the night with Lucia ..." Jessa turned around and saw the anguish on Shara's face. "Nothing happened, Shara. Now that you've heard the piece, you know how much it features a solo violin. I was working with Lucia on that until four in the morning. I've known her since I was eight and we'd shared rooms, even beds, as friends, countless times in our early twenties, long after our affair was over. It was only because Stephanie was jealous of her that we stopped being close. It would have been silly for one of us to try to sleep on a sofa when we were both so knackered and had such a full day ahead of us. It would have made even less sense for one of us to take over your bed, when I had no idea when you'd be home, so we shared my bed. I was wrong not to make that clear at the time, but I was so hurt and angry over your spending the night with Derek ..."

"I'm so sorry, Jessa ..."

"So what now?"

"Now you know how I feel ..."

"Do I?" Jessa was still afraid to believe what Shara's confession implied.

"I've missed you, Jessa. I've been empty without you." She stepped closer until she was so close that her body brushed against Jessa's. She deliberately untied the sash on the robe and raised one hand to caress Jessa's cheek. "Please don't turn me away."

"I can't," Jessa said simply, before her mouth covered Shara's in a hungry kiss. "I love you too much."

PART TWENTY-FIVE

I can't stop touching you ..." Shara said softly. She laughed self-consciously, but her voice had broken on the last syllable and she struggled to hold back tears.

Jessa looked at her kiss-swollen lips and flushed skin and replied, "I'm not complaining. I like having you touch me ... and I like looking at you." And she did. She couldn't get enough of Shara Quinn.

Now she knew that Shara was especially sensitive there, the left side of her neck had acquired a special, delicious significance and looking at it made Jessa smile. Unable to resist, she trailed a finger over Shara's skin, making her shiver. Their eyes met and Jessa whispered, "You're gorgeous. I'm totally in love with you. Do you know that?"

"I knew that when I heard *A Walk in the Rain*. And do you know how much I love you?"

"Do you?" Jessa couldn't hide her insecurity.

"I love you," Shara said it slowly, deliberately. "I thought I'd just shown you how much ..." As she spoke, the finger that had been slowly circling Jessa's nipple brushed softly over it, making Jessa gasp.

"I remember," she said. "It's just hard for me to accept that I haven't imagined it. I've loved you and wanted you for so long that it's hard for me to believe I'm here with you ... like this."

In response, Shara moved one foot sensually up Jessa's calf. "It feels a bit like a waking dream to me, too. Why didn't you tell me?"

Jessa frowned, distracted by the movement of Shara's foot and by the finger that still flirted dangerously close to her nipple, causing it to harden ... again. "Tell you what?" Arousal seemed to be causing a rapid drop in her IQ, despite the fact that Shara was barely touching her and that they'd already made love twice that night.

"That it would be like this," Shara replied huskily, moving so that she was lying on her side facing Jessa, who still lay on her back. "That it would be this good." As she spoke, three more fingers joined the first in caressing Jessa's breast while avoiding the jutting nipple. "That I would want you ... so much ... that I couldn't get enough of you." Her words were punctuated by kisses: soft, open-mouthed kisses placed strategically around the nipple of Jessa's other breast. Jessa moaned, because when Shara stopped speaking, it was so her open mouth could cover the nipple and her tongue could swirl softly around it. Shara didn't close her mouth and when she breathed in, the sensation of heat and wetness Jessa felt from her tongue was followed by the bite of cool air. The resultant surge of arousal caused Jessa's back to arch off the bed.

Shara lifted her head and looked into Jessa's eyes, which were half-closed and dazed. "Why didn't you tell me ... that you could want me this much?" she asked hoarsely and her hand swept roughly over Jessa's breast and her stomach to her pubis.

Jessa had been surprised to find that Shara was a vocal lover. The woman was so reluctant to verbalize her feelings outside the bedroom that it had first disconcerted, then delighted, Jessa to find that this was one of the inhibitions Shara lost when it came to sex. In fact, she seemed to lose every possible inhibition, which was just fine by Jessa. To make it even more erotic, Shara didn't talk "dirty" in any stereotypical way, she just said whatever was on her mind – and Jessa had discovered in just a few hours, that Shara Quinn had a very inventive mind. Shara made her feel more beautiful than any lover had in the past. It was impossible to doubt the softly spoken words of praise preceding the kisses and touches that demonstrated physical appreciation of Jessa's body. Jessa's touch, the taste of her, her responsiveness and her physical beauty were all recipients of Shara's vocal tributes, some of which were delivered in a whimper or a breathless moan.

It was Jessa's turn to moan as Shara's fingers slipped between Jessa's labia and Shara said softly, "I love the way you get so wet for me . . ." She leaned forward and kissed Jessa, swallowing her helpless moan as her fingers began a slow, relentless pressure that conspired with the taste of her mouth and the sight of her heavy-lidded eyes to overwhelm Jessa's senses.

Jessa knew that if she didn't stop Shara at that moment she would be lost and there was more she wanted to share with Shara before the inevitable and shattering orgasm that would make her as helpless as a baby in Shara's arms. She gathered her strength and with no little effort, she pulled away from Shara's kiss and at the same time shifted on the bed so that she was straddling Shara. She almost gave up her efforts when Shara smiled seductively at her and demonstrated that her new position gave her even better access to Jessa's body.

Jessa squeezed her eyes shut and for a few seconds allowed herself to savor the sensation of Shara's fingers sliding into her body.

Eventually, she managed to say "No!", although the word emerged somewhat breathlessly. She pulled Shara's hand away and pinned it above her head. She moved to lie more fully on top of Shara and slid one thigh between both of Shara's, resting her full weight on Shara to keep her from moving – or at least to try to keep her from moving.

Shara was fit – and a lot stronger than she looked. She chuckled, a wicked, teasing sound that sent shivers down Jessa's spine. Then she parted her legs further, trying to get leverage on the bed to push Jessa into a more submissive position so that she could continue what she'd started. But she achieved a different, unintended consequence. As she shifted her hips on the bed, Jessa let go of her hand so she could push her upper body away from Shara's to pin her with her hips. That, combined with Shara's movement, caused Jessa's swollen clit to slide deliciously against Shara's, which made them both gasp.

Shara looked up at Jessa, saw the look of wonder at the shock that had gone through her body and said, "I like that." She wasn't sure what it was she liked most: Jessa, leaning over her with bruised lips and red marks on her skin from her teeth and nails, the expression of complete, helpless horniness that dilated Jessa's pupils and made her look almost pained, or that unbelievable sensation of Jessa's body pressing against hers so intimately and knowing that the small movement of her hips had given Jessa as much pleasure as it had given her.

To test herself, Shara moved again, feeling a lightning bolt of sensation go through her as swollen, aroused flesh was ground against similarly aroused flesh. She closed her eyes and moaned, throwing back her head. Her arching back broke the contact between their two bodies and Jessa thrust her hips forward to regain it. That movement intensified both the contact and the sensation and Shara moaned. To prevent Jessa from thinking that the moan had signified anything except near-unbearable pleasure, Shara put both hands on Jessa's buttocks and pulled her forward, urging her to repeat what she'd just done.

Jessa did and this time they both moaned. Jessa needed no further urging and together they built up a rhythm that made Shara feel as though the rest of the world had fallen away, leaving all her senses to be completely dominated by Jessa. She could feel the pressure building in her belly. Both she and Jessa were making sounds that might have indicated affection, or just mind-expanding pleasure, and she could see from Jessa's half-closed eyes and dazed expression that she, too, was close to the edge. Jessa's hair was wet, and both their bodies glistened with sweat as their movements became faster. But no matter how desperately they strained towards the inevitable, they had to control their thrusts, or risk losing that heavenly contact. The concentration required seemed to intensify the sensations, because it meant that Shara was completely aware of Jessa: the woman she loved, the woman who loved her, the woman who was loving her.

"I've never ... come ... this way before," Jessa gasped. Her arms were trembling and her movements were slightly jerky, spurring Shara to hold her hips more tightly.

Jessa watched the way the light played on the Shara's sweat-slicked skin and the way her stomach muscles bunched visibly and then relaxed with each thrust and she didn't think any sexual moment could be more powerful or more perfect than the one she was experiencing. She didn't think that there could be anything more perfect than making love with Shara Quinn.

Shara looked into the eyes of the woman she loved more than she'd thought it possible to love. The woman whose body she worshiped. She watched the sway of Jessa's breasts and felt the play of strong muscles in her buttocks. She wanted the moment to last forever, but she knew that her body was racing toward fulfillment and she could not hold back – not with Jessa. She lifted her head off the bed and Jessa obeyed the wordless request and kissed her deeply. As their mouths moved apart, Shara moaned into Jessa's ear, "Come with me ... please ... now ..."

Jessa couldn't believe the effect that Shara's words had. As though conjured from the depths of her soul, an orgasm like nothing she'd felt before wracked her body and as it did, it seemed to communicate directly with Shara's body and she felt Shara come at the same time. As Shara bucked against her, she heard a low, growling sound, but she wasn't sure who made it. It was a guttural sound of animal satisfaction, but it accompanied a sating of emotional, as well as physical, desire. Neither woman had closed her eyes; they'd chosen instead to watch the sensation build in each other's bodies before feeling it explode between them.

Jessa collapsed onto Shara, her tears mingling with the sweat on Shara's temple and soaking into Shara's hair. Shara stroked Jessa's back with a hand that trembled. As she felt Jessa's weight on her and her heart and breathing gradually slowed, a feeling of safety and satisfaction stole quietly into her soul. For the first time in more than thirty-six hours, she slept.

PART TWENTY-SIX

When Shara woke up, it was light outside and for a few seconds she couldn't remember where she was. Then it all came flooding back – the frantic transcontinental and transatlantic flights, the hours spent standing in the cold waiting for Jessa, Jessa coming home, quarreling with her and then taking such wonderful care of her when she was feeling ill. And finally, the night spent in Jessa's bed. She was still there, but Jessa wasn't. She smiled and stretched, enjoying the feeling of the cotton sheets against her sensitized flesh. She felt well loved, completely relaxed and hungry. She entertained a guilty hope that Jessa was out there somewhere, preparing food.

She lifted her head and looked around for a clock. There wasn't one, but her watch was on the bedside table. *Two o'clock!* She couldn't believe she'd been asleep for at least ten hours. She flushed when she realized that she'd fallen asleep within seconds of making love with Jessa. She remembered having read somewhere that women liked to be cuddled after sex and felt as though she'd failed a major test of lesbianism. Perhaps because she'd never feel such a deep emotional bond with any of her partners, she'd always wondered why other women objected to husbands and boyfriends going right to sleep. *I'll make it up to her* she vowed immediately and grinned when she acknowledged that her motives weren't completely altruistic. Not ever having had a particularly strong sex drive, she was surprised by what she felt now and even more so by what she'd felt and done the night before.

She pulled Jessa's pillow towards her and hugged it, inhaling deeply and feeling intoxicated by the smell of her lover. She closed her eyes and continued to smile to herself. She was in love. She had never been so much in love. Jessa Hanson made her soul content. *And she doesn't do too badly by my body, either.*

Suddenly filled with a longing to see the woman who dominated her thoughts and filled her heart, Shara looked around for the robe she'd worn the night before. Her smile widened when she remembered that it had been abandoned on the living room floor. Jessa's white shirt had been dropped on the floor by the bedroom door, so she pulled that on, enjoying the way Jessa's perfume still clung to the white fabric.

The first thing she noticed when she walked into the living room was the music. It was *Signore, ascolta!* from Puccini's *Turandot*. Shara remembered the scene well: the slave girl Liù was begging Calaf not to risk his life in a quest for the love of the unfeeling princess. She had already admitted that all her sacrifices in caring for his father had been inspired by a single smile from Calaf, which had made her fall in love with him. It was a beautiful love song, even though Liù knew that the society in which she lived would not allow her love to have a happy ending. Shara shivered as she realized that her love, too, would be frowned upon by some segments of society. She shrugged off the feeling and looked around until she saw Jessa, mouthing the words to the Italian love song and stirring something in a bowl.

As though sensing that she was being watched, Jessa looked up and when she saw Shara, she smiled. Looking at Jessa's smile, Shara completely understood how Liù had felt, because that smile was one major reason why she was so much in love. Of course the ruffled hair, big brown eyes and gorgeous body didn't hurt, nor did the intelligence, compassion, kindness and incredible talent *on the podium and in the bedroom*, Shara's suddenly sex-obsessed mind acknowledged. Jessa was wearing silk pajama bottoms and a white t-shirt and Shara wanted to do nothing more than drag her back into the bedroom and take them off, despite her growling stomach.

Jessa had decided that Shara deserved a big breakfast, but one that was reasonably healthy. She'd been smiling almost constantly from the moment she'd woken up to find Shara still in her bed. Shara must have been exhausted, because she'd fallen asleep immediately after making love, with one arm still around Jessa and their legs still in a sweaty tangle. Jessa had extricated herself without causing so much as a flicker of one of Shara's eyelids. After a bit of searching, she'd found the duvet on top of the pillows on the floor and retrieved everything before pulling the duvet over both of them and falling asleep herself. During the night she'd woken to find Shara snuggled against her with one hand on her breast. She'd grinned and wondered what kind of dream Shara had been having, before falling asleep again.

That morning, Shara had been lying with one arm and one leg over Jessa, as though she'd been afraid that Jessa would escape while she slept. When Jessa had first tried to move, she'd tightened her grip and Jessa had given in and just stayed in bed to enjoy the weight of Shara's warm body against hers under the covers. The sun had been coming up on a new morning and Jessa had felt as though her world was complete. *Christmas.* She didn't need trees decorated with baubles or twinkling lights; the warmth that filled her at that moment could have lit up an entire city.

She must have fallen asleep for a few more hours, because when she woke again, the room was bright. Shara had moved her leg, so Jessa was able to get up without waking her. After a brief stop in the bathroom, she'd pulled on some clothes and answered the call of an uncomfortably empty stomach by starting breakfast. She turned on the stereo and requested random tracks while she worked.

She'd been shocked to see the time and she wasn't surprised when she looked up just as she started to mix the pancake batter, to find that Shara had emerged from the bedroom. Shara was wearing her white shirt and nothing else and Jessa felt as though her body temperature had gone up a few degrees. *How can anybody be so beautiful?* Jessa wondered. The shirt came just to the tops of Shara's thighs and she hadn't managed to get the right buttons in the right holes. Even her short hair was out of place and her eyes were smoky gray and sleepy. Jessa wanted to do nothing more than put down the bowl she was holding and drag Shara back to bed.

As their eyes met, a smile slowly spread across Shara's face. Although still heavy-lidded, her eyes lit up and she started walking towards Jessa as though pulled by an invisible force. There was so much love in her expression that Jessa felt her stomach do a little flip. She put down the bowl and opened her arms so Shara could walk into them. She remembered doing the same thing in New York, but so much had changed since then. This time, the woman who wrapped her arms around her waist, snuggled into her body and nuzzled her neck was the woman who loved her.

"Merry Christmas, sweetheart," Shara murmured against Jessa's neck.

"Yes, yes it is," Jessa replied softly. "Thank you. And merry Christmas to you, too." She kissed Shara's forehead and the tip of her nose. Shara closed her eyes and tilted her face up and Jessa smiled at the silent invitation before accepting it.

As their lips met, Shara made a little squeaky noise that Jessa was learning to love and when Jessa would have pulled away, she went on tiptoe and pressed forward so the kiss would continue. Jessa's head was spinning. Shara felt so good in her arms and the kiss was a languid, sensual exploration that was almost sleepy. It wasn't really foreplay – it wasn't intended to lead anywhere – but it heightened all her senses and made her body heavy with arousal, so that she just wanted to stay there and kiss Shara forever. She let her hands wander over Shara's back, feeling the cotton shirt sliding over smooth skin and firm muscle. Her hands shaped Shara's bottom, eliciting another squeaky moan and causing Shara to grind her hips against hers while caressing the back of Jessa's head, threading her fingers through the riotous curls at the nape of her neck.

The steady hum of arousal between them was interrupted by the loud growl of Shara's stomach, last night's soup and bread now being no more than a distant memory. Jessa pulled away and chuckled. "Sounds as though I have to feed my woman . . ."

Shara inhaled sharply and when Jessa looked at her, her heart seemed to swell up in her chest and tears filled her eyes. Shara's expression was one of naked adoration. "I love being your woman," she told Jessa softly.

Jessa gulped. "I'm not sure what I did to deserve you, but I'm glad I did it – whatever it was."

"You won't be saying that if you don't feed me soon. I'll be passing out again and making a complete prat of myself, as I did last night."

"You didn't make a prat of yourself, but I have to say you have a unique way of getting a girl's attention . . ."

Shara smacked her on the bottom. "Well, as I recall, you seemed to be enjoying giving me your attention."

Jessa grinned mischievously, "Hmm, you *do* have a wonderful way of rewarding someone for a cup of tea and the use of her washing machine."

Shara raised an eyebrow and flashed her a seductive look. "You should see what's on offer for a full breakfast . . ."

"Will pancakes and real maple syrup, scrambled eggs, fresh fruit, yoghurt and freshly brewed coffee do? There are other menu options . . ."

Shara groaned. "Baby, I promise you that the pancakes and coffee alone will buy you a *lot* of sexual favors."

Jessa was still laughing when she returned to the pancake batter with a lot more enthusiasm than she'd felt before Shara had come out of the bedroom.

PART TWENTY-SEVEN

The month of January passed in a blissful blur. Shara rented a flat in South Kensington and made noises about needing to buy a place, since she'd sold her half of the Highgate house to Derek, but she seemed to be in no hurry. More and more articles of her clothing showed up in Jessa's wardrobe and, far from minding, they made Jessa feel warm inside every time she saw them. Sometimes, if they had dinner in West London, they'd spend the night in Shara's flat, but it was obvious that Jessa's place felt more like home to both of them than the temporary accommodation, furnished tastefully and impersonally by decorators, while Shara's possessions remained in storage.

London was cold, gray and blustery, but Jessa couldn't remember ever having enjoyed it more. The days developed a lazy, repetitive and somehow comforting, sameness, punctuated by adventurous, exhilarating lovemaking that made her wonder how her body had survived being deprived of it before she'd met Shara.

In general, Jessa woke up early. Occasionally she lingered in bed with Shara and they made love, but other times she got up and did what Shara called "those mysterious morning things" like meditating at home, going to the Dharma center or working out in her home gym. If she'd been up late composing, she'd sometimes go for a run, have a shower and then get back into bed before Shara had stirred. Those were some of her favorite mornings when, tired and relaxed, she would cuddle up to Shara. Sometimes Shara would wake and wrap her in her arms before they both went back to sleep.

Most mornings there wasn't a lot of conversation, since Shara was cute, but hardly communicative, before noon. Each would wander off to do her own thing: Jessa playing the piano and scribbling or poring over scores, Shara reading scripts or using the gym in contemplative solitude. At some point they'd both read one or the other of the two newspapers Jessa had delivered whenever she was home. No matter what they did, there was always music – even if it was listened to in wireless headphones by one so as not to disturb the other.

By lunchtime they usually both managed to be showered and dressed and after laconic discussions about what each felt like having, they'd wander out to sample the wares of one of the restaurants in Clerkenwell or, if they had dinner reservations or plans, they'd make something quick for themselves. Both had months of fan mail to catch up on, so sometimes they tackled some of that in the afternoons – especially if the weather was particularly miserable.

Some afternoons they went shopping or ran errands and Jessa discovered that Shara had an almost pathological compulsion to buy shoes. A few times they strolled through art galleries and once they attended a special exhibition at the Tate Britain. No matter how ordinary the activity, it took on new significance when they did it together. Both admitted that the best afternoons were the ones where they just stayed in and made love.

Jessa had met Elise and Shara had met a few a Jessa's friends, but since most were somehow involved in music, they either traveled or were based where the work was. They saw Lisa more than anyone else and the first time they'd had dinner with her and her partner, Paul, she couldn't stop smiling when she looked at them.

It was early February and it had been one of Shara's favorite kinds of days: she'd woken around 7:30 when Jessa got back into bed, smelling of shower gel and with her hair slightly damp. She'd either been running or she'd gone to yoga – either way, she smelled and felt wonderful. Shara assumed she looked wonderful, but she hadn't been able to summon the energy to open her eyes. When she'd woken again, Jessa was still asleep, so she'd woken her by making love to her. They'd had a late breakfast and Jessa had turned on the stereo before stretching out on the couch with a book. Shara noted that it was a collection of Jackie Kay short stories that she hadn't read yet, so she made a mental note to borrow it when Jessa finished it. After a quick shower she'd gone out for a manicure and facial.

When she got back, the stereo was still playing and Maria Callas was singing an aria from Saint-Saëns *Samson et Dalila*. It was one of Shara's favorites: *Mon coeur s'ouvre à ta voix*, "My heart, at your voice, unfolds and rejoices, Like a flower when dawn is smiling". Until she'd met Jessa, she'd never experienced anything like that. Now, when they were apart and Jessa rang her on her mobile, she completely lost the plot when she heard Jessa's voice. It was so bad that Elise had given Jessa instructions not to ring when they were having lunch together.

Shara and Jessa had seen the Saint-Saëns opera performed at Covent Garden in the first week of the new year and when the young mezzo-soprano singing the part of Dalila had performed that aria, tears had flowed down Shara's cheeks. She closely identified with the emotion that the song described, so she'd been deeply affected by the storyline where it was sung to lure and betray a lover. It had been the last classical performance they'd been to, because that night had been disrupted when they were recognized during the interval and surrounded by fans. They'd been nice enough, asking polite questions and congratulating Jessa on the success of *Rain*, but the physical closeness Shara and Jessa had enjoyed in the first act, thighs touching and hands discreetly clasped under their jackets, had come to an abrupt end. Jessa had obviously had trouble concentrating on the opera afterwards, fidgeting like a small child, and Shara had reacted in the opposite way – concentrating on the action on the stage to quiet her panicked reaction to the encounter.

Jessa now appeared to be deep in thought and she wondered if it was because the music reminded her of the only time they'd been recognized by members of the public when out together. She had no doubt that the staff at some of the restaurants they ate at recognized them, so they'd tried not to go to the same one twice. The result had been a month-long gastronomic tour of London, but it couldn't last forever.

"Hiya, sweetheart. You okay?"

Jessa smiled weakly. "Yeah. I was thinking that I'll be conducting this opera for the first time in Buenos Aires and I'm a bit nervous."

Shara sat next to her. "Just about conducting?"

Jessa offered her a crooked smile. "How come you know me so well?"

"I love you," Shara said simply. "So what's bothering you?"

"We've been invited to a Valentine's Day party." Before Shara could react, she rushed on. "Steve, he's a cellist with the LSO, he has this party every year. He says it's the one place you can have a good time on Valentine's night, whether you're coupled up or not, and all his friends make a special effort to attend. Most of their partners don't even mind after the first time, because, while it might not be particularly romantic, it delivers on the fun and he plays enough slow tunes for those who are so inclined to . . ."

Shara put a finger up to Jessa's lips to stop the flow of words. "Shh . . . I'll go. I'd love to go."

Jessa looked doubtful. "I don't want you to be uncomfortable . . ."

"Is he some kind of ogre?" Shara was teasing. She knew why Jessa had doubts. Jessa couldn't control who would be at the party and Shara might be recognized by someone who had no reason to be discreet about the fact that she was romantically involved with Jessa. But she couldn't ask Jessa to socialize only in completely closed environments, just to make sure she was comfortable. If she was honest with herself, she'd have to admit that she was terrified by the thought of what might happen. Her breakup with Derek had finally faded from the gossip pages, but any hint of a lesbian relationship would make the tabloid press redouble its efforts to turn her entire life into fodder for a manufactured scandal. She was also sure that Derek would be only too pleased to provide grist for the mill. But that was her problem and she couldn't ask Jessa to isolate herself because of it. Jessa was so good to her and expected so little in return that it made her want to give all of herself.

"No, of course not or I wouldn't . . ." She realized Shara was teasing and gave a mock growl before grabbing her and pinning her to the couch. "I should punish you for taking the piss . . ."

"Mmm, what punishment did you have in mind?" Shara was completely undaunted by the threat. This was one aspect of their relationship where she knew she could be good to Jessa. Sex with men paled into insignificance when compared to what she'd found in Jessa Hanson's bed and she knew that Jessa, too, thought what they had was extraordinary.

Jessa stared at her, entranced. Shara had taken off her coat and boots and was wearing black trousers and a teal jumper that emphasized the gray-green of her eyes. Her hair had started to grow and the dark rinse had faded leaving it a shining mahogany that brushed softly against her cheek as she smiled provocatively at Jessa. There was something about her teasing expression that made Jessa want to surprise her. The thought caused a feeling of excitement in Jessa that was not completely related to physical arousal.

Still holding Shara's wrist firmly, she got off the couch and pulled her to her feet. "Come," she commanded.

"You'll have to do better than just telling me to do it," Shara's smile widened, but her heart rate had quickened because she'd seen the purposeful look on Jessa's face.

When they got into the bedroom, Jessa pushed her unceremoniously onto the bed and asked, "Do you feel safe with me?"

Intrigued, Shara replied slowly, "Yes . . ."

With a frown and a serious expression, Jessa said, "If at any time you don't feel safe, I want you to say a word which I'll interpret as a cue to stop whatever I'm doing. That word can't be *stop* or *wait* because those are things that might become part of the game."

Shara could feel a steady throb between her legs that mimicked her racing heart and Jessa wasn't even touching her. "Petula", she said softly.

Jessa grinned, looking positively dangerous, and Shara wondered if she was ready for this. Before she could reconsider, Jessa walked over to a drawer and came back with something black and silky clutched in her fist. As Jessa unfurled it, Shara realized it was some kind of blindfold, which Jessa proceeded to tie securely over her eyes. "Lie back," she instructed softly and Shara did.

With exquisite gentleness, she undressed Shara. As each article of clothing was removed, she covered the bare skin in light, teasing kisses, making Shara's skin sensitized to her slightest touch. Every time Shara reached out to caress her in return or even to touch her, she stopped and pinned Shara's hands to the bed almost roughly, repeating some variation of "No, you are *not* in control of what happens here. This is your punishment."

When Shara was stripped down to her panties, she felt the mattress shift as Jessa got up. She knew better than to ask what Jessa was doing – whatever it was, was out of her control. The bed gave as Jessa returned. She lifted Shara's hand, then Shara felt pressure on her wrist and heard a quiet click. Jessa repeated the action with the other wrist and then Shara felt her arms being raised above her head until her body was stretched almost to the point of discomfort. "Wait," she said, nervously but Jessa ignored her. A mixture of apprehension and excitement filled Shara as she realized that she had been handcuffed to the bed.

PART TWENTY-EIGHT

Jessa, hurry up!" They were expected at the Valentine's party in an hour and Jessa still had not gone in to the shower. Shara had reluctantly showered alone and she was wearing Jessa's robe, her wet hair dripping onto the shoulders as she smiled indulgently at Jessa.

"I just want to get a few more done. I've been really bad about this and I'm starting to feel guilty." As she spoke, she furiously signed a stack of publicity photographs. The incoming fan mail was in four neat piles and Shara knew that it didn't include requests for autographed photos. Those received a standard response, along with one of the photos that Jessa was now signing.

"I know, sweetheart, but you promised you'd be early so that Steve could spend some time with you before the rest of the guests arrived."

Jessa looked up and smiled. "Yeah, right. He just wants to meet you. He's a fan, you know."

"He won't be after he meets me," she grimaced. "A grown woman who plays make-believe for a living."

"Hardly. Your job brings works of art to life and allows people to appreciate them who wouldn't have had a chance otherwise. In a way, conducting is a lot like acting – we interpret the artistic creations of others."

"Yeah, but you're interpreting Beethoven and Puccini and I'm probably interpreting a spotty-faced social outcast with paranoid delusions, who *happens* to be able to write scripts that the public wants to see played out on a screen."

Jessa winked. "If you promise to make mad, passionate love to me, I won't tell Peter Garofolo what you really think of him."

"You know he isn't at all like that. In fact, he's quite a ladies' man."

"Voice of experience?"

"Might have been, if I hadn't been in love with a temperamental composer at the time."

"I'm not at all temperamental. Just ask," she looked down at a letter that was on top of one of the piles on her desk, "Susan from Wiltshire. I intend to send her a nice long letter in response to her lovely note about my admirable temperament and charm . . ."

"Not to mention your breasts . . ."

Jessa pretended to be indignant. Shara stuck out her tongue at her and walked further into the spare bedroom which Jessa had converted into a study. "So what are these piles for?" She gestured towards the mail on the desk.

"Lisa's secretary sorts my incoming post, pulls out the obviously mad ones and the ones that can be sent a standard response. Lisa then goes through them once more and deals with any business issues that don't need my personal attention, then she sorts the rest into four groups. The first one is all business: offers of collaboration, invitations to perform, that sort of thing. The next one is all charitable stuff, requests to lend my name, support things in person, or just give money. By the time I get them, Lisa has made sure they're all legitimate and she knows my politics well enough to know what I won't even consider supporting." Shara grinned, because her assistant, Cassie, did exactly the same thing for her. "The third pile is all so-called fan mail that Lisa thinks I ought to read. Some of it is critical and some of it doesn't even require a response. In a lot of ways, it's the most important pile."

She looked sheepish. "The last stack is always the smallest and Lisa always replies to it. She only sends it on to me because I won't let her send on the explicit sexual letters, so she amuses herself by imagining my reaction to them. She says I don't have to read them if I don't want to, but you do, don't you?"

"What are they about?"

"They're from people who want my genes."

"As in trousers?"

"As in DNA."

"What?"

"A few years ago it was just from fertility clinics, usually the kind that offer sperm from Nobel Prize winners. Then it started coming in from couples who wanted a 'designer' baby with musical talent, so they decided that my genes would fit the bill nicely. Then those couples started including lesbian couples and some single women who tend to attach a few strings . . . . "

"And you don't answer them?"

"Lisa sends out a letter saying no, thanks, that I would never consider mothering a child solely for his or her musical potential and any child that carries my genes will be personally brought up by me."

"Are you sure it's all to do with your musical talent and not because you're gorgeous and they think your baby will be, too?" Shara's voice was teasing. As they'd been talking she'd crossed the room to stand next to Jessa and she slipped her fingers through Jessa's short curls as she spoke.

Jessa swiveled the chair around to face Shara. "Darling, if you really believe that, all *you* have to do is ask, because I'd rather it be you and not some faceless lesbian from Santa Cruz, California."

To Jessa's surprise, Shara seemed to freeze and she moved away, turning towards the window.

"Shara?" Jessa was confused by her reaction.

She pushed the chair away from the desk, stood up and walked towards Shara, putting a hand on her shoulder. "Look, babe, I'm sorry if it's too much, too soon. We've been together less than two months, so I shouldn't even be talking about ba . . ."

Shara turned towards her and put a finger on her lips to stop her from speaking. "No, it's not that. This isn't about how long we've been together or my commitment to you." She waited for Jessa to meet her eyes and said deliberately. "You mean everything to me, Jessa. I want to spend the rest of my life with you."

Jessa inhaled sharply, feeling a sweet ache in her heart as Shara said the words. She wanted to respond in kind but she found herself unable to speak. Shara smiled, understanding that her declaration had thrown Jessa completely off-balance. It made her a bit sad to see that, because she knew it was because she so seldom told Jessa how she felt about her. It wasn't fair to Jessa and she hoped to get better over time, but it was hard to change the emotional habits of a lifetime. As Jessa continued to stare adoringly at her, Shara stood on tiptoe and pressed her lips to Jessa's.

The gentle pressure seemed to reanimate Jessa and she opened her mouth in welcome. Shara parted her lips and moaned as Jessa's tongue thrust softly into her mouth. It still amazed her how affected she was when she kissed Jessa. Jessa's arms went around her and her hands roamed restlessly over Shara's back before moving down to cup her bottom. Feeling her body beginning to fall prey to the desperate attraction she felt for Jessa, Shara pulled back to say softly against her lips, "We're gonna be late . . ."

Jessa reached down to untie the sash of the robe. She cupped Shara's breasts and stroked her thumbs over Shara's nipples, smiling as she felt the shudder that went through Shara's body when she did it. "Yes," she replied huskily, before lowering her head so their mouths could meet again.

The theme of the party was "1967 to 1973" so the music was from those years and the guests were expected to wear period dress. Jessa was wearing a lime green halter top that wrapped twice around her waist, with tight white hipster bell-bottoms and thonged sandals. She was also wearing a wig, so her hair looked straight and black and hung down to her waist. A thin bandana with a Native American pattern was tied across her forehead to complete the ensemble. Shara had looked at her when she was fully dressed and asked if they could just stay in for the evening.

Looking back at Shara, the hardest thing Jessa had ever had to do was insist that Steve was waiting for them. Shara was wearing an indecently short vinyl mini-skirt with a translucent white blouse that had long sleeves, yet exposed most of her torso by ending in a knot just below her breasts. Stockings with a zigzag pattern clung to the curves of her thighs before disappearing into knee-high boots with four-inch heels and impressive platforms. She grinned when she noticed Jessa's slack-jawed stare and did a small twirl for her. Jessa noticed that despite the snugness of the skirt, she had no visible panty-line and gulped.

"We'd better leave now," Jessa said desperately, turning away from Shara to look for her bag, because she didn't trust her self-control.

Shara was smiling politely at something Steve was saying, but looking at Jessa. She knew that it was probably impolite not to look at her host while he spoke, but she couldn't help herself. The song was *Keep on Truckin'* by Eddie Kendricks and Jessa was dancing with someone who Shara thought might be a percussionist with some London orchestra, but whose name she'd forgotten. He was a good dancer and Jessa was obviously enjoying dancing with him. As her body moved in time to the music, Shara watched the play of muscles in her shoulders and arms and the sway of her hips. The wig had been taken off soon after they'd arrived at the party and the headband was now threaded through Jessa's natural curls, making her look untamed. Shara licked her lips and imagined what she could do to tame her. She turned and Shara was treated to a perfect view of her arse and moaned, temporarily forgetting that she was supposed to be listening to Steve.

"You really are in a bad way, aren't you?"

His question forced her attention back to him and she was horrified by her own bad manners.

"Oh god, I'm so sorry." She raised her hands to her suddenly hot cheeks and then immediately dropped them to her sides when she realized she was doing a bad impression of Macaulay Culkin.

Steve laughed. "Don't worry about it. I spent at least two years with a similar look on my face. To make it worse, Jessa was dating Stephanie at the time. At least in your case she looks at you the same way. My only excuse is that I was seventeen at the time." He put a reassuring hand on Shara's shoulder. "It's nice to see someone that much in love with Jessa. She deserves it."

Before Shara could think of something suitable to say to him in response, another guest called out to him and he'd melted back into the crowd.

Jessa turned again on the dance floor and caught sight of Shara. *She's mine.* The thought was intriguing, barely believable and probably not-quite-feminist, but it brought a huge grin to Jessa's face. Shara saw her looking her way and waved.

The song ended and Smokey Robinson's *I Second That Emotion* started. "C'mon, let's dance." Paul, Lisa's partner, grabbed Shara around the waist and pulled her onto the dance floor.

Shara knew that Jessa was looking at her, so she put on a show. Paul laughed, enjoying himself. Like Lisa, he'd been witness to the trials of Jessa's life and he was thrilled to see her in such a loving relationship. He wasn't surprised when Jessa cut in as Marvin Gaye started singing *Too Busy Thinking About My Baby*. Most other people on the floor were dancing apart, but Shara immediately pulled Jessa into the circle of her arms. They danced well together, moving smoothly to the beat and forgetting about the rest of the world as they listened to the lyrics and stared into each other's eyes. Jessa put her mouth just above Shara's ear and said, "I'm glad you're not starting another film until the spring, I'm not sure I could be very productive if you're not close to me. I really do think about you all the time when we're apart."

"I think about you, too. And you already know what it does to me to hear your voice on the phone."

Jessa grinned. "Yeah, Elise told me. I like that."

"Egomaniac."

"Anything but. I'm terrified of losing you, Shara. Love has never gone right for me in the past."

"And I've never been in love before now," Shara said simply, making Jessa pull her even closer so that their bare bellies were pressed together. The action made both of them sigh.

"Look, Shara, I'm sorry if I made you panic earlier by talking about . . . you know."

Shara pulled away slightly so Jessa could see her face, then realizing that with the music so loud, Jessa couldn't possibly see and hear her at the same time, she took her by the hand and led her off the dance floor to the kitchen. Finding it crowded, she pulled her down a darkened corridor that led to the bedroom where they'd left their coats. The room was dimly lit and deserted. Shara closed the door and took both of Jessa's hands. "Jessa, when you talked about . . . a baby, I know you think you frightened me. I *was* frightened, but not for the reason you thought. When you talked about some lesbian in America wanting to have your baby it made me . . ." she looked away, unable to meet Jessa's eyes as she said the word, "jealous."

"All I could think was that if anybody was going to give you a baby, it was going to be me. I know it's absolutely the wrong reason to want a baby, but I knew that the moment I told you I was pregnant with your baby was the moment that would bind you to me in a way that would last the rest of our lives. And I so desperately want that that it made me panic." She met Jessa's stunned gaze. "The strength of what I feel for you terrifies me, Jessa."

Jessa's hand shook as she reached out to tuck Shara's hair behind her ear. Then she cupped Shara's cheek, tears filling her eyes as Shara covered her hand with both of hers, turned her face to her palm, inhaling the scent of her before kissing the sensitive skin. "Shara, I can't deny or explain the primitive longing I feel at the thought of you carrying my baby, but we don't need a baby as insurance. I love you. I will always love you."

"Do you promise?" Shara's voice cracked as she asked the question. A feeling of dread suddenly filled her and she desperately needed Jessa's reassurance.

"Yes," Jessa replied, hugging Shara close and inhaling her perfume and the scent of her skin. "I promise." Then she pulled back to look at Shara. "Do you like Pablo Neruda?"

"Yes. I love his writing."

Before Shara could ask Jessa why she'd asked, Jessa quoted from a Neruda poem that Shara vaguely remembered and whose sentiments she had not truly understood until Jessa quoted softly to her from Neruda's *If You Forget Me*:

> *my love feeds on your love, beloved,*
> *and as long as you live it will be in your arms*
> *without leaving mine.*

PART TWENTY-NINE

S hara, we really need to talk about what happened."

Shara didn't look at Jessa, but continued to stare at a speaker from which Renée Fleming's exquisite voice delivered the aria *Un bel di vedremo*, the optimistic song of a woman who believed, absolutely, that she did not love in vain. "There's nothing to talk about, is there? It's the nature of what I, we, do for a living: publicity, photographers, satisfying public curiosity, they are requirements of the job."

"But they're not always easy to deal with and they ruined what had been a perfect evening."

At that, Shara did look up. "In hindsight, it was still a great evening, now that enough time has passed to let me ignore how it ended."

"If it was such a great evening, why is it so difficult to get you to leave the flat nowadays?"

Shara smiled faintly, but it didn't reach her eyes. "Would you believe, because I don't want to be away from you, since we have this dwindling time together when neither of us is working?"

Jessa sat next to her on the couch and took one limp hand in both of hers. "I like being alone at home with you as well, you know that. But you won't even go out when I go out. I know it's awful that one of Steve's guests called the paparazzi and it was terrible the way they behaved, but you can't just go into hiding because of it. Believe me, that just makes you an elusive target whose photographs will go up in value." Jessa's voice was filled with the conviction that comes from first-hand experience.

Shara wanted to be reassured, but her mind went back to the events that had followed the Valentine's party and she shuddered. After they'd emerged from the bedroom, she and Jessa had been completely engrossed in one another. She remembered gyrating on the dance floor to The Archies' *Sugar Sugar* and the Shondells' *Mony Mony*. She also remembered holding Jessa close and fighting back tears as Roberta Flack sang *The First Time Ever I Saw Your Face*.

The crowd had started to thin by the time they'd thanked Steve and made their way to the front door, still holding hands and looking forward to the moment they could close the door to Jessa's flat and be alone together. So they could make love and reaffirm the promises they'd made to each other. They had just stepped out onto the pavement when the first flashbulb went off. Shara had shielded her eyes and Jessa had turned her face away, only to be blinded by three more flashes from photographers who'd been standing off to the side.

"Was it a good party, Miss Hanson?"

"Miss Quinn, what is your relationship with Jessa Hanson?"

"Hey, Jessa, wanna pose for a few pictures?"

"Jessa, are you dating Shara Quinn, or are you two just friends?"

"Shara, did you meet Jessa Hanson while you were filming her life story?"

"Can I get a smile over here?"

The questions had come almost simultaneously, none of the men, and they were all men, allowing his prey to answer even one, before the next had been fired off. They'd also moved close enough to the two women to be physically intimidating, which prompted Shara to grab Jessa's arm so hard that her nails dug into the flesh, even through Jessa's winter jacket. "E-excuse me," she'd stuttered, her voice barely audible over the shouted questions and clicking, whirring cameras.

"Don't any of you people have a conscience?" Jessa's angry voice had temporarily stopped the barrage of questions. "We are friends who went to a party at the home of a mutual friend. Now we'd like to get into our taxi and go home without having to break away from a bloody scrum!" She grabbed a camera whose flash had gone off less than a foot from her nose while she'd been speaking, twisting it away from her and almost choking the owner to whom it had been attached by a strap around his neck.

"Hey!" He'd protested as loudly as he could, "We're just trying to earn a living. No need to get violent." The statement had been echoed by several of his colleagues as the moment was being captured by at least three other cameras.

Knowing immediately that she'd made a tactical mistake, Jessa had forced herself to calm down. "You want to know what's going on? All you had to do was ask, instead of behaving like idiots." She pointed at the photographer farthest back in the small crowd "You! You seem to be almost civilized. You've got three minutes with me for as many photos as you can take and as much as you can get me to say. Give me your card. My manager will ring you in the morning to sort it out." They'd all temporarily stopped taking photos, stunned by her about-face. The photographer at the back had handed her his card with eager gratitude, then she'd put her hand on Shara's arm and guided her towards the curb where a mini-cab had been waiting with its engine running. The action seemed to bring the other photographers to their senses and the flash photography had resumed, continuing to light the darkness until well after the taxi and its occupants were out of range.

Jessa had kept her word and given the interview, patiently repeating her claim that Shara was a friend, admitting they'd known each other before the filming of *Maestra* had begun and confirming they'd been at a mutual friend's party on Valentine's night. Unfortunately, that had not stopped the dogged presence of freelance paparazzi on her doorstep and in the park across the street from Shara's South Kensington flat. After a few days of that, Shara and Jessa had given up, loaded up Dusty and headed for Jessa's cottage.

That week had defined the expression 'time out of time'. With the exception of Harry, they'd seen nobody but each other, literally or figuratively. Shara had got a lot of reading done, finishing *Sophie's World* and *Smilla's Sense of Snow*, two books she'd bought almost a year earlier and had been delighted to learn that Jessa also owned, and devouring the poetry of Pablo Neruda and Octavio

Paz. Earlier in the year, when they'd been walking around Clerkenwell, she'd recommended *How Proust Can Change Your Life* to Jessa and she was pleased to see Jessa reading it on a rainy afternoon at the cottage as they'd shared the sofa closest to the fireplace in the living room.

They'd walked a lot and talked about the lives they'd lived before they'd met, but not about the future. It had seemed natural; after all, they were still getting to know each other, but looking back on it, Jessa felt uneasy.

When they'd returned to London, Shara had become increasingly withdrawn. Jessa had thought at first that she was imagining it, because she was starting to get wrapped up in her own work as she prepared for her trip to Argentina, but as the days wore on, she'd been forced to admit that something was troubling Shara and it was something Shara refused to discuss with her. She'd come to the conclusion that whatever it was had been triggered by the events following the party and the subsequent behavior of the British tabloid press.

Jessa had grown used to ignoring photographers and going about her daily business, having decided during the Stephanie scandal that strangers only had the power over her life that she gave them and she would not give tabloid photographers more power than they could grab. She wanted to reassure Shara, but part of her also wanted to tell her to get on with it. Shara was strong and had worked in the public eye for a decade. Jessa wondered if she was being unreasonable in her expectations of the woman she adored.

As though reading her mind, Shara said, "I know you wish I'd just snap out of this, but there's really no way out, is there? As you've pointed out, the more I hide from them, the more intrigued they seem to become, but I really don't have the stomach for confrontation . . ."

"Darling, it doesn't have to be confrontational."

"Doesn't it?" Shara's eyes looked smoky gray and haunted. Before Jessa could reply, she rushed on. "Even if I quit – just give up acting – that would only make me a tragic figure who can't, or won't, do the work she's trained for and is finally getting recognition for. It would make them even worse!"

Jessa was shocked. It had never occurred to her that Shara would consider giving up her profession. Surely Shara had dealt with the tabloid press before, after all, her breakup with Derek had been quite public. "Oh darling. Come here." She pulled Shara into her arms and leaned back on the sofa so that they were both half-lying on it and could hold each other.

"Shara, you shouldn't even think of giving up. I know you joke about the fact that so many of the major projects you're offered are about nothing significant, but the money lets you do things like the Irish documentary you funded and narrated, not to mention your charity work . . ."

"Personally, I don't need the money," Shara continued quietly, as though talking to herself, "I live simply, anyway. The only people who will suffer are those who are helped by the money I give to charity. But it would be so much easier to just give up . . ."

"*No*," Jessa said firmly. "Don't even think like that. No inconsiderate tabloid hack is worth it." She turned Shara's face so she could look at her.

Shara stared at her, wondering what it was like to be so sure. While filming *Maestra*, it had been brought home to her how much Jessa had suffered when the press had turned its vindictive attention on her. Jessa had stoically endured the name-calling and the bags of hate-mail, she'd risen above the trick interview questions and offered no more than an angry look when she'd been spat at during a demonstration organized by a religious group. Even pretending to be Jessa and having the freedom to walk away when the director said "Cut", had been almost too much for her. She loved Jessa and the more she knew of Jessa the more she admired her. But she wasn't *like* Jessa and she knew she couldn't handle the press with the same degree of grace or dignity. She'd acted out the events without first discussing them with Jessa, because she'd wanted to play the scenes with the near-panic of immediacy rather than the calm of hindsight. It was ironic that now she was facing her own public "outing" and was living through the near-panic again.

Unable to voice all the doubts and conflicts that churned through her mind and soured her stomach, Shara reached out for the one thing that could make her forget everything bad in the world. She put her hand behind Jessa's head and caressed the soft, looping curls, before opening her mouth over Jessa's and kissing her deeply. The kiss lasted for several minutes and they shifted on the couch, trying to get more contact with each other's bodies. Eventually, Shara pulled back and looked at the surprise and arousal in Jessa's wide brown eyes. "Make love to me," she pleaded, knowing that, even if Jessa didn't understand the reason for her urgency, it would nevertheless be a request that she'd be powerless to resist. Shara offered a silent prayer of thanks that her feelings for Jessa were reciprocated, because she had never needed anyone or anything so much.

PART THIRTY

The kiss on the couch surprised her. Just a moment earlier, Shara had seemed so lost when she'd talked about dealing with the press. Neither of them had mentioned that the issue was exacerbated by the fact that Shara's new relationship was a lesbian one and therefore of special interest to gossips and those with a prurient bent. It terrified Jessa that Shara was prepared to sacrifice her career to protect her privacy, because she knew it would be entirely less complicated to sacrifice their relationship. She also felt guilty and worried that Shara would end up hating her.

In the midst of all that jumbled emotion, Shara suddenly kissed her. Not a friendly or reassuring kiss, but a hot, carnal, kiss.

Shara plunged her tongue into Jessa's mouth and rubbed her body sinuously against Jessa's. By the time she pulled away, Jessa had temporarily lost the power of speech. She had no recollection of how one of her hands had managed to find itself on Shara's thigh, apparently having lifted Shara's leg to rest it on her hip, so one of her thighs was pressed against Shara's crotch.

Jessa's train of thought had been completely derailed even before Shara's demand, yet the words, "make love to me", huskily spoken and betraying profound need, had unleashed something in Jessa. She wanted to make Shara forget about pushy reporters, disapproving strangers and everything that didn't directly concern the spiraling heat between their bodies.

Shara was wearing a pale pink blouse with pearl buttons and with deliberate savageness, Jessa ripped it open, sending some of the buttons clattering to the floor. Shara's eyes widened, but not from fear. Her pupils dilated and her breath shortened. Jessa initiated the next kiss, stroking Shara's tongue with her own and pushing her body up so that Shara could reach down and release the drawstring on her trousers.

She groaned against Shara's mouth as Shara's fingers slipped into her panties and then slid two of them between her labia and over her clit. She allowed her weight to fall onto Shara's arm, trapping her hand, but as she lifted herself away from Shara and expertly unclasped her bra with one hand, Shara's fingers continued to move, the tiny, restricted movements increasing the pressure, so that Jessa found herself parting her legs further, despite the awkwardness of their positions on the couch.

"I want you so much," Shara moaned against Jessa's mouth.

"I know." Jessa pulled down Shara's bra. The movement dislodged Shara's hand and trapped both of her arms by her sides. As the bra scraped over Shara's nipples on its way down, she whimpered. Jessa made a hungry, growling noise as Shara arched her back, pushing her peaked nipples towards Jessa's open mouth.

When Jessa's mouth closed over one hard nipple and she flicked her tongue against it, Shara groaned, "Oh *god*."

Jessa sucked the nipple deep into her mouth and unsnapped Shara's waistband. She was drunk on the feel and the taste of Shara Quinn and as she listened to the helpless noises being emitted from Shara's throat, she knew that what they had between them was special and no outside influence could make it go away.

She lifted her mouth from Shara's breast and trailed open-mouthed kisses over her chest to her neck, making circles with her tongue on the sensitive skin just below Shara's ear and moving lower towards her shoulder, as Shara writhed against her.

"Harder," Shara begged.

"I'll mark you," Jessa warned, before scraping her teeth along Shara's skin and then sucking the red mark that she'd created.

"I want you to mark me."

Jessa moaned at the physical surrender inherent in the reply. At the same time she started to pull Shara's jeans over her hips, having already released the button fly with a single, rough jerk. Shara's short nails scraped across Jessa's shoulders, almost drawing blood and Jessa shuddered, the unexpected pain mixing with her growing arousal and making her want more. "And *you're* marking *me* . . ." she admitted, the satisfaction she felt twisting itself through her body and into her heart.

"Please . . ." Shara's voice shook as she lifted her hips so that Jessa could peel her jeans down.

"What do you want?"

"I want you to fuck me."

Just thinking about it made Jessa's blood warm, although her body would probably be sore tomorrow. *So will Shara's*, she thought with a smile.

The first time on the couch was wonderful, athletic, hot, hard and satisfying. They fell onto the floor near the end. Jessa was amazed that Shara was still so lucid and well coordinated after an orgasm that had made her sink her teeth into Jessa's shoulder when it quaked through her body.

"You have extremely talented fingers, Miss Hanson," she croaked, her voice hoarse from telling Jessa exactly how much she liked what was being done to her.

Jessa did no more than smile in response when Shara went on purposefully, "And such talent should always be rewarded." Then, with uncharacteristically silent intensity, she proceeded to make love to Jessa. Jessa was already close to climax just from making love to Shara and she'd expected it to go quickly, but Shara had other ideas. She teased, tasted, sucked and licked Jessa almost to the point of madness, each time pulling back just before Jessa achieved climax. When it finally happened, Jessa cried.

Afterwards, Shara held her tight and stroked her hair as her tears fell.

"You're amazing," Jessa said softly, although, even though she knew right away that no words could express what she felt.

Jessa collapsed on top of Shara and fought to catch her breath. Twilight lengthened the shadows in the bedroom, but she was barely aware of the passage of time. Not since their first night together had she and Shara made love so many times and with such ferocity.

"Sweetheart, are you awake?" Shara's voice interrupted Jessa's thoughts.

"Mmm, I think so. But I'm too relaxed to know for certain."

Shara chuckled. "Do you mind if I use that thing, even if you're not with me?"

Jessa laughed. "It won't be nearly as much fun . . ."

"I don't doubt it." She heaved a contented sigh. "Jessa, does it bother you that I slept with men? I wonder sometimes, since you've always known who you were and it took *you* to make me see who I am."

"Darling, in the words of Neruda: *I am not jealous, / we shall always be alone, we shall always be you and I alone on earth.*"

Shara hugged her tighter. "I like it when you do that."

"Quote Neruda?"

"Yes. Quote Neruda about us. As though I, our relationship, brings his poetry to the front of your mind and you never have to make an effort to find a poem or a stanza that describes what we have."

Jessa looked at her, seeing the shadows of evening softening her features and threatening to hide the love that filled her eyes and was revealed in her voice. "No mortal man's words can describe what we have," Jessa said quietly.

The fading day could not obscure the tears that slipped down Shara's cheeks when she said it.

Every time I think I cannot possibly love you any more than I do, you say something ridiculously romantic and I feel myself falling for you all over again. Shara brushed her hand over Jessa's wild curls. *I want a baby with your hair.*

Jessa saw the expression on Shara's face and felt as though she'd been punched in the stomach. She closed her eyes and fought to get the longing under control, but when she opened them again, Shara was still looking at her, eyes roaming over her features, hands still caressing her hair. She moved away from Shara and when Shara thought she was getting off the bed, she leaned down and kissed Shara's belly and then turned her face to the side and rested her head on Shara. "I sometimes wish I didn't feel so much," she murmured in a voice so low that Shara could barely hear it. "And I wish I didn't know you so well." Shara wasn't sure what she meant and she was too moved by Jessa's actions to speak.

She lay there quietly, listening to the gurgling noises in Shara's stomach. "You're always hungry." There was a smile in her voice.

"I have an active lifestyle." Shara defended.

Jessa smiled. "Yeah, running on the treadmill, lifting weights and shagging. The most action you can get without going outdoors."

"Like you're complaining," Shara was smiling, too.

"I can't wait to take you to my favorite restaurants in Buenos Aires. Lucia and I trained with a guy called Fernando, who's now running a nightclub that has gay tango nights. It will be great to catch up with him and I know he'll be thrilled to meet you."

Suddenly, Shara was tense. "Jessa, I can't come with you to Argentina."

Jessa lifted her head and stared at her for several uncomprehending seconds. "What?"

"It's too much. They'll be waiting in the airport and then I'll be leaving the country and they'll be swarming all over my family, especially my father. He's still getting calls about Derek and he can't go ex-directory because he's a minister."

"So what are you saying? That for the convenience of your father you won't live your life as you want to? Or is the convenience your own? I understand that you might not want to be romantically associated with a dyke, but you should at least have the courage to say so, instead of using your father as an excuse – after all, you've openly admitted that the two of you aren't close."

"In case you hadn't noticed, I am a dyke, as you so charmingly put it, or didn't it count when I told you I loved you, or when I made love with you?" Shara was hurt and angry.

"That's easy enough to do behind closed doors, isn't it? But you want the outside world to continue to grant you your heterosexual privileges . . ."

"It isn't about that! It's about wanting to keep my private life private."

Jessa got up and started to pull on her clothes. "Now, where have

I heard that before? Oh, that's right. I heard it from Stephanie. For six years, we were *private* and *discreet* because I believed her when she told me it was the right thing to do. Well, you've just walked in my shoes for the cameras, so I don't have to tell you how *that* turned out." By the time she finished speaking, she was dressed, although her hair stuck out at odd angles. She grabbed a jacket, took her purse and keys out of the bowl on the table and headed for the door.

"Where are you going?"

"I need to think and I can't do it here."

PART THIRTY-ONE

Jessa walked blindly along Clerkenwell Road before turning right and heading north towards St. Pancras. Then she turned east and followed the crooked streets uphill towards the Angel. The streets were lined with the odd mixture of small businesses, council housing and luxury flat conversions that characterized south Islington, but all she could see were the images that had surfaced in her head. Images that moved her to the kind of hurt and anger that she thought she'd left behind almost a decade earlier.

She and Stephanie had met after a concert at the Royal Festival Hall. Jessa had already been working as a second violin with the London Symphony Orchestra and had been given permission to appear as a soloist for the special performance of a youth orchestra. Stephanie had been a mediocre cellist, who'd been forced to attend the concert by her parents in the hope that she'd be inspired to practice more. The only thing that had inspired Stephanie had been her first glimpse of Jessa Hanson. And practicing the cello had not been what she'd been inspired to do.

Jessa had just lived through two years of upheaval. At sixteen, she'd been filling in for a second violinist with the LSO when she'd met Daphne. Daphne had been twenty-five and stunning. The product of an Asian father and an Irish-American mother, she'd been modeling from the age of fourteen and she'd been the most gorgeous, sophisticated creature Jessa had ever seen. Daphne had decided that a little lesbian fling was just what she'd needed to while away the month she was forced to spend in London for a two-minute appearance in a James Bond film and Jessa had been eager to oblige. Daphne had assumed that Jessa was at least twenty and Jessa had decided that the assumption was harmless enough.

Jessa's father had kept a flat in the Barbican since he'd worked in the City part-time after retiring from the Royal Navy. Jessa had stolen the spare keys from her father's study and would meet Daphne at the flat in the middle of the afternoon, when she did not have to account for her whereabouts. The affair had been mutually satisfying and Daphne had been expressing that satisfaction quite loudly the day Jessa's father walked in on them.

It would probably have been a lot worse for Jessa and Daphne if he had not had his mistress with him at the time. His indignation at finding his daughter's head buried between another woman's legs had been mitigated by the red lipstick smeared around his mouth and on his neck. Jessa's mother had been given an edited version of events at the flat and Jessa went to live with Lisa until she was eighteen. The shouting and recrimination that had preceded her departure had faded into insignificance in Jessa's memory, but she still remembered the feeling of mutual betrayal she'd exchanged with her father that day at the flat.

Betrayal.

She'd never thought that Stephanie could betray her. Stephanie had never had any issues about her own lesbianism. She'd come out to her parents at fifteen and ignored their disapproval until they'd stopped expressing it. She'd assumed that Jessa was a socially awkward, sexually inexperienced, classical musician, like those with whom her cello had forced her to associate for years, and had literally licked her lips at the thought of seducing her. Jessa had assumed that Stephanie was a "bi-curious" socialite with no clue about what she'd been inviting when she'd flirted with, and then propositioned, her, so their first time together had been surprising to both. They'd often laughed about it in the years that followed.

Jessa had been surprised when Stephanie had asked her to keep their relationship a secret, but she had not objected. It had been easy enough on the music scene, where, with the exception of a few soloists, classical musicians remained anonymous to everyone except those in the industry. Neither had expected Jessa to make a name as one of those soloists, despite her prodigious talent and the fact that she'd occasionally performed as a soloist with major orchestras. She'd always been labeled a "prodigy" and she'd cynically explained to Stephanie that the title would be outgrown as her age took away the novelty of her talent. She'd decided that she wanted a career as a conductor anyway, so the angst of being pulled between her two favorite instruments would stop tearing her apart.

"Jess, I think you should hire a publicist."

"Stephanie, I don't need a publicist. My calendar is full, I've got a recording contract with a big label," *although nothing much has come of it yet*, "and Lisa is doing an excellent job of managing my career. Besides, you're always complaining that I'm on the road too much as it is."

"You're twenty years old and you've done more in your life than most people three times your age, yet nobody who isn't a classical music enthusiast even knows your name or what you look like."

"So?"

"So, if you became a household name, you'd sell more recordings, make more money and get even more opportunities."

"I don't need more money. I've conducted five different orchestras, including the LSO. Don't you think it would be greedy of me to want more opportunities at my age? I'm more than happy to have the career I'm having now. Even if most of my year is still spent playing the violin, there are people I studied with who would give their eyeteeth to perform violin concertos with the orchestras I've played with."

"Okay, so maybe the money isn't a factor, but public demand to see you on the podium can drive the move from musician to conductor . . ."

"I'm not sure, babe." Jessa had frowned, feeling butterflies in her stomach and a sense of apprehension. "Fame brings its own pressures and you're the one who doesn't want me to out myself as a dyke."

Stephanie had dismissed Jessa's concern with a wave of her hand. "A publicist would handle that, so you didn't have to worry about it. And if you're trying to become a household name, it would be even more important for you to keep your sexuality a secret, so that Middle England could relate to you."

That conversation had set off a series of events that still had the power to make Jessa's gut hurt. The value of the publicist in advancing her career had probably been negligible, because the people who became familiar with her image and name were unlikely to attend classical concerts or buy classical music CD's, but Jessa Hanson became a London "it girl" and Stephanie became her "best friend". Jessa "dated" male models and actors and went to film premieres and trendy nightclubs. While all this was going on, she struggled to find enough time to practice both of her instruments and eventually gave up performing the piano, because the public demand for her as a solo violinist was greater.

Lisa had warned her that her image as a party girl was hampering her attempts to get conducting jobs, because her age and sex already counted against her and she was beginning to give the impression that she fit the very stereotype she was trying to break away from. But Jessa had paid no attention to Lisa because she'd been in love with Stephanie and she'd been starting to enjoy some of the forbidden pleasures of the London, New York, Milan and Berlin party scenes. The day she rolled her Porsche down an embankment in Italy had been the day it all came to an abrupt end.

"You scared me, Jessa." There had been tears in Lisa's eyes as she'd sat by Jessa's bed, holding her hand. "I know I've kept my comments about your life on a completely professional level, but I'm really worried about you. I love you so much and I don't like the way you're treating yourself. Now you're hurt and I wonder if there's anything I could have said or done to prevent it from happening."

She'd thought that Jessa had been unconscious, but Jessa had been waking up and she'd heard. She'd realized at that point just how much she'd cut Lisa out of her life, when Lisa had been more parent than manager to her from the time she'd been hired when Jessa had been twelve. She'd opened her eyes and lifted her other hand weakly to touch Lisa's cheek. "It was not your fault, Lisa. I made choices – bad ones. I love you." She'd fallen asleep after that, without asking or wondering where Stephanie had been. Stephanie wasn't good in a crisis, so she had not been surprised that her visits to the hospital had only happened several days after Jessa came out of intensive care and when her biggest worries had been the pain of her broken ribs, the cast on her leg and her shaved head.

"The doctor says it's a miracle your hands weren't injured," Stephanie had told Jessa during her first visit and for some reason that statement had made Jessa cry.

It had taken six months for Jessa to have the stamina and dexterity to work again, but once she'd started, she'd ignored everything else, to the dismay of Stephanie and the publicist. She'd found that she got many more opportunities to conduct in Asia, so she'd toured there extensively, but after a three-month stint, she'd found herself uncharacteristically homesick and she'd canceled her appearance at a reception and caught an earlier flight back to London. The last thing she'd expected when she'd walked into to the flat she'd shared with Stephanie had been to find a woman she didn't know, making tea.

"I'm sorry, Jess."

"What about? That you were shagging somebody else while I was busy having the career you wanted me to have? Or that you were living with her *in my home* while I was working my arse off and living the life of a transient, in countries where I barely speak the language? Why are you sorry?" Jessa's voice had steadily risen as she'd spoken and the last question had been shouted.

"I never meant to hurt you. But I was so lonely. You're gone most of the time and I'm so isolated."

"I'm gone because of *your* ambition, not my own! And of course you're isolated. You're the one who chose the straight life for both of us! We can't get socially close to anyone who isn't chosen by that bastard publicist and has as many secrets to keep as we do. As a couple we can't have close friends who really know us, because we're so much in the public eye that just knowing us is worth money on the open market."

"I can't believe you're talking like this. Since you began taking my career advice, you've become famous! You were *nobody* when I met you!"

"You're wrong there, Stephanie. I might not have been the somebody you wanted to be with, but I was somebody: to my old friends and to Lisa. Now all I have is a fake life, with fake friends who don't even know who I am!"

"You mean old friends like Lucia?" Contempt had dripped from Stephanie's voice. "She just had you as a fuck-buddy – a convenience when you were both in the same city."

Jessa remembered the searing pain of the accusation, because at that point she'd had no idea whom, or what, she could trust in her life. She'd haphazardly started throwing her things into whatever bags she could find in the flat, relieved that she hadn't had a chance to unpack before discovering Stephanie's betrayal.

"Where do you think you're going?"

"Away from you," Jessa had said, with a voice that shook.

"To what? Your old friends? Come on, Jessa, you rejected them six years ago, do you think they're waiting for you to go crawling back to them? Or maybe you'll run back to Lisa, using her in the childish way you've always used her."

"Shut up!" Jessa had known that her response was as childish as Stephanie was accusing her of being, but she'd felt as though she was in some sort of fugue and she'd been worried that she might be having a mental breakdown. "Leave Lisa out of this! Unlike you, she's always put my interests first and she's never betrayed me."

"Your interests? Don't make me laugh. She hated your hiring a publicist and left to her, you'd be an infamous dyke with no real career to speak of – although I'm sure she'd still take ten per cent of whatever you earn. Face it, Jessa, she's paid to pretend she cares about you." When Jessa had ignored her, she'd continued in a spiteful tone. "Fine. Run away because I made one slip, but we'll see how your precious Lisa handles it when all her dreams come true."

Jessa had stopped what she was doing. "One slip?" The enormity of that misrepresentation stunned her. The woman's clothes had been in the bedroom cupboard and she'd obviously been sleeping in their bed for weeks, if not months. "You're fucking delusional, do you know that?" In her outrage, she had paid no attention to the comment about Lisa's dreams coming true.

She'd phoned Lisa from the back of a taxi. Before she could say anything, Lisa had said, "Jessa! Welcome back to Blighty. I heard you'd skipped that reception to catch an earlier flight home and I can't blame you. You must be exhausted. I have some great news for you and you must be dying for a visit to a chippy. Why don't you come over when you've had a chance to catch up on your sleep? We'll have tea and a chin wag, and then I'll buy you a big, greasy bag of chips."

The thoughtfulness, the love in Lisa's voice and the welcoming tone had done what Stephanie's spitefulness had not managed to do: Jessa had burst into tears. In between hiccupping sobs she'd told Lisa a shortened version of what had happened. Lisa had immediately insisted that Jessa abandon plans to book into a hotel and tell the driver to drop her off at her home. After tea and sympathy, she'd told Jessa the news that she'd been offered the job of principal conductor with the London Philharmonic.

The next day, when she'd signed the contract, she'd found out what Stephanie had meant about all Lisa's dreams coming true. It had always bothered Stephanie that Lisa disapproved of Jessa's decision to keep her sexual orientation a secret, initially saying that if Jessa treated it as a non-issue, most other people would do the same.

The headlines ran from the factual *New Conductor is Gay* and *Lesbian Appointed Conductor of Philharmonic*, to the sensational *Homosexuals Increase Influence on British Culture* and *Parents Worried About Gays in Classical Music*. There could be no doubt as to who had planted the stories. There were horrible "rumors" of deviant sex and threesomes, some accompanied by photos of Jessa, Stephanie and female socialites that Jessa knew had come from Stephanie's private collection. Photos of their home, including their bedroom, and even one of Stephanie by Jessa's hospital bed in Italy, were published in subsequent weeks, the latter when the story of Jessa's near-fatal crash had been dredged up. This time there had been more strident insinuations about cocaine and alcohol having been factors in the accident.

Jet-lagged and emotionally traumatized, Jessa had initially had to be sedated when the scandal hit. Within a few days, her fiery temperament had come to the fore and she'd wanted to kill Stephanie. She'd insisted to Lisa that she could plead provocation and the law would allow her to go free. "No, Jessa, the law would consider it pre-meditated murder and lock you up for life. And can you imagine what the tabloid press would consider it?"

Jessa had insisted that Lisa offer the Philharmonic the chance to rescind their offer and eventually she'd done so, tagging on a small financial penalty despite Jessa's objections. To their surprise, the Philharmonic had refused, because they'd found that quite a lot of the correspondence they'd received from people who actually attended performances had been positive. Nevertheless, they'd insisted that Jessa deal directly with the issue, appearing on chat and news shows to talk about, and defuse, some of the wilder accusations in the press. Stephanie had done her work well and everything, from the juvenile affairs with Lucia and Daphne to her estrangement from her parents, had become the subject of public discourse.

Jessa had done the publicity circuit, often mildly sedated, hanging on to her dignity and her temper by a thread, forcing herself to speak of things she considered beneath contempt, because the Orchestra had stood by her and she'd owed them that much. After those public appearances, sometimes where the questions and fellow guests were chosen with the specific intent to humiliate or anger her, she'd gone back to Lisa and Paul to rant angrily or, after the worse ones, to sob like a baby. After one crying jag, she'd lifted swollen eyes to Lisa's and said earnestly, "Never again, Lisa. Never again. I'm never going to lie about who or what I am. Anyone who keeps a secret for you holds incalculable power over you. If Stephanie could do this to me after all those years together, then there is no safety. No level to which human beings will not sink."

"Jessa, don't think like that. There will always be trustworthy people in the world. Stephanie just wasn't one of them. Don't give up on people just because of her or the people she surrounded herself with. Think of all the people who have been kind and supportive, even through all of this." Jessa had said nothing, but fresh tears had flowed down her cheeks. "You should follow your instincts to be honest about your life, but you should also follow the ones that tell you to let someone get close to you. That probably won't happen right away because of what you've just gone through, but don't shut yourself down."

Eventually, the press had lost interest, but in the meantime, the Philharmonic got more donations, publicity and conservative censure than they could possibly have anticipated when they'd decided to hire their first female conductor. Jessa had fired her publicist and became a star.

Now, as she walked past the restaurants of Upper Street and realized that she was miles from home and reeking of sex, she remembered Lisa's advice and wondered how she could handle a situation where her instincts to trust someone and to be honest with the world seemed to be in direct conflict with each other.

PART THIRTY-TWO

When Jessa walked in, the flat was in darkness. She turned on a lamp and was surprised to see Shara sitting on the sofa, wearing jeans, a jumper and a blank expression.

"Is this how it's going to be, Jessa? When we have a disagreement, you'll walk out on me instead of talking about it?" She didn't tell Jessa that she'd grown up with a father who had subjected her to angry silence or "jobs" he had to do with members of his congregation that took him away from home for hours, whenever she'd displeased him. When she'd been small, he'd called in a woman from the village to stay with her, but once he'd decided that she was safe on her own, he'd simply walked out whenever she committed some transgression or in any way annoyed him. Shara had always consoled herself that he'd never been physically or verbally abusive like some other parents, but as an adult she'd become less generous in her assessment of his parenting.

"I needed to think." Jessa was immediately defensive.

"And you couldn't share your thoughts?" Shara hid her pain under a veneer of calm, because it wasn't Jessa's fault she'd triggered so many terrible childhood memories.

"I think that maybe it's all been too much, too soon," Jessa said, not looking at Shara. She shrugged out of her jacket and dropped it on a chair. "We met in summer, but then we didn't see each other for months. And from the time we saw each other again, we've been practically living together."

Because she was walking towards the fridge to get a drink, she missed the look of unbearable pain that twisted Shara's features at her words. It took Shara every ounce of her training not to cry out at the feeling of betrayal. She wanted to ask Jessa to explain what she'd meant, but emotionally she knew that no matter what Jessa said, her heart had heard a message of rejection. "Fine," she replied in a voice that was strained to breaking point, "I can solve that problem. There's no need for you to leave your own home for hours just to be able to think. I'll leave."

Jessa swung around to face her, realizing for the first time what Shara thought she'd meant. "That's not the solution, Shara. You know I love being here with you . . ." Her eyes filled with tears, because she had heard Shara's emotional withdrawal in her tone of voice.

"But . . .?"

"There's no 'but'. I enjoy being here with you. No conditions. I also want you to travel with me when you're not working and I'd assumed you'd want me to travel with you when I'm not working." She looked away again and opened a bottle of beer. "I admit that I feel like a fool for being so presumptuous." Anger crept into her voice, disguising the hurt that her pride prevented her from expressing.

"That's not it!" Shara stood up and walked towards her. "How could you even *think* I don't want to be with you?"

"Because you said so?" Jessa asked sarcastically.

"I just need time, Jessa, and that's about the media and how I cope with them, it's not about you."

"Oh come on. You've been coping with the media for more than ten years! Don't you dare insult me by pretending it has nothing to do with me and your new *lesbian* relationship!"

"Of course it has to do with the fact that I'm in a lesbian relationship. All I'm asking you for is what I won't get from them: a chance to adjust to the fact and deal with how I tell the world . . . On my terms."

"And your terms are to keep me and our relationship hidden? To lie about what we do together and deny . . ." As she spoke, her voice grew hoarse with pain and she stopped herself from finishing the thought that burned into her brain. *You want to deny our love.*

"I just need time, Jessa. I'm not ready." *I'm not strong enough right now to do it.*

"You won't be alone."

"You don't understand. Less than a year ago, my life was all mapped out for me: I was going to marry the man I loved, I knew what to expect. Now everything is different and I need to find my own way. I need to think things through. I can't do that with flash bulbs exploding in my face."

"What's there to think about, if you're committed to our relationship?"

Shara made a frustrated sound. "This isn't about my commitment! Jessa, if I didn't feel the way I do, do you think I could have been with you this way, said the things I've said?"

"I've been here before, Shara. A relationship needs affirmation. It's the reason straight people get married and make vows to each other in public. You tell me you love me and I believe it, but a woman lived with me for six years in secret and said exactly the same, then she betrayed me in every conceivable way. Afterwards I accepted my share of the blame because I agreed to live the lie. Now I know that I can't be with someone who is ashamed to be with me. It erodes my self-respect and weakens our relationship."

Shara's eyes filled with tears. "Do you really think it's fair to compare me to Stephanie? I know what you went through because of her . . ."

"You know nothing!" Jessa cut her off, angrily. "All you want is an easy life. If you won't even deal with the hassle of some yobs with cameras in order to acknowledge me, how can I have any confidence that when things get really rough you'll want to be bothered?"

"I'm not gonna stay here and take this." Shara stalked off.

"Yeah, that's it. The first time we don't agree on something you walk out."

Shara turned back to her, her expression incredulous. "You're a fine one to talk! The difference between us is that *you* went off in a strop because I dared to make an independent decision about what I want to do with my life in the next few weeks. *I'm* leaving because of the things you're saying to me. Whether you want to accept it or not, Jessa, I did read about what happened to you. It wasn't just yobs with cameras who made your life, and the lives of everyone you knew, a misery. I admire the fact that it didn't affect you very much and you're comfortable and so on with your life, your sexual orientation and your public image, but *I'm not ready!*" With that she turned and walked towards the bedroom.

"Didn't affect ..." Jessa could not believe what Shara had just said. It had taken years, and near perfection of the art of meditation, before she'd felt like a human being again. It had also taken the love of Paul, Lisa and the friends who Stephanie had said would never have her back. She was barely recognizable to herself as the person she'd been before Stephanie threw her to the wolves, yet Shara had just stood there with a straight face and said that it *hadn't affected* her? "Shara, wait."

"No, Jessa," she said without looking back, "I grew up with a bully who walked out on me when he was angry and who never thought I could make a decision on my own and I'm not going to stay here while you behave like that." There were tears streaming down her face as she started pulling things out of drawers and cupboards.

Jessa followed, looking at her helplessly.

"It *did* affect me."

Shara looked up, surprised to find Jessa standing in the bedroom doorway.

It devastated me. Everything I believed in was ripped away and there was nowhere to hide from that fact. Every bolt hole I'd ever had was blocked by the press. Every sympathetic shoulder I thought I could count on turned me away. The only people who were there for me were the people I thought had abandoned me, because I'd abandoned them. "You think you know what happened because you read a book and a script, but you don't." *Have you noticed that there's almost no reference to Lisa in either? It's because Lisa's role in my life isn't dramatic — it doesn't make for literary tension or good cinema, yet she saved my life.* "But I survived it all. And when I did, I decided that I could not be in a relationship with a woman who wasn't proud to be in a relationship with me."

She looked angry and, at the same time, defeated. "I won't stop you from leaving, because it's obvious that, despite what you feel for me, you're not willing to be that woman. Perhaps it's an emotional weakness in me that I can't be with someone unless she loves me enough to shout it from the rooftops, but that's a weakness that we're both going to have to live with."

She was gone as quietly as she'd arrived, leaving Shara to stare at the empty doorway. Shara sat on the bed, her mind and heart in turmoil. She loved Jessa beyond all reason, but she wasn't the woman Jessa wanted. Jessa wanted someone who was courageous. A woman who was self-assured and confident enough to stare down the mob. Someone as strong and well-balanced as she was. Shara knew she wasn't that woman and her misjudgment of what Jessa had gone through with Stephanie made her feel even worse.

She found one of Jessa's suitcases and started folding her clothes neatly and placing them into it. As she packed, she picked up a jumper Jessa had worn the day before and placed it with her own clothes. It would smell like Jessa and she knew she'd need that, if she was going to get through the next few days. She managed to control her voice long enough to ring for a taxi, then she heard it and started to cry again: Jessa was playing Chopin's *Raindrop*. Shara wasn't even sure Jessa realized what she was doing. Whenever Jessa was troubled, she sat at the piano and her fingers ran restlessly over the keys. As if in confirmation, there was a crash of the keys, as though Jessa had come to her senses and slammed her hand down on them.

Shara pulled the suitcase behind her as she headed for the front door of the flat. Jessa sat at the piano and stared at her, but even across the room she could see that Jessa, too, had been crying.

"I . . ." Shara didn't know what to say. She decided that honesty was as good an approach as any. "I know it's a lot to ask, but please don't give up on me, Jessa."

Before Jessa could respond, she'd opened the door and slipped out.

PART THIRTY-THREE

S hara looked at herself critically in the mirror. If she breathed in, she could count her ribs. It wasn't a good look for her and she thought she looked every one of her thirty years. *Maestra* would be going into wide release in three weeks, but it had premiered on the opening night of the Toronto International Film Festival the previous week.

In the months since she'd seen Jessa, she had learned to survive, but it hadn't been easy. This time, it had not been her decision to stay away; Jessa refused to see her. She was torn between calling a press conference and announcing her own lesbianism – doing anything to get Jessa's attention and try to win back her love – and taking out an advert in a classical music magazine just to tell Jessa Hanson to fuck off. To shout at her for showing her what it was like to be loved the way Jessa loved and then to withdraw that love, leaving a devastating emptiness that was tearing her apart.

There'd been a break in the filming of her current project that coincided with the film festival, whose importance in the industry calendar was growing every year. *Maestra* had been nominated for multiple awards and she was expected to promote it, when all she wanted to do was hide.

She was in the same city as Jessa and she wasn't sure she could handle bumping into her, especially if it meant seeing her with another woman. Even the thought of it brought fresh pain to her stomach and her chest. The doctor had said it was an ulcer, but Shara knew it was just heartache.

She slowly began to get dressed. She knew that what she was about to do was completely mad, but she couldn't help herself. She'd got a friend to buy her a returned ticket and she was going to see Jessa conducting at Roy Thomson Hall. It was the only performance by the TSO that week, because the Hall had been converted for the screening of films during the festival. It had been converted back into a concert venue for that night's orchestral concert and for the most coveted ticket in town: the awards ceremony on the final night of the festival, and Shara dreaded that most of all.

It was the first time in her career that she did not want to be recognized for a performance, but her contract stipulated that she put in an appearance. "Not that I think you're the type, Shara," Peter had said almost apologetically, "but I've learned from bitter experience that actors get bouts of shyness come awards time and there are a few places I'll need you to show up if we're featured or nominated: Cannes, Sundance, Toronto, Golden Globes, People's Choice and, of course, the Oscars." At the time it had seemed like the least she could do and she had told her agent she'd accept the clause. She hoped this near-phobia of news cameras would not get worse as time went on. She didn't yet have the career to pull off a Garbo.

She dressed casually in black trousers and a black t-shirt, taking along a black linen jacket in case the air-conditioning got to be too much for her. Her hair was shoulder-length now and she pulled it back into a ponytail, secured with a scrunchie. She put on glasses with clear lenses and tortoiseshell frames, because she had yet to be recognized when she wore them.

That night's concert was to feature Sibelius and Holst. She'd read the review in the newspaper that had been delivered to her room along with the breakfast tray that she'd ignored, so she knew that Jessa's interpretations of *Finlandia* and *Planets* had been well-received by the critics.

Hearing *Mars: the Bringer of War* performed live would have been a thrilling experience anyway, but with Jessa conducting, it gave Shara goose bumps and caused her heart to pound. The accuracy of the dramatic closing bars was stunning and made Shara want to stand up and cheer. After that, the delicacy with which the orchestra handled *Venus: the Bringer of Peace* was amazingly touching. Shara imagined that in ordinary circumstances, she would have found it profoundly calming, but when Lucia Scattaglia stood up as the featured violinist, she couldn't get the image out of her mind of Lucia emerging almost naked from Jessa's bedroom. *They work together now. Have they resumed their relationship? Is she the one who falls asleep holding Jessa and gets to make love to her and hear that little growling noise she makes?*

The painful memories and questions consumed Shara to such an extent that she completely missed the delicately nuanced performance of *Mercury* and when she again focused on the concert, the orchestra was performing *Jupiter* with the tongue-in-cheek precision it deserved.

As much as she tried not to stare, again and again her eyes were drawn to Jessa and she wondered if, on some level, Jessa could sense her presence in the room. Surely a love as strong as the one she felt would communicate itself to the heart and soul of the beloved? Yet she knew that Jessa's concentration was absolute. From her seat in the first balcony, just to the right of the stage, she caught glimpses of Jessa's profile, and sometimes her whole face, when she turned to her right to instruct or encourage the double basses or the cellos. Jessa was perspiring and Shara shivered as she got a vivid flashback of Jessa's naked body pressed against hers in the aftermath of lovemaking, Jessa's damp hair clinging to her forehead in that same way, but her expression lethargic with satisfaction.

They had progressed to *Saturn*, with its overtones of inevitability. *Things move on and often we have no control over them.* Shara had tried to adjust to her lack of control over her future, but not an hour went by that she did not wish something unsaid or undone in her relationship with Jessa. She knew that her decision not to go to Buenos Aires had been the right one at the time for many reasons, but she had never so bitterly regretted anything in her life. Living with it was destroying her from the inside out and, no matter what the doctors thought, that had nothing to do with an ulcer.

She felt immense pride as she watched Jessa lead the orchestra through the complex harmonies and tempi of *Uranus: the Magician*. She could have been imagining it, but she thought the orchestra looked at Jessa a lot more than normal. She supposed that might be because of the complexity of the piece, but she suspected it was because Jessa so perfectly anticipated where every instrument should be at every split second of the performance. Jessa conducted with boundless energy and complete empathy with the musicians, yet she remained immersed in the music itself, so her movements were graceful, beautiful and her expression sometimes entranced, with her eyes half-closed.

When the final, haunting notes of *Neptune: the Mystic* faded away, the audience rose to its feet as one and the applause was thunderous. As Jessa turned to bow in acknowledgement, tears welled up in Shara's eyes, because she saw how thin Jessa was. *I did that*, she thought. *She told me that love had never worked out for her in the past and she asked me to show her that it would be different with me — simply staying with her would have been proof enough. But I let her down. It's really no wonder that she won't see me or take my calls. That has devastated me, yet I understand it. How can she trust me? But Jessa is suffering too, and she doesn't deserve that.*

Suddenly needing air, Shara hurried out of the auditorium. As she stepped out into the warm evening, a taxi was cruising by with its light on and she quickly hailed it. She wanted nothing more than to be back in her hotel room to cope in private with all the happy, painful memories that seeing Jessa had evoked.

She was surprised to see the message light blinking on the phone in her room. She dialed into voicemail and was jolted by the sound of her father's gruff voice. "Shara, I know this is a surprise, but I wanted to wish you good luck. You deserve to win. You deserve good things in your life and if this Jessa Hanson can't see how lucky she is, then she's a fool."

Shara's hand shook as she replaced the receiver in its cradle. Two months. It had been two months since she'd walked out of his house in a cold, almost dispassionate rage. She'd been filming on location in Budapest when it had hit her like a blow to the body, that almost every important decision she'd made in her adult life had been influenced by the man who had brought her up after her mother had died. She didn't even like to think of him as her father, although he'd fed, clothed and sheltered her until she'd reached the age of majority. She had a vague childhood memory, that she'd sometimes thought had been a dream, of him hugging her so tightly that she couldn't breathe. She supposed there must have been other overt demonstrations of physical affection from him, but all the hugs and kisses she remembered receiving when she'd been growing up had come from family friends or relatives.

She'd caught a flight to Ireland and shown up unannounced on his doorstep. He'd been shocked to see her, but had stepped aside wordlessly to let her in. "To what do I owe the honor?" he'd asked, after he'd closed the door behind her.

"Why did you never show me love? Why did you never once tell me that you loved me? I was a little girl. What could I possibly have done to deserve your dislike?"

He'd stopped moving, remaining facing the closed door for several seconds, before turning to face her. "Good afternoon to you, too, lass."

"I'm not here to exchange pleasantries. I'm here because I'm tired of screwing up my life by going out of my way to avoid anything that I associate with you."

"I didn't dislike you, Shara. Far from it. You represented everything I'd dreamed of with your mother. It's just that in my dreams, she was always there, too. I did my best."

"Your *best*? Is that what you tell yourself?" Years of impotent pain manifested themselves in the shimmering rage under the words.

"Yes. But I don't always believe it."

"Well, you shouldn't. All it would have taken would have been a kind word or some sign of affection. Some indication that I was capable of doing something of which you could approve, never mind being proud of."

He looked away from her, but said nothing.

"Is that all I'm gonna get after all these years? More silence?"

"I'm not sure what you want."

"Some acknowledgement, for a start."

"Okay, I wasn't the perfect father. There, are you happy now?" He'd sounded exasperated.

"No," she'd replied quietly, "I'm not. But I'm sick to the back teeth of your perceived approval being part of that equation. And apparently the only person who's gonna help me get past that is me. I don't know why I wasted my time coming here!"

"Why did you?" he'd asked angrily. She could seldom remember having elicited that much emotion from him at any time in the past.

"Because I've fallen in love. I've found someone I want to spend my life with, but we're not together because the only thing growing up with you taught me to do was to be emotionally isolated. I worked so hard to show love in every way I could, but when it came down to it, I was too afraid. Afraid that I would give you even more to disapprove of. Afraid that giving my love in the innocent way a child loves would end with the same result: rejection and silence. It's so fucked up that now I see it, I can't believe I allowed it to happen." The profanity slipped from her lips in a way that would normally have appalled her in her father's presence. "I'm incompetent when it comes to real love, because I have no reference point to go by." She laughed bitterly. "You know, you don't have to say anything – I think I got what I came here for."

With that she turned on her heel and headed for the door. The question hit her between her shoulder blades. "What's her name?"

"How did you . . .?"

"I might not be the most demonstrative person, Shara, but I know my daughter. Those young men who have paraded through your life have never even scratched the surface of the woman you are. After a while, I asked myself why."

"Her name is Jessa Hanson. And now, if you'll excuse me, I need to find out if she'll have me back."

She stared numbly at the phone. She'd tried to reach Jessa, but Jessa had refused to return her calls. She'd completely surrendered her pride and contacted Lisa. Lisa had told her as kindly as she could that Jessa did not want to see her.

There was no way she could have predicted that, for the first time in her life, her father would not only indirectly admit that he was closely following her career, but that he would almost sound as though he did not disapprove of her lesbianism. *Was it always the way that when you stopped needing something, it came into your life?* She hoped that wasn't some sort of rule, because she would always need Jessa.

PART THIRTY-FOUR

Lisa and Jessa were having an early dinner on the patio behind Jessa's house. The house was east of downtown Toronto, situated just where the city gave way to the Scarborough Bluffs. Several feet beyond the patio, there was a wooden railing and a steep staircase that led down to a stretch of pebbled beach. The waves of Lake Ontario lapped at the pebbles a mere ten feet from the bottom of the steps, but Jessa loved that miniature beach, because although it was only about twenty yards long and legally owned by the province, it was completely isolated and accessible only via the steps from her rented property.

It was warm, even though afternoon had begun to yield to evening, and Lisa was glad of the partial shade of the trees overhead, despite the fact that there was a squirrel in one of them who insisted on pelting the two women with acorns when they least expected it.

When she'd moved to Toronto, Jessa had declined the offers of luxury high-rise apartments and Lisa knew it was because they reminded her of Shara. She had also decided not to live in Rosedale, the moneyed, tree-lined enclave in the middle of Toronto, where many of the Orchestra's major financial sponsors resided. She'd chosen, instead, to rent a house that was beyond the trendy, yuppie, Beaches community, but not quite in Scarborough with its myriad immigrant communities. The house was hidden from the street by old-growth trees, but had a wonderful view of the lake from the rooms at the back, a small patio with faded terra-cotta tiles and an outdoor Jacuzzi that she had yet to use.

"I had lunch with Shara yesterday," Lisa said casually, and Jessa almost choked. "I have no idea how she knew I was in Toronto or how she managed to get my suite number at the hotel, but there was a knock on the door and when I opened it, she was standing there."

"What did she want?" Jessa tried for a casual tone and failed.

"What difference does it make to you?"

Jessa said nothing and stared at a catamaran that was skimming across the lake, several hundred yards from the shore.

When it became obvious that Jessa wasn't going to comment, Lisa asked, "Jessa, when are you going to stop punishing her for whatever it was she did?"

"I'm not punishing her. I just don't trust her." She took a sip of her wine. "Has she found herself a boyfriend yet?"

"Why would you even ask something like that? You don't believe she's still interested in you?"

"Maybe if it's convenient and looks innocent and tabloid-friendly," Jessa sneered. "Look, can we change the subject? I don't trust her. End of story."

Lisa ignored her. "She asked about what happened with Stephanie. Why haven't you told her? Don't you think it could have made all the difference to the way she reacted to the press?"

Jessa laughed mirthlessly. "Her fear of what the press and the public could do to her was apparently stronger than her love for me. And that was *before* she knew how vicious the bastards could actually be. Do you really think that, if I told her the full horror of it, like the fact that one of them actually broke into my home, that it would make her *more* likely to take them on? Or do you think that if I told her they turned me into a blubbering mess who had to be sedated so she wouldn't wake up screaming in the middle of the night, that that would somehow make me more attractive?"

"So your lack of trust obviously pre-dated whatever it was she did, otherwise you'd have told her, instead of taking that macho stance that makes her believe you're some invulnerable paragon." Lisa's voice was as cold as Jessa had ever heard it, but she was tired of standing back as Jessa entered another self-destructive spiral, possibly worse than the one that had landed her in an Italian hospital.

"She can't possibly believe that," Jessa said dismissively, acutely aware of her vulnerability where Shara Quinn was concerned. "I opened myself completely to her, Lisa. I held nothing back and she knew it. There is nothing *macho* about the way I love her." She grimaced at her own weakness. "There was a time before she refused to go with me to Buenos Aires, when I considered sending *her* one of those type-four letters." She looked down at the table and attempted a disparaging smile, but her lips trembled. "Tell me what's macho about wanting her baby? Not that I told her ... Because it stemmed from my own insecurity about her feelings for me ... even though I'd reassured her about mine for her ... Anyway, god knows there are already too many children in the world who were conceived through fear: fear of loneliness, fear of mortality, fear that there'd be nothing left if a lover walked out of the door ..." She stopped talking abruptly, as though deciding she'd said too much, and poured more wine for herself. "There's sod all that's macho about the way I love her," she repeated lamely, before drinking deeply from her glass.

Lisa noticed that Jessa spoke in the present tense and responded the same way. "And what about the way she loves you? I've never got the impression that you two are separated because either of you doesn't love the other, but please correct me if I'm wrong ..."

Jessa put down her glass, pushed her chair away from the table and stood up. "Shara said she loved me, but I thought she'd have moved on by now ..."

"Because Stephanie moved on the first time you left her alone for a few months? Jessa, Shara isn't Stephanie, but you're treating her as though she is."

"She wanted to keep our relationship a secret." It was a relief for Jessa to talk about it. "She was actually using the same words Stephanie had used. I saw my future turning into more years of *discretion* and lies." She crossed thin arms protectively over her body. "It was a nightmare: convoluted lies to the press and to people I met, avoiding friends I'd had for years because they're queer and it would raise questions ... I lived in an artificial world and eventually

I started obeying its twisted rules . . . which almost killed me. Then I found out Stephanie had her own reasons for wanting our relationship to be a secret." Even so many years later, the remembered pain in her voice seemed to chill the summer evening.

"And you believe Shara has similar reasons? Is that why you asked about a boyfriend?"

"No . . . I don't know." She sat down again and looked helplessly at Lisa. "I only know that there was something she wasn't telling me. I know her and she was scared, but not of some wankers from the press. She wasn't going with me and she wasn't being honest with me about why. In my experience that only leads to one thing . . ."

"So you thought you'd do it to her before she did it to you . . ."

The sentence hung between them and Jessa considered it for several seconds. Had she been unfair to Shara? Was she making them both pay for something Stephanie had done? *If I was wrong, could Shara possibly forgive me?* The question made her stomach twist painfully.

"How is she?" She asked, finally, in a quiet voice.

"A bit like you: beautiful, too thin, haunted. You can see for yourself – she should be on TV in half an hour or so. They're broadcasting the film festival awards ceremony and she's been nominated."

Shara wanted to be anywhere except where she was. She was dressed for it, in a form-fitting bronze evening gown whose spaghetti straps revealed smooth, golden shoulders and a fine gold necklace with a diamond droplet pendant. Her hair was pinned up loosely and her makeup had been professionally applied, but she was simply not in the mood to face so many people.

Since she'd had lunch with Lisa the day before, and following the message from her father, she'd been re-thinking her reaction to Jessa and trying desperately to understand Jessa's response to her decision to keep their relationship a secret, even for a short time.

It was through Tony's contacts that she'd been able to confront Lisa. The meeting and subsequent lunch had been good, because the time together had reminded both of them that they genuinely liked each other, but maddening because it had moved Shara no further forward in understanding why Jessa had reacted so strongly to what she'd said that day in February.

She was frustrated that Lisa wouldn't give her the details of Jessa's past, except to say that the biographer had only scratched the surface of the harassment Jessa had endured and that Jessa's public reaction had been very different from what she'd gone through in private. Lisa had insisted that Jessa should be the one to talk to her about it, which made Shara want to scream, since they both knew that Jessa was refusing to see or speak to her and she could think of no way around that.

She knew that, if she could only speak to Jessa and explain the childish fears that had driven her actions, they could probably make peace with each other. After all, Jessa's behavior had been as over the top as hers. Walking away from a relationship as deliriously happy and emotionally intense as theirs had been was irrational, but they'd both been wary of it well before that had happened, when, on the surface, nothing either of them had done had given the other reason to be so unsure. It was just her own bad luck that she'd fallen for someone more pig-headed than she was and that was making it impossible to resolve their problems.

"Miss Quinn! Miss Quinn, can I get a smile over here?" The photographer's voice broke through Shara's reverie and she automatically complied with the request.

"Shara! Do you think you'll win?" another voice shouted from behind her.

"I'm not sure I'm worthy, but I hope *Maestra* does well. It's a wonderful film and was a great opportunity for me."

The shouted questions continued to come across the velvet ropes and Shara answered the reporters who were closest to her or whose questions were simple enough to allow for a one-liner. After several minutes, a security officer announced to the press and the fans that she had to go and he escorted her the rest of the way along the red carpet and into Roy Thomson Hall.

As Shara disappeared through the doors, Jessa tore her gaze away from the television screen. "What's so funny?" she asked impatiently, when she caught sight of Lisa's huge grin.

"You. You're hilarious. You know, you could have got a really good seat in the auditorium, since you're so interested. All you had to do was ask."

"Piss off," Jessa replied rudely and Lisa's grin turned into a giggle.

"Why don't I dish up dessert and we can eat it in front of the TV."

"Bring the rest of the bottle of wine as well, while you're at it," Jessa muttered, before deciding to fetch it herself.

While she was up, she cleared the remains of their dinner from the table outside, rinsed the dishes and put them into the dishwasher and was starting a major cleaning job in the kitchen, when Lisa shouted, "Will you *please* stop faffing about and come and sit down?"

Reluctantly, Jessa joined Lisa on the sofa. Taking pity on her, Lisa changed the subject and started to fill Jessa in on Paul's latest exploits. He was a writer for a London radio program that prided itself on early-morning madness and she was convinced that he only did it because he wasn't quite sane. By regaling her with stories of Paul's so-called research, she almost managed to hold Jessa's attention until the festival's "Most memorable performance" nominees were announced.

Despite everything that had happened, Jessa stood up and cheered when Shara was named as the winner. Lisa was happy for Shara as well, but Jessa looked so proud that she wanted to hug her. Lisa believed that Shara and Jessa really would be hilarious if they weren't so damned tragic.

Shara walked carefully onto the stage, cocooned in the insulating feeling that she was observing her own actions from a distance. She welcomed the resulting numbness, knowing that if she fully acknowledged what was happening, she'd panic. She took the small plaque from the legendary producer and accepted kisses on both cheeks before stepping up to the microphone. *I've won.* The words meant nothing. *I'm standing in front of everyone who matters in the film industry and I think my armpits are starting to sweat.* Suddenly the sea of faces started to swim into focus and as she recognized one set of features after another, she felt a rising sense of panic. She struggled to think of something that would calm her down and one particular person immediately came to mind. *Jessa.*

All at once, she recognized the opportunity that the occasion presented. Members of the press from every country that had a film industry were there. The ceremony was being broadcast live on Canadian television and the highlights would appear on news and entertainment shows all over the world.

A sense of calm descended on her and she began to smile. "Thank you for voting for me, although I'm sure this award has more to do with the superb writing, direction, photography and design of *Maestra*, than anything I've done," she said, the huskiness of her voice and the pronounced Irish accent the only hints of her emotional state as she smoothly reminded the audience of the other categories in which the film had been nominated. "Nevertheless, I am grateful for this award and even more grateful to have had the opportunity to do this film. I'm especially grateful that doing research for the part gave me the opportunity to meet ... and fall in love with ... the subject of the film, Jessa Hanson."

There was a collective gasp and the audience started to murmur excitedly. As gossip went, it didn't get much bigger than that.

Shara looked into the camera directly in front of her. "Things might not have worked out quite the way I wanted them to, but sweetheart, this is for you." She lifted the plaque. "From the rooftops."

PART THIRTY-FIVE

S hara was shaking as the security guard led her out of the back entrance of Roy Thomson Hall to where Tony waited in the car. She felt drained and exhausted, but she had no regrets. The impromptu press conference that had followed the ceremony had lasted for almost twenty minutes. She'd declined to answer any questions about Jessa except those detailing how and when they'd met, but she'd spoken cautiously about her own feelings. She'd tried to be honest and rigidly factual, even though it had gone against her nature and her instinct to be private. She was hoping to defuse any attempt to mine her friends, family or acquaintances for information by saying flatly that there was no story; she had met and fallen in love with Jessa and then they'd gone their separate ways. When asked about the nature of their relationship with questions that contained euphemisms for sex, she'd replied firmly and repeatedly, "Jessa became one of my closest friends. I hope we'll always be friends."

"Well, Miss Shara, will we be going to the reception at the Four Seasons?" Tony asked, when she was comfortably settled in the car.

Shara sighed. "I suppose. Having given the press free rein to cross-examine me, I might as well offer the same chance to my peers. It's hard to believe it's been less than two hours since my big announcement. I feel as though my life has changed."

"It's because only one thing in your life matters to those people you've been speaking to since then. It will be back to normal when you spend time with your normal friends. Too bad the stores are closed or I would offer to take you shoe-shopping to make yourself feel better."

Shara smiled. It was good to be around someone who didn't perceive a change in her just because she loved Jessa, even if he insisted on calling her *Miss* when he was working. She got the feeling that all the men backstage at Roy Thomson Hall had been mentally undressing her and then placing her in imaginary sexual scenarios with their favorite fantasy females. She wasn't sure which was more unsettling, that she was right and men in the industry were all lecherous, or that she was wrong and had turned into a raving paranoiac during her first hour as an out lesbian.

The car turned left onto University Avenue, heading north towards the Four Seasons Hotel. They drove past the new opera house and past "hospital row" to Queen's Park, with its floodlit provincial parliament building. When they stopped for a red light, Shara admired the greenery and the dignified University of Toronto buildings that characterized that part of the city. In January, she had looked forward to living here with Jessa and her heart ached as they drove past the Royal Ontario Museum, which they'd talked last summer about stealing away to visit, before Derek had announced his imminent arrival and ruined the trip.

Photographers surrounded the car as soon as it pulled up outside the hotel, although it was not a flashy stretch limousine, so Shara knew that their counterparts at Roy Thomson Hall must have managed to alert them. She smiled and allowed Tony to help her out of the back seat, then kept the smile plastered to her face as hotel security pushed back the photographers and escorted her through the main doors.

The first person she recognized when she got inside was Lucia. "Shara!"

I'm not ready for this, Shara thought, but she could hardly snub Lucia. "Hi, Lucia. Nice to see you fully clothed," she added under her breath as Lucia kissed her on both cheeks.

"Oooo, meow!" There was genuine amusement in Lucia's tone, even a touch of admiration. "Let me be the first to officially welcome you to the sisterhood. Unfortunately, despite what that Ellen

DeGeneres said, there is no toaster."

Shara couldn't help it, she laughed. "Thank you. And if you think that making me like you is going to mean I won't fight for Jessa, you've got another think coming," she said, sweetly.

"Brava! I would expect no less, or you would not deserve Jessica. But you should not regard me as competition – she has no romantic interest in me, nor I in her. She is, however, one of my closest friends, so I am pleased to see that you have finally come to your senses and admitted to the world how you feel."

The security guard cleared his throat, hinting that Shara was supposed to be at the reception, not hanging around outside the banquet hall talking to people he didn't know. That annoyed Shara. "May I escort you into the den of superficiality that awaits?" She held out an elbow and Lucia took it with a wicked laugh.

The cocktail reception was made surreal not just by the bizarre conversations that followed Shara's "outing" of herself, but by the fact that, whenever someone began crowding Shara or asking questions that were too intrusive, Lucia was always on hand to rescue her. That had been especially useful when an award-winning actress wanted to know if Shara would consider sleeping with a man again, should she be required to play a heterosexual woman in the future, and Shara had already balled her hand into a fist to punch her. It was a relief when huge wooden panels along one wall slid back, signaling the end of the cocktail hour and the start of the main festivities: the celebratory dance.

"Another glass of champagne?" Peter Garofolo had been fussing over her from the time the party had begun, hyperactive with glee as he was from *Maestra* winning three awards. He almost seemed to think that Shara's newfound lesbianism was a special favor to him, to help promote his film.

"If it will send you off to the bar for a few minutes to fetch it," she replied, rolling her eyes. He'd been like a big puppy all evening and she imagined that's what he'd be like as a baby brother, although he was several years older than she was.

"Dance with me before that American gets back," Lucia demanded. "I love this song and I'm not sure, but I think he pinched my bum."

Shara laughed. "It might have been him, or it might have been dozens of other men. It's a very nice bum in a very tight dress in a room full of men with a sense of entitlement."

"You like my bum?" Lucia did a little twirl.

"What can I say? Jessa has good taste," Shara replied cheekily.

"Egoïste," Lucia accused.

"Tu m'appelles?" Shara raised an inquiring eyebrow and they both started to giggle tipsily as they walked to the dance floor. They turned quite a few heads as they danced and they were still smiling and exhilarated as they wended their way through the crowd to the bar before the song had even ended.

"Are you trying to pick up my woman, Lucia?" Both women turned in surprise towards the sound of Jessa's voice.

Shara and Jessa stared at each other as though unable to tear their eyes away. Shara felt on the verge of tears; it had been so long since she'd looked into those eyes she loved so much.

Jessa was dressed elegantly in a honey-colored trouser suit that complemented her tan and a bronze blouse that was almost transparent, worn with a bra that must have been the same color as her skin because she looked naked under the blouse. She wasn't wearing any jewelry that Shara could see, but she was wearing makeup. Her cheekbones were highlighted in bronze and she wore a frosted lipstick that Shara immediately wanted to kiss off. Her eyes looked like molten cinnamon as they roved over Shara's face and body, warming her as though she'd touched her.

"*Is* she your woman?" Neither of them looked away when Lucia asked the question.

"Yes," Jessa said quietly. "If we never met again, she would still be my woman." It was stated confidently, but with a tenderness that precluded arrogance.

"Well, that's as it should be, isn't it?" Shara asked softly.

"Is it?" Lucia tried to sound skeptical, but her smile was too wide for her to be in any way convincing.

"It is," Shara said, still looking at Jessa, "because her heart belongs to me. It always will."

Jessa smiled. "I've requested a song. Dance with me?"

As though on cue, the music slowed and Sarah McLachlan's *Fumbling Towards Ecstasy* began to play. Shara moved easily into Jessa's arms and, although they did not bother to go onto the dance floor, the crowd parted and allowed them space to dance.

Lucia had the feeling that it would not have mattered what the people around them thought or did, but it was nice that they all stepped back, even if they did stare shamelessly.

As the couple moved slowly together to the beat of the music, Shara put her arms around Jessa's neck and Jessa's hands rested lightly on Shara's back. Their eyes were closed as they savored the feeling of being in each other's arms.

Later, each would apologize for rashness, fear, lack of faith. Later, they would talk about pain from the past that they would not allow to ruin the future. Later, they would affirm their relationship by making love and then they would hold each other and cry. But as the song played and the warmth flowed between them, they said little. As the buzz went through the crowd that Jessa Hanson was at the party and dancing with the woman who had become the story of the festival, cameras started to click, beep and whir, despite the fact that flash photography was forbidden.

"Shara Quinn, will you live with me and be my love? Will you spend the rest of your life with me?"

Shara pulled back so she could look at Jessa's face. Her eyes showed the overwhelming love that filled her because she was there with Jessa and everything was going to be okay. Then Jessa's words sank in. She shouldn't have been surprised; she knew Jessa well enough to know that, after her gesture at the awards, Jessa would want to demonstrate a similar commitment to her. "Jessa Hanson, are you asking me to marry you?"

"Yes."

"Yes."

Jessa lowered her head so their lips could meet. A cheer went up from the crowd, but neither Shara nor Jessa noticed it. One ballad faded into the next and Gloria Estefan began to sing *Más Allá*.

From the side of the room, Lisa gave a satisfied smile.

THE END

An excerpt from
Forbidden Passion
by
Ruth Gogoll

Tiny letters danced across the screen in front of Kim's eyes. Exhausted, she rubbed at her eyelids. Working at a computer for hours at a stretch wasn't exactly restful. But when she could work no more, she went to one particular Internet site, where she could relax a little. There were stories there that she read again and again. Very special stories. From woman to woman.

Slowly, Kim let herself slip into the story. The woman with the chestnut brown hair sank back on the couch, and the other woman leaned over her –

"Ms. Wolff?"

Kim spun around. Her boss stood in the doorway. Silky chestnut brown hair fell across her shoulders, shiny and seductive. Kim swallowed.

"Are you working on something urgent?" her boss asked. "Or could you come see me right now?"

"I can ... come," Kim managed with an effort. That was certainly true. She probably almost could've.

Sonja Kantner, Department Head and object of Kim's restless dreams, glanced briefly at the screen, but she was too far away, the screen stood at too sharp an angle, and the letters were too small. Kim thanked all the goddesses in heaven for that.

"I'll just save this quickly," Kim commented, feeling warm in the face. Hopefully, she hadn't turned beet red. But she didn't really tend to. That was lucky for her. At least at this particular moment.

"Good, do that," Sonja Kantner confirmed with a nod, then turned away.

Kim watched her luscious backside disappear from the doorway. Did she have to be so attractive? It was a daily torture.

SIX WEEKS EARLIER

When Kim had seen her new boss for the first time, at her intro-
duction in the conference room six weeks ago, Kim had nearly
fainted. She immediately worked out a plan for how, for reasons of
strategic importance to the company, she could move the department head's office – normally immediately adjacent to her own –
to the other end of the hall, or better yet, to another floor. Or even
better still, to another building.

"Why don't you start by introducing yourself, Ms. Kantner," the
CEO invited after relating a few of the career highlights of his new
department head.

He drew back, and Sonja Kantner stepped forward. She repeated,
in slightly different form, what he'd already said about her, but that
didn't interest Kim in any case. What interested her, Sonja Kantner
said right at the start: married, no children.

"Yet," she added with a charming smile.

She'd guessed right. Kim almost sighed when she received confirmation of what she'd already known anyhow. Sonja Kantner was
straight, and solidly so. But what good would it have done if things
had been otherwise? Kim brooded some more over her plan to ship
her off to another building. Didn't they have branch offices in other
countries, too? Couldn't Sonja Kantner perhaps be assigned there?

Kim knew one thing, at least: She wouldn't be able to stand having Sonja Kantner so close to her for long, everyday, almost every
minute. Perhaps Kim would get used to her and the attraction
would fade with time? Kim mustered Sonja Kantner's body once
more from head to toe as she spoke. – No. – No, the chances of
that were exceedingly slim. The opposite was more likely to occur.

When the assembly started to break up, Kim was about to leave
when the CEO waved in her direction. "Ms. Wolff? Would you
come over here for a moment?"

Kim took a deep breath and squared her shoulders. Courage! She
went over to the two of them, and he introduced her with a smile.
"This, Ms. Kantner, is your closest coworker, Ms. Wolff."

Sonja Kantner smiled likewise and offered Kim her hand. Kim
would rather not have touched her, but she could hardly avoid that,

after all. Sonja Kantner's hand was soft and warm in hers. For preference, Kim would never have let go, but Ms. Kantner drew back after the appropriate interval, as was proper.

"I'm glad to meet you, Ms. Wolff," she said. "I hope we'll work well together."

Work together? thought Kim, but aloud, she responded with what was expected of her: "I hope so, too, and I'm looking forward to it as well." She smiled in a way that she hoped came across as confident. The tingling that had slowly spread from her hand throughout her entire body somewhat hindered her ability to control her reactions.

"You'll take Ms. Kantner on a tour of the company and show her everything, won't you, Ms. Wolff?" her CEO surmised in a tone of friendly command.

Kim tried not to gulp. "Yes," she replied, the effort required to control her voice making it sound very soft, "of course. I'll show her everything." If only that were possible! What all Kim would've liked to show her . . . !

Sonja Kantner laughed. "But not until tomorrow! Today, I still have to tour the executive floor."

The CEO melted at her charming smile just as Kim had, only he was permitted to let that show; Kim wasn't. *One day's reprieve! At least she had that!*

"Then until tomorrow," Sonja Kantner smiled at Kim once more. "When will you be here?"

"At eight," Kim forced out.

"Good," smiled Ms. Kantner. "I'll be here at seven."

CR&SO

"This really wasn't necessary, Ms. Wolff," Ms. Kantner greeted her, beaming.

Already in such a good mood this early in the morning – this was going to be something! When had she gotten up? Kim had been punctual, but Sonja Kantner was already sitting at the desk when

Kim entered her office.

She came over to Kim and extended her hand. "Good morning," she said when she'd reached Kim, and her eyes delved into Kim's with an irresistible gaze.

She probably had no idea what effect that had on Kim . . . she had on Kim —

"You could just as well have come in at eight," Ms. Kantner continued. "I know I get on everyone's nerves by being such an early riser. But I like to catch up on things in peace and quiet first thing in the morning. When no one is here yet. Otherwise one never gets to some things." Her laugh was enormously likeable.

She'd only just started. What was there for her to catch up on? Kim nudged herself into an understanding smile and withdrew her hand, which Ms. Kantner still held. "You're right about that," she agreed. "Although I prefer to do it in the evening, when everyone else is gone."

Sonja Kantner laughed once more and went back to her desk. "To each her own," she said. She turned to face Kim. "How late do you stay at the office in the evenings?" she asked.

"Sometimes until ten," answered Kim, "but I usually don't come in until —" She broke off. Perhaps she shouldn't reveal to her new boss what time she normally came in in the morning.

Sonja Kantner smiled. She was too clever to be led so easily astray. "You don't normally come in at seven or at eight, do you?"

Kim sighed. "No," she admitted. "But I'll change that, of course," she added hastily. "If you're here at seven, I will be, too."

"That's not necessary," replied Sonja Kantner. "As I said at the beginning: I know I get on everyone's nerves by being such an early bird, but I don't demand it of anyone else." She kept smiling. "Although by ten o'clock in the evening, I'm usually already in bed. So we ought to agree on some time in between."

In bed? Kim looked at her. How seductive must she look lying in bed, if she was already this attractive during the day? She was sure to have wonderful negligees for nighttime . . . and if she wore nothing at all . . .?

"When's the earliest you can be here?" Sonja Kantner was now asking as she paged through a file on her desk, which her predecessor must've left behind.

Kim first had to tear herself away from her thoughts. "Eight-thirty?" she suggested then. She could probably just about manage that.

Sonja Kantner looked up. "Fine," she said. Then she smiled once more in that unbelievably likeable, almost loving way. "And if it's more like nine sometimes, that's not a problem. I suspect that was the time you really wanted to suggest, am I right?"

She must've graduated from a great many leadership seminars, to be this good. "Yes," Kim admitted.

"We'll thrash it out together eventually!" laughed Sonja Kantner. "Will you show me around the company now?"

Thrash it out together — what a nice image, Kim thought for a moment, before she yielded to Sonja Kantner and they left the office.

An excerpt from

L as in Love

by

Ruth Gogoll

AT SAPPHO

"**Y**ou're not serious!" Sabrina's eyes flew open. "She was there when you got home?"

"She's got a lot of nerve," said Carolin.

"I . . ." Anita wrung her hands and looked at the floor. "I can't just send her away."

"Why not?" Sabrina shook her head. "After all the liberties she's taken with you, I thought you'd finally figured this out."

"She . . . she needs me," Anita said softly. "She said so."

"Is that a new record, or has it been playing for awhile now?" Carolin sighed.

"One cappuccino, one latte, and one fresh-squeezed vitamin bomb," Melly smiled as she set down their order.

"What would you say, Melly?" Carolin asked. "Marlene showed up at Anita's place again . . . after not being around for a week."

"Right, she hasn't been around here, either." Even though Melly nodded as she spoke, she didn't appear particularly interested.

"We have to do something," Carolin said.

"About Marlene?" Melly laughed. "She's not all that bad. You just have to let her know the score."

Sabrina raised an eyebrow. Melly headed back to the counter. Sabrina got up and walked after her. "You had something with Marlene, too?" she asked.

Melly shrugged. "When I first came to the café, a long time ago," she said.

Sabrina involuntarily glanced at Melly's ample breasts, clearly visible under her tight, sleeveless top.

Melly laughed. "Yes, that's what she's into." She glanced over at the table. "Of course I can't compete with Anita."

"Why . . ." Sabrina frowned. "Why would you take up with her?"

"Oh, she has a certain . . . robust charm," Melly replied with a laugh.

"Charm? Marlene?" Sabrina looked dumbfounded.

"I don't think she was as unhappy then as she is now. She was still working as a truck driver, so she only came in now and then."

"Chris told me that she used to drive trucks."

"That was her dream job. Ever since they took away her driver's license, though, she's stuck in an office. I think that's what makes her so short-tempered," Melly offered.

"Why did they take away her driver's license?"

"What do you think?" Melly rolled her eyes.

"Alcohol?"

"Yes, of course. She drinks way too much." Melly took a couple of bottles out of the refrigerator and began to mix a cocktail. "I told her as much, too, but she listens to no one when it comes to that subject."

"I don't think you can get her to listen when it comes to any subject," Sabrina said. She glanced over at Anita, who was talking with Carolin.

"I wouldn't say that." Melly filled the cocktail shaker with ice. "You just have to find the right starting point with her."

Sabrina laughed skeptically. "And how do you find that? Maybe I can give Anita some sort of tip."

"Anita . . ." Melly looked over at the table. "There's no sense in that. Women like Anita are deadly for Marlene. They bring out the worst in her."

Sabrina stared at her, speechless, for a moment. "You're telling me it's Anita's fault?" she finally managed in stunned disbelief.

"No one is at fault; that's not what I said," Melly countered. She decorated the cocktail and delivered it to a table.

Still mulling things over, Sabrina returned to Carolin and Anita.

"Take the key away from her," she heard Carolin say.

"I can't do that." Anita's forehead was furrowed with concern.

"You have to." Carolin appeared outraged. "She can't just come and go as she pleases. In your apartment."

"Don't get yourself worked up, Carolin," Sabrina said. "Anita has to decide these things for herself."

Carolin looked at her aghast.

"What is it you like so much about Marlene?" Sabrina asked Anita. "Carolin and I obviously can't comprehend it, but something about her must appeal to you."

"She's so . . . ," a ready smile spread across Anita's face, "strong."

"Does she hit you?" Carolin blurted out, before Sabrina could stop her.

Anita's eyes widened. "No," she said. "She's never hit me."

"But others have?" asked Sabrina. "Other women you were with?"

Anita lowered her gaze.

"So it's true?" Carolin pressed.

"No." Anita's voice was barely a breath.

Carolin looked at Sabrina. Sabrina shook her head. "Did you see there's a reading coming up at the alternative bookstore?" Sabrina asked, being sure to sound relaxed. "I'd love to go. Rumor has it the author is the new Rita Mae Brown."

"I hate Rita Mae Brown," Carolin said. "You couldn't pay me to read her books!"

"So that means I'll have to manage without you," Sabrina sighed. "How about you, Anita?"

Anita lifted her head. "I'd love to go," she smiled shyly.

"Everyone having fun?" Chris gave Sabrina a kiss in greeting, and sat down with them. "I just ran into Rick. They ought to be here any second."

"They?" Carolin looked at her in surprise.

Just then, the door opened and Rick and Thea walked in.

Chris grinned. "Yes, 'they'," she said.

Carolin raised an eyebrow in interest and regarded Thea thoroughly.

"Hello people," said Rick. She pulled up a chair and sat down across from Chris.

"Aren't you going to offer your girlfriend a seat?" Sabrina asked, smiling.

Rick looked up and stood again. "Oh, sorry," she said to Thea.

"Have a seat."

Thea smiled at her and sat down. Rick dragged over another chair.

"And you're not planning to introduce your girlfriend to us, either," Carolin added with a grin.

"My name is Thea," the woman said, smiling. Rick appeared both confused and exhausted. "I'm a journalist."

"Ah, so you interviewed Rick . . . in that capacity?" Carolin asked.

"Y-yes. Yes, you could call it that," replied Thea with an even wider smile.

Carolin and Sabrina grinned. "How was your day, honey?" Sabrina asked Chris, running her hand lovingly along her leg. "Hard?"

"It was okay." Chris leaned back.

Melly came to their table, glanced briefly at Rick, and then nodded at Chris. "What would you like to drink?"

"A champagne cocktail!" Chris laughed. "No, bring me a Proud Mary, please."

"Coffee," Thea said. "I'm totally wiped out. A quadruple espresso or something." She reattached herself to Rick and cuddled up to her.

"I could offer you two doubles," Melly responded.

"Ricky, don't you want something?" Thea caressed Rick's cheek.

"Umm . . . a beer," Rick replied quickly.

"I think coffee would be more appropriate," said Thea. "Beer makes you tired, and I'd like it better if you stayed a little frisky." She nibbled tenderly on Rick's earlobe and looked up at Melly. "Cancel the beer and bring her the same as me."

Melly started to raise her eyebrows, but quickly caught herself. "All right," she said, and went back to the counter.

"Thea," said Sabrina thoughtfully. "Thea Funk?" Thea nodded. "I know your show," Sabrina continued. "I listen to it sometimes."

"And? Do you like it?" she asked, briefly releasing Rick.

"Very amusing," Sabrina said.

"That means you don't like it?"

"When you have guests in the studio that you're interviewing I find it very interesting," said Sabrina. "I like the live atmosphere."

"That's when it's the most exciting, too," said Thea. "Usually I cut together several interviews before the broadcast and just play them back; that can be kind of boring. But when I have live guests, something unexpected could happen at anytime." She let her hand glide across Rick's shirt, opened a button, and slid it inside. Rick didn't seem to appreciate it, but said nothing.

"Have you known Rick for long?" Chris asked, feigning innocence. She knew differently, as she'd spoken to Rick a week ago, and there hadn't been any Thea mentioned.

"Forever!" Thea laughed. "It seems like it, anyway. Isn't that so, darling?" She stroked Rick's breast under her shirt, as everyone could clearly see.

"A week," Rick said laboriously.

Chris could barely suppress a grin. "And you're just now introducing her to us?" she asked.

"We were . . . busy," Rick said, as she sat up, causing Thea's hand to slide out of her shirt, which she was quick to button back up.

"Oh, yes . . ." Thea confirmed, smiling. "Rick has qualities that people don't see at first glance."

Rick gave her a chastising look. "Would you please stop that," she said.

"But darling." Rick leaned forward and Thea snuggled up against her back. "We've had so much fun. Aren't your friends allowed to know that?"

Melly produced two large cups filled with a pitch black liquid. "Quadruple," she said placing them down and handing Chris her cocktail.

Rick suddenly reached for Thea and kissed her deeply and passionately running her hands up and down along Thea's body.

Melly turned around and walked quickly toward the kitchen.

Sabrina put her lips to Chris's ear. "Oh, man, here we go," she whispered merrily. "Who do you think is going to win this one?"

An excerpt from

Ruth Gogoll's Christmas Carol

By

Ruth Gogoll

It was late when Michaela headed home that evening. The streets were deserted. She entered her apartment where everything looked exactly as it always did. There were no Christmas decorations, no burning candles. Michaela missed none of it. What was all that humbug for anyway?

The apartment had only sparse furnishing; there was nothing unnecessary. Michaela's idea of superfluous included a coffee machine, a refrigerator and a television. She had none of those.

She had moved into the apartment with the few pieces of furniture remaining from the previous tenant. She had been forced to sell her family's house after she had inherited the company and discovered that she was nearly bankrupt. Her father had needed only a few months to ruin what had taken her grandfather decades and a lot of effort to build. At that moment, she had taken a solemn oath never to become like her father. Yes, he had always been everybody's darling. However, Michaela was not after that. Popularity had no value. Money was the only thing that counted, never having to rely on anybody.

She crossed her apartment in the weak light streaming through the window from a street lamp. Why should she turn on a light? She knew where everything was. There was hardly any furniture, so there was not much opportunity to run into anything. She did not have to pay for the street lamp – although, that was not entirely true either, her taxes paid for it, much to her annoyance.

She just wanted to change out of her clothes, brush her teeth and fall into her bed. She had no use for Christmas. She did not notice that the light through the window seemed to be brighter that night because the street lamp was supported by the many colored lights shining out from the surrounding windows. Had she noticed, she would not have cared. At worst, she would have gotten upset about people's wastefulness. Those people somehow felt the need to illuminate the street, which was a waste if they were inside.

She yawned and went to bed, shivering when her body hit the cold sheets. There was no heat in her bedroom. It would get warm under the blanket in a moment, as always. She was still waiting for all of her toes to adjust to the surrounding temperature when she started to drift off.

She had a strange dream. What was even stranger: She usually did not dream at all. While she was dreaming, she was not aware of that, of course.

She was running through a long corridor, searching for something, though she would not have been able to say what exactly she was looking for. She opened every door, of which there were incredibly many on the seemingly endless corridor, and looked inside. She found herself in front of storage rooms, bricked-up doors and windows, never finding what she was searching for. Once there seemed to be a room flooded with light behind one door, but when she wanted to look inside to see what kind of room it was, the door closed, and she was back in the dimly lit corridor. She noticed she was starting to panic. She knew, she had to find it … it … it … whatever it was.

"Mike … Mike …" A voice drifted through her dream. "Mike …"

She opened her eyes and peered into the darkness. Her bedroom faced the courtyard; not even the street lamps could cast a glow here. Still, her eyes adjusted quickly to the absence of light, and it was as if shadows populated the room, formless, faceless shadows.

"Mike …"

It sounded like an echo, a faraway echo without any substance, as if coming from nowhere, as if it had no origin.

Michaela set up straight in her bed. It could not be that she was just imagining this! She had never had nightmares. There had to be some real cause. A burglar maybe?

She scanned the room – as much as she could see. She was not prepared for a situation like this. To be honest, she had always thought there was nothing to steal in her apartment – which was probably true – and that she could neglect any kind of security. She had an ordinary lock on her front door. That was it. She had no weapons, neither for defense nor for offense. She knew her grandfather had had a pistol, a souvenir from the war, and she knew that pistol still had to be somewhere. But, even if she were to find it, it was not likely that it would still fire.

A flashlight on her bedside table would have been very useful now. It would have provided light, and she could have used it as a weapon. Unfortunately, Michaela had thought that investment was unnecessary too.

She lay down again and tried to calm herself. She could hear the sound of her own breathing and her rapidly pounding heart. With difficulty, she tried to get both into a slower rhythm.

A rustle. She held her breath. She knew there had to be something in the room.

She stared into the darkness, unable to move. The little bit of light in the room seemed to change, as if suddenly a street lamp was switched on outside. This could not have been, after all, there were no street lamps in the courtyard.

No, the light did not come from outside, it came from inside. Michaela sat up again; and this time she got out of bed. If there was something there, she wanted to face it upright. The air was freezing, but she did not feel it, even though her feet tried to call her attention to it.

"Mike . . . " One of the formless shadows glided towards her.

Michaela shrank back, startled, but then stopped. She was hallucinating; that was all.

The shadow hovered in the air in front of her and then suddenly took shape – a female shape. A face peeled itself out of the darkness, strangely familiar and unfamiliar at the same time. Suddenly Michaela recognized something very familiar. "Karina?"

The shadow with Karina's shape smiled.

Michaela took a deep breath. What was that woman thinking? "Did you use your key again, even though I told you not to?" she asked with irritation in her voice. Then she scowled. Had she not taken the key from Karina?

With an unusual expression on her face, rather angelically inno-cent and a small halo around her head, Karina answered, "I didn't need to. Not this time." She smiled a shadowy smile.

Michaela wanted to say something but shut her mouth again right away. She was confused, because Karina was so different. She did not know her like this. "Why are you here, in the middle of the night?" she asked when the shadow did not seem to want to move.

"It is a very special night," Karina whispered, the angelic smile still on her face.

"It is a very cold night!" Michaela snapped. Suddenly she became aware of the frostbite threatening her bare feet standing on the bare floor. She fumbled for her slippers and put them on. Unfortunate-ly, they were also cold.

"It's as cold a night as it has to be," Karina said. "As it always is."

"Why are you out and about then? Don't you have a bed at home?" A knowing smile spread over Michaela's face. "Or is your bed empty? Are you alone and looking for company?" Now she knew what was up. She recalled that Karina could not stand being alone. Her bed was rarely empty. And today – on Christmas – all of her lovers were busy elsewhere – all except Michaela. So Karina had come over.

"You are the one looking for something, not I," said Karina.

Michaela remembered her dream. "How do you –?" She started to feel spooked.

"I know everything," Karina replied, "but there's a lot that you don't know yet – or no longer. That's why you will have visitors tonight."

"What? More visitors? Do you want to have an orgy?" Michaela laughed.

"You just don't understand," Karina said. "I'm not the one you think I am. I'm just a messenger."

"I rather think you're a bad dream caused by my upset stomach," Michaela replied. "Or you're playing a trick on me." She waved her hand dismissively. "Leave me alone. I have to sleep. It'll be morn-ing soon, and I have to go to work." She crawled into her bed and pulled the blanket up over her shoulders. My god, that was cold!

"Tomorrow can wait," Karina said, "but you might not."

"Don't talk in riddles!" Michaela got upset. "That's not your style." Indeed, Karina was the most direct person she knew. She never hid what she wanted. Why was she doing it now?

"You are capable of making even an apparition like me sigh," Karina said. "You don't believe in what you see. You walk through the world with your eyes shut, without looking around you. Do you never stop?"

"Stop and smell the roses, you mean?" Michaela laughed with chattering teeth as she shivered under her blanket. "Are you Satan offering me a single moment that's so beautiful I'd want it to last forever in exchange for the world?" She propped herself up. "All right, make me an offer. I'll think about it."

"I'm not the devil." Karina glided away. "Like I said, I'm just a messenger. The others will come. Be ready."

"The others? What others?" Michaela stared confused into the darkness that started to spread out again. The light coming from Karina's shape waned. "What others?" Michaela yelled into the silence that followed the darkness.

But there was no reply.

Check out these exciting books and more at

www.elles-books.com

www.ingramcontent.com/pod-product-compliance
Lightning Source LLC
Chambersburg PA
CBHW020321260626
47156CB00004B/1316